I0545888

HOWLER

TERROR IN THE OZARKS

EDWARD J. MCFADDEN III

SEVERED**PRESS**

HOWLER

Copyright © 2025 Edward J. McFadden III

WWW.SEVEREDPRESS.COM

ISBN: 978-1-923165-54-0

"But come what may, I do adore thee so
That danger shall seem sport, and I will go."
— William Shakespeare

1

Borderland Game Preserve, Ozark Mountains, Arkansas, U.S.
8:06 PM CST, August 16th, 2022

Jake Kahn tracked the Howler as it fled through the dusk-shrouded evergreens.

One person's folly is another's profit, and bills come due regardless of intentions, hard work, or fortunes. The beast had disturbed the rich folks sitting in their comfortable tree stands, and the call to bring home a ceremonial pelt had come just in time.

Fate is a merciless hunter.

Kahn squeezed the Honda Recon's throttle gently and its engine gurgled as the quad's knobby tires crunched and popped over stones and twigs, kicking up clouds of dust and grit. He bit his lip as the sounds of his passage carried through the woods. Kahn had been hunting since he could walk, and he knew that no matter how stealthy he was, the Ozark Howler would sense him. Still, there was no reason to make himself an easy target. The wind was out of the west, which meant his bodily stink was being pushed away from the Howler, so at least he had that going for him.

In the aftermath of his family fracturing nature became his refuge and hunting his trade. Exile had stripped away his old life, leaving him adrift, and the Ozarks provided the perfect place to disappear. Kahn embraced the wild with the fervor of a man seeking redemption. He missed his daughter deeply, but each trophy claimed helped him carve a path of hope for Jenna's future, and that gave purpose to his lost life. A life destroyed by circumstance, poor decisions, weakness, anger, and arrogance.

The woods were alive, breathing with the rhythm of the whispering wind and the creaking trees. Wildflowers bloomed defiantly along the edges of the trail, where the ghosts of past hunters lingered, urging those who followed to listen to the stories the mountains told. The forest never failed to ease Kahn's troubled mind and loosen the worry and sorrow that constantly knotted his neck and back.

A gentle breeze pushed down the trail that ran along the preserve's boundary, the sharp undercurrent of gasoline just below the sweet scent of evergreens mixed with moist earth. The faint hum of I-49 carried through the white oaks and shortleaf pines as the orchestra of chirping crickets, hooting owls, howling coyotes, and buzzing katydids tuned-up for the evening's performance.

The trees murmured and the creatures went still. A piercing wolf-like howl mixed with a manic hyena-like laugh, followed by the sharp crack of a breaking branch echoed down the trail. Then came a low, menacing growl, and a harsh, guttural tapping that sounded like the rattle of a chain being dragged over metal.

Shadows danced in the woods as the last rays of the setting sun angled through the tree canopy and cast spotlights on the densely packed underbrush. Tendrils of darkness leaked through the forest, blending into the creeping dusk as the oaks' pale green leaves turned black, and the evergreens became one with the growing night as the rolling hills faded into darkness.

He brought the ATV to a stop and killed the engine.

Massive four-toed footprints stretched down the center of the path, forming a distinct double track. At the tip of each toe, deep three-inch gashes marked where sharp claws had sliced into the earth. In the dusky light ahead, two glowing yellow eyes hovered above the hulking silhouette of a shadowy figure, its form barely discernible in the gloom.

Kahn had been tracking the Howler for days, and his back ached and his stomach gurgled as it demanded whiskey and food. He had been hired by the staties after a hunter was killed during a guided luxury excursion, by what was being described as a rabid bear. Three days before the killing, what Kahn and Deputy Sheriff Misty Connelly believed to be a Howler had attacked two hunters in their stand, though the guests escaped unharmed.

The Borderland Game Preserve was a private club, and strangers were kept at a distance, but the sheriff insisted on outside involvement and Kahn needed the money. His summer nuisance contracts were coming to an end, leaving him without a steady source of income. He sent most of his modest earnings to Evelyn to support Jenna, which meant he'd be living on a steady diet of spaghetti for the next few months, supplemented with venison and whatever other game he could kill and keep.

He eased the Remington from its scabbard, put its stock to his shoulder, and pressed his eye to the scope. The rifle was a bolt-action rifle equipped with a three-round internal magazine, and there was a round in the firing chamber.

Branches laden with pine needles drooped over the trail, partially obscuring his view. As the hash marks within the sight's crosshairs came alive with a vivid green light, Kahn adjusted his aim as he searched for his target. He focused on the shifting shadows cast by the trees.

When Kahn found the yellow eyes, he eased the rifle's safety into the fire position as he breathed deeply.

A low gurgle carried down the trail and the eyes disappeared.

He let the tip of the rifle dip as he jerked his head back. The Howler was on the move. He thumbed the safety back on, slipped the gun into the scabbard, and fired up the quad.

The Honda whined as Kahn pinned the throttle, the ATV's wheels spinning and kicking up dirt and rocks as it surged forward. He kept the headlights off, and moonlight angled through the trees as blackness filled all the empty spaces. The narrow trail bent east, the buzz of I-49 growing, heat spreading through Kahn as unease stroked his nerves.

If the beast went up to the highway… He didn't want to think about that, especially after the tragic accident the prior year. The massive multi-car pile-up had taken weeks to untangle, and though it hadn't been mentioned by anyone—not even the local conspiracy nuts, Kahn believed a Howler had something to do with the crash. He had no evidence, only vague suspicions fueled by the fact that he was one of the rare few who had actually seen an Ozark Howler.

The Honda vibrated beneath Kahn as he gripped the handlebars. The path cut through a thick patch of underbrush as it twisted and turned, revealing the dark outlines of a steep cliffside and rocky outcropping.

Kahn took a deep pull of fresh air. He hadn't intended to stay long in the Ozarks. Just a weekend to clear his head, but the mountains had wrapped their tendrils around him, and he had nowhere else to go anyway.

But that had been just the start.

When he heard the stories whispered at the local diner—tales of the Ozark Howler, a creature said to terrorize the region, a beast with a haunting cry that could chill even the most hardened naturalist, he was intrigued. Most folks dismissed Howlers as folklore, a figment of overactive imaginations fueled by moonlit nights and the mysteries of the forest, but Kahn knew better, and that was why Misty had recommended him, and the sheriff had chosen him.

Kahn rounded a bend as a cold breeze swept through the trees, and goosebumps broke out on his skin. The night creatures fell silent, and even the rustling leaves seemed to hold their breath. Shadows flitted amidst the trees, but other than the beast's tracks there was no sign of the Howler.

The trail gave way to a clearing, revealing a dark vista of rolling hills and dense woods. He followed the path, but as the field ended and he entered the woods Kahn spotted the outline of the Howler crouched in the underbrush. His heart raced as he slowed the ATV to a crawl. The shadows shifted, and Kahn caught a glimpse of glowing eyes staring at him, unblinking.

Another bone-chilling howl pierced the night as the beast threw back its head, its long dark snout silhouetted against the corpse light leaking through the tree canopy.

As fast as the beast had appeared, it was gone again.

Kahn thumbed the throttle, and the quad roared beneath him, adrenaline flooding his veins. Trees blurred past him, shadows writhing in his peripheral vision as sweat dripped down his forehead and dampened his armpits. Branches scraped the ATV like skeletal fingers, and the thrill of the hunt morphed into a nagging sense of dread.

The path bent sharply, and Kahn worked the handlebars, narrowly avoiding a tree that leaned precariously over the trail. Branches whipped his face, the quad's engine grumbled, and Kahn couldn't shake the feeling that he was the one being hunted.

An Ozark Howler with black matted fur and glowing yellow eyes surged from the undergrowth, its mouth stretched wide, rows of razor-sharp teeth glowing in the starlight. The cryptid growled as its powerful jaws snapped closed and the beast overshot its target, skidding to a stop on the trail.

Kahn swerved, but the Howler was too close.

The creature bounded into the ATV, knocking Kahn off balance, and sharp pain surged through him as claws raked across his arm. He gasped, struggling to maintain control of the quad as one of the front wheels caught a stone. The four-wheeler shuddered and metal bent as the handlebars twisted out of Kahn's grasp and the Honda shrieked as it flipped.

Kahn was tossed from his seat and the Howler swiped at him with one of its baseball mitt-sized front paws. The air sizzled as the knife-like claws raked the air inches from his face. He hit the ground hard, and the chanting of the beast's labored breathing rose above the ringing in his head.

The Ozark Howler's muscular frame rippled with raw power, its eyes glinting like shards of glass as it clawed the ground as if spoiling to run. It was a grotesque mix of feline and bear, a hulking mass of fur and muscle with twisted horns.

He searched for the rifle but then remembered his Beretta. Kahn was dazed but he managed to roll onto his side, protecting his injured arm as he pulled the 9 MM. Pain surged through him as he prepared the gun to fire and aimed it at the Howler.

Moonlight painted the world in harsh black and white and the Howler turned tail and ran.

Kahn fired until the Beretta clicked empty, the gun bucking slightly as he held the weapon in a singlehanded grip. The sharp tang of gun smoke filled the air, and Kahn's eyes stung and his head rang as he rolled onto his back, his backpack digging into his spine. He stared at the thin clouds streaking across the star-dappled sky, his arm throbbing with pain as hot blood trickled down its length.

A cackling laugh-like howl squealed through the darkness.

2

Kahn struggled to one knee before pushing himself to his feet, his arm pulsing in sync with the pounding of his heart, the sharp ringing in his head softening into a persistent throb. He pulled a spare magazine from his Kevlar-reinforced hunting vest and swapped out the empty magazine before holstering the Beretta. The vest also held night vision binoculars, a rangefinder, a utility knife, firestarter rods, his cellphone, and a GPS beacon. He retrieved the binoculars and pressed them to his eyes.

Nothing moved on the trail ahead except the swaying of evergreen branches, their gentle tapping arguing with the breeze.

He dropped his pack and fished out a first aid kit and a Maglite from the collection of supplies that included a field dressing kit, a water bottle, power bars, a flask, scent blocker spray, and various calls and scent lures.

The LED Maglite was overly bright, so he dampened it with a leaf as he examined his wounds. A series of deep, jagged gashes ran down the length of his forearm, where claws had sliced through the flesh. The skin around the wounds was torn, and muscles and tendons glistened and twitched. Blood dripped in dark splatters, and in places, bone was exposed.

The scent of blood and raw meat clouded the air, metallic and pungent. White-hot pain raced up Kahn's arm like fire licked the edges of the wounds. He flexed his hand, and all his fingers were not only there, but functioning.

Kahn pulled the ten-inch high-carbon stainless-steel knife from its sheath on his left leg, its curved edge glinting faintly. The blade was a drop point design, and the spine sloped gently away from the black rubber handle toward the curved tip.

The sleeve of his woodland camouflage shirt was in tatters, and Kahn carefully cut away the fabric. He would have the wounds professionally dressed when he got back to the lodge and maybe take some stitches, but for now, he needed to do everything he could to stop the cuts from getting infected.

Kahn sheathed his hunting knife and went to work with the first aid kit. As he cleaned the gashes with alcohol pads, Kahn's rubber boots squeaked as he shifted on his feet, trying to keep his fleeing adrenaline from tightening his muscles. The pain was excruciating, but the wounds felt better after he applied the healing ointment and bandages. He flexed his arm and lifted it in the air. Range of motion was limited, but he could tolerate the pain, so he decided against jerry-rigging a sling.

An owl cooed and crickets sang as Kahn packed his gear, his gaze shifting from the path to the ATV. The Honda lay on its side, and the handlebars were bent beneath the machine. Its engine had stalled and the right front control arm, which connected the wheel hub to the quad's frame, was twisted. There was a bent tie rod, and the damaged wheel assembly's shock absorber was broken from its mount. The Honda wouldn't be going anywhere except on a trailer.

The Remington's stock had broken off, and Kahn jerked the gun free of its scabbard and held the broken rifle like a pistol. He shook his head and punched the gun back into its holster.

Cars buzzed faintly along I-49, their distant hum barely cutting through the night chorus. He switched off the Maglite, and darkness closed in around him. As his eyes adjusted, Kahn pulled out his phone. The lodge had a signal booster, so Kahn wasn't surprised to find he had a weak cellphone signal.

A horn blast carried through the woods. He knew how to get to the highway. It would take an hour, but once there he could flag down a car for help. Kahn stared at the image of Jenna on his phone's main screen. Or he could call Mad Maddox, the game preserve's Lodge Master, or Deputy Sheriff Misty Connelly.

He tapped his watch, and a cloud of luminescent green light leaked through the darkness. It was 8:34 PM, and Misty was probably three deep at The Red Robin, and Mad Maddox wouldn't rush to help him. The guy had made it known more than once that Kahn was on his own, and he wasn't wanted. His guides could deal with the problem, and his resisting the incursion of outsiders would only be supported by Kahn's injury and lack of results.

Still, what choice did he have? The game preserve was four thousand seven hundred and sixty-two acres of raw wilderness, and he was in the northeastern quadrant which cut into Borderland Pass. It was a long walk back to the lodge. He was tired and hungry, his arm ached, and the nearest hunting stand was at least half an hour's walk away, and all he'd find there was an empty blind.

Kahn cracked his neck and called Maddox.

The phone rang six times before Mad picked up. "Yes, Kahn. What is it? Do you know what time—did you get it?"

Kahn swallowed his anger and frustration. "I'm on its trail, but I've had a bit of a—setback."

Maddox sniffed but said nothing, his derision and disappointment revealed with that one simple sound.

7

Though he considered himself to be an honest person, Kahn had fallen off the tightrope of truth more than once. He tended to temper his comments based on who he was speaking to, and he realized he didn't owe Mad Maddox the truth, or even an explanation. He flipped the script and went on offense, the bullshit flowing like wine.

"Who maintains your ATVs?" Kahn said. He didn't allow Maddox to respond. "Whoever they are haven't been doing a good job and my arm is all torn up thanks to their incompetence." He breathed deep, the weight of embarrassment lifting from him.

"Are you alright?"

Mad could have been asking what time it was, and Kahn's stomach burned, but he took a deep breath. At least it had been the jerk's first question. "I'll live."

"I assume since you've called me, that your quad is nonoperational?"

"You could say that."

A loud, obnoxious sigh.

Kahn wanted to reach through the phone and grab the man's neck, and venom poured from his mouth. "Are you giving me shit right now? I was on the Howler's ass, and thanks to your shit equipment I've got a damaged wing, and the beast got away. So, save your crap for one of your employees."

Maddox said nothing.

"You there?"

"Yes, I'm here. The Honda you were issued is two years old, Kahn, so how about you tell me what really happened?" Maddox said.

Kahn licked his lips as he shook his head. It pained him how easily Mad saw through him, but the damage was done and there was only one path left to travel; deny until you die. "I don't know what you're talking about. Are you going to send someone out to get me, or not?"

A coyote barked, and the call was answered by two others.

"You know what? Forget it," Kahn said. "I'll call the deputy sheriff and tell her you're not cooperating, and she'll call the staties. Do you know what that means?"

Maddox stayed silent.

"You'll have the state police crawling up your ass and scouring your precious preserve. What will your high-dollar customers do then? I wonder how much money the lodge will lose when word gets out about the attacks. You got lucky with the murder so far, but, you know, I'm feeling talkative."

"Don't have a coronary," Maddox said. "Text me your coordinates and I'll send someone out for you."

"I've activated my beacon. That will give you my exact location in case—"

A branch snapped and a low gurgle stroked Kahn's last nerve.

"What is it? What?" Maddox said. He was fully awake and paying attention now.

"It's nothing. Get someone out here." Kahn killed the connection.

Moonlight filtered through the tree canopy, and shadows frolicked in the undergrowth as Kahn pressed the binoculars to his eyes.

Through the eerie green glow of night vision, the Ozark woods transformed into a surreal, shadowy landscape. Trees that appeared solid and towering during the day were skeletal outlines, their branches twisting like fingers. The dense undergrowth, normally lush with earthy greens and browns, was washed out, and replaced by an ethereal monochrome. Leaves and pine needles shimmered faintly as they caught the wind, their movements magnified and glowing green.

Chipmunks, squirrels, and foxes, normally invisible to the naked eye, flitted through his field of vision. Their eyes glowed like embers, stark beacons against the backdrop of swirling shadows. An intense ruffling of branches and leaves rippled through the forest, followed by the haggard panting of an animal exerting itself.

A sharp staccato cry pierced the darkness, abruptly silencing the night symphony. The echo of the wail lingered in Kahn's head, refusing to fade away as it joined the chorus of cracking branches reminiscent of breaking bones. Each creak and snap amplified the haunting cry, and Kahn's nerves danced just beneath his skin as he surged into motion.

Kahn knew he should wait for a guide to pick him up, but he felt the Howler mocking him, egging him on. As he jogged down the trail, Beretta in a doublehanded grip, he caught a glimpse of a slithering shadow at the edge of his vision moving fast between the trees. Kahn froze, his breath catching in his throat as he aimed the Beretta at nothing.

An absence of light leaked from the underbrush, slowly taking shape as the beast stepped into a shaft of moonlight that sliced through the forest. Bathed in a silvery glow, the Howler stood on its hind legs, its blazing eyes eight feet above the ground.

Kahn's pulse quickened. The Ozark Howler was massive, its body covered in thick, bristling black fur that absorbed the moonlight. Its shoulders were broad, its arms unnaturally long, and its hands—clawed and wicked—were up in fighting position. But it was the moonlit face that rooted Kahn's feet to the ground. The creature's head was a grotesque blend of mountain lion and bear, with a long snout and jaws full of jagged teeth. Two twisted horns protruded from its head, adding to the beast's demonic presence. Its eyes, glowing a deep, fiery yellow, locked on Kahn, holding him in place with primal fear and shock.

The Howler let out a low, rumbling growl that vibrated through the trees as Kahn's gut went nuclear. He should fire, but he was stiff with shock and there were many branches between him and his target. Time slowed as he inched forward, searching for a clear shot, pine needles brushing his face.

Then the beast moved, impossibly fast, darting back into the shadows of the forest with the fluidity of water.

Kahn stood alone in the dark, heart pounding as he stared after the beast. The wind gusted and brought the murmur of I-49 as he turned on the flashlight and held it on top of the Beretta like a sight as he eased through the woods.

He hadn't gone far before he paused, looking back at the gray ribbon of gloom that was the path as it trailed through the dark forest. If he strayed far from the path, he doubted Maddox's people would look for him. His arm throbbed with constant pain, and the bandages were crimson, but he wasn't doing any further damage to his arm, and if he could kill the Howler right here and right now—

That was just wishful thinking. Kahn had first encountered a Howler on the eastern side of I-49 by an abandoned homestead. He'd seen two others in the months that followed, one of which didn't have horns, and based on his observations Kahn surmised that only male Howlers grew horns.

Shadows raced through the forest and Kahn fired, slowly squeezing the trigger as bullets peppered tree trunks and zipped through the undergrowth. When he'd fired ten times he stopped. He had plenty of 9 MM parabellums in his backpack, but he only had one spare magazine, and it was empty and would take time to reload.

If Kahn hit the Howler the beast gave no sign. He searched the area with the night vision binoculars and found the glowing form of the creature charging through the forest, heading east toward the interstate.

He started forward again, despite the alarms flashing all over his mental dashboard.

Hunting was usually a waiting game. That's what had drawn him to the sport. Sitting in a tree stand or blind with nothing to do except stare at nature and wait for prey to mosey along sounded like a snoozefest to most people, but to Kahn, it was the ultimate form of relaxation. Nobody asked questions when he was hunting, and nature proved the only high he needed. Well, the forest and a little Jack Daniels. Hunting was hours of waiting punctuated by a few thrilling moments followed by a great deal of bloody work.

But hunting the Howler was far from standard procedure. He had been wandering the preserve, looking for signs of the Howler so he could set up a tree stand, but the Ozark Howler was a cunning beast, and it usually left very little evidence of its passage.

He turned off the Maglite and let his eyes adjust as he listened for an incoming ATV, but there was nothing but the screeching, bleating, and howling of the night creatures, the gentle hum of I-49, and the push of the chill wind.

Kahn pressed through the underbrush and came to a steep slope of tumbled stones. The moon hung like a silver egg in the sky, casting long shadows that danced across the gnarled trees and jagged rocks. His eyes narrowed as he scanned the landscape with the binoculars.

Ahead there was a shallow dell carved into the forest floor, and at its center a stream trickled over smooth stones, the sound nearly drowned out by the night symphony. Kahn shifted his position and crouched low in the underbrush, his breathing slow and measured, the Ozark night wrapping him in its cool embrace. His heart thudded in his chest, not from fear this time, but from the thrill of the hunt.

Through the ghostly green lens of night vision, the dell came alive in sharp contrast. Shadows flickered unnaturally, and Kahn smiled when he caught sight of the Howler.

3

The Ozark Howler squatted at the edge of the stream, its massive body low and hunched as it dipped its head to drink, its dark fur blending with the surroundings. It moved with an eerie grace as if every muscle was perfectly attuned. The beast's broad, wolf-like head turned, exposing the glint of glowing eyes. Even through the binoculars, Kahn saw the glimmer of intelligence—or malice—in those eyes.

Seeing the Howler now, bathed in the monochrome green, the beast felt more dangerous than the tales suggested. This wasn't just a mindless predator; it was something more calculating, something primeval.

Kahn remained motionless, watching as the creature lapped at the stream, its broad shoulders twitching. If he had his rifle he might've taken a shot, though he doubted he would be able to hit the Howler. He was in an elevated position, which helped, but the distance was at least two hundred yards, which was out of his range.

One wrong move, one stray sound, and the predator would vanish back into the shadows. The night was young, and he was patient, but as patient as the Howler? He didn't know, and he had to ask himself what purpose his patience would serve. The wind was out of the west, so he could creep closer and try to get a shot with the Beretta, or...

He pulled his phone and attempted to get pictures in night mode with full zoom, but all he got was a bright glowing blob.

Kahn had seen an extreme closeup picture of an eagle on social media and the photographer explained how she'd used a technique called digiscoping to capture the image. The wind argued with the crickets as Kahn held his cellphone's camera lens to the binoculars' eyepiece, shifting it around until it was focused on the beast. There was a little more detail, but the image was useless, and Kahn gave up.

It was time to back off. That much was clear. If he pressed the issue now and scared off the Howler, it might not come back to this spot for a long time. Letting the beast drink its fill was the move, and then he could build a blind or set a trap at this watering spot.

The sites where the hunter had been killed and the pair attacked were useless because Mad's crew had trampled all over them, contaminating the scenes and leaving their scent everywhere. As he watched the Howler, he thought about the murder scene and tried to put together puzzle pieces that didn't fit.

Kahn had been called in after the preliminary investigation of the hunter's murder. He wasn't a crime scene investigator or even a trained law-enforcement officer, but the preserve's story didn't sit right with him from the start. The deputy sheriff agreed, but there was no evidence to support any other story except the one told by hunting guide Tanner Slade, which was supported by Maddox and his people.

The murder scene, if you could call some blood splatters a scene, didn't tell him much, but Kahn knew the Howler better than most, and he recognized signs others did not.

Slade claimed he and his guest, Greg Aldridge, a contractor from Fayetteville, left their quads behind and hiked into a deep section of the forest. This appeared to be true, because there were no ATV tracks at or around the murder scene, and Kahn was able to verify the location where the guide claimed to have left the machines. Aldridge wasn't a member of the lodge and had been 'gifted' the hunt by a rich land developer who he'd done extensive work for, and this complicated matters but also simplified things for the lodge. The contractor was divorced, with no children, and his kin accepted the story of his hunting death as though they'd expected it and put up very little fuss.

The area where Aldridge was killed was marked off with red flags, but all there was to be seen therein were splatters of dried blood. Smudged animal tracks mixed with boot prints indicated that a large animal had been present, but if anyone else noticed the three-inch gashes that made up part of the paw prints, they didn't let on. The facts concerning the actual attack were where things got shifty.

Slade claimed he left Aldridge alone for five minutes so he could take a leak and spray scent spray to lure in a bear or deer, and that's when the attack occurred. The guide claimed to have heard nothing, and he returned to find Aldridge gone, and a trail of blood leading into the undergrowth.

Said trail of blood was there, a dried brown stripe covering bent weeds. Slade found Aldridge's corpse, minus a leg and an arm, fifty yards deep in the brush. The body was covered with claw marks and bites, and pictures verified this. Mad and the preserve called the attack a random hunting accident, most likely a bear the likes of which could be found all over the Ozarks. When Kahn pointed out that bears rarely attacked humans, especially in the summer months when there was plenty of food, Mad had said, "Maybe it was rabid."

The story might have made sense, and the cops might have moved on, if not for puzzle pieces that stuck in Kahn's mind like fishhooks.

First was the NDA Aldridge signed. Researching this led down a rabbit hole, and Kahn learned there were several types of Non-Disclosure Agreements. An NDA is a legally binding contract designed to protect confidential information shared between parties. It ensured that sensitive details discussed or shared—whether related to business strategies, intellectual property, client lists, or proprietary data—remained private and were not disclosed to third parties without consent. There were three types: Unilateral NDAs were very common. In a U-NDA only one party agrees to keep the shared information confidential. This usually occurs when one party, like an employee, contractor, or customer receives proprietary information. A Mutual NDA requires both parties to share confidential information and agree to protect each other's data, and a Multilateral NDA involves three or more parties.

Aldridge had signed a U-NDA, and when Kahn asked what proprietary information was shared with Aldridge, Mad said it was just a legal formality to protect the preserve from lawsuits. While the U-NDA did provide legal recourse for Aldridge's kin, its existence raised multiple red flags. Hunting was dangerous. Everyone above ten years old knew that, so a signed liability waiver would normally be used to protect the party providing the service. In this case, the lodge was more concerned with Aldridge not talking about what he had seen.

The second puzzle piece that bothered Kahn was Slade's inopportune bathroom break. Like the tollbooth operator who ducked inside his booth when Sunny arrived at his murder scene in The Godfather, he was supposed to believe Slade just happened to go to the bathroom when the attack occurred? That was possible, if unlikely. But hearing nothing? Kahn couldn't buy that.

Kahn had requested a meeting with Slade, but Mad declined, saying the guide had already spoken to the deputy sheriff and Kahn was just a hired slaughterjack, which was true. He didn't push the issue because Misty said the guy just read from his written statement when she interviewed him.

Then there was the general feeling—and Misty appeared to sense it also, that Mad didn't want the Howler killed.

Kahn crouched on the lip of the dell, the rolling wilderness of ancient mountains, thick forests, and silent valleys stretching out before him. He scanned the hollow one last time with the night vision binoculars and saw the beast lounging beside the stream, its eyes like signals in the darkness.

The scene was deceptively peaceful. Owls cooed, crickets tittered, and frogs bleated, their songs a quiet backdrop to the rustle of leaves and the buzz of I-49. Kahn traced the course of the glowing stream, noting the game trails that crisscrossed its banks. It was a natural predator's paradise. It was perfect for him.

Knowing it was time to leave, Kahn crept through the underbrush, his boots crunching softly on dry leaves as he left the Howler behind.

14

Shadows stretched through the forest, blending with the dark thoughts that always haunted Kahn.

Technically, exile had been his choice, and yet each step away from his old life felt like a sentence he hadn't expected. Out here, away from the minutia of daily life, away from the people who knew his name, Kahn could almost pretend the world had forgotten him. Almost.

The trek back to the main trail meandered through thick underbrush, weaving up and down rocky inclines. Every muscle ached, but out here Kahn couldn't afford to let his guard down, and he held the Beretta at his side as he pushed through vegetation as silently as he could. The distant call of a hawk carried through the forest, easing the nerves that knotted his neck so tightly he'd forgotten the pain beating through his arm like a second heart.

Kahn reached the trail and found that he was north of where he'd left the path. The trail bent west at the point where I-49 curved, and he double-checked his bearings using his cellphone. He didn't hear an ATV approaching and he shook his head as he cursed Mad. The guy was such a dipshit Kahn started thinking of ways to mess with the man, but that wasn't his way, at least not anymore.

Whenever Kahn had thoughts of revenge or antagonism, he reminded himself that he didn't have the luxury of being a nozzle. He had to fly below the radar and go unseen. Going after Maddox would bring increased scrutiny for everyone, and that wasn't what Kahn wanted. Misty knew his story, and she understood, though the deputy sheriff disagreed with how Kahn was handling his personal life. He figured she had a point, yet he felt powerless to do anything about it. Jenna was where she needed to be, and there was nothing Kahn could do to help her except provide money for her support.

He headed south along the path, flashlight on. Eyes glowed in the darkness ahead, but they were low to the ground and scattered as Kahn approached.

Though he didn't like to think about it, he'd once been a successful business owner. His

security guard company hadn't been making him rich, but the Kahn clan had been doing O.K. That was until his family's world imploded and he started drinking heavily. Kahn had been good at making excuses back then, and there was plenty of bad to focus on, yet he'd failed to see the damage he was doing not only to himself but to his family. He'd let his daughter down when she'd needed him the most, and the thought of it charred his stomach and sent bile racing up his throat.

Kahn stopped walking and tuned out the night symphony.

The faint gurgle of an approaching ATV echoed down the trail as a cloud of light leaked through the forest. Critters ran for home, and the trees and undergrowth swayed in the gentle breeze that brought the faint scent of animal waste.

As the forest exploded with light Kahn checked his gear, making sure everything was tucked away. He didn't holster the Beretta, though he was one hundred percent confident the ATV had been sent by Maddox—but maybe that was why he kept his gun ready. Kahn didn't trust Mad as far as he could throw him, and Kahn probably couldn't lift the overweight ass off the ground. If something was going on, to what length would Mad go to stop Kahn from discovering the truth?

Two headlights momentarily blinded Kahn, and he couldn't see the face of the quad's rider. With a cough and sputter, the machine went still, and its rider dismounted. "Kahn?"

It was a female voice, and as the woman stepped into the light Kahn saw it was Blair Stone, and he breathed a sigh of relief. Blair was a good egg, and she would do right by him. She had her hair tied back in a ponytail, and she wore jeans, an orange hunting vest, and a black Stetson which she always wore. A rifle hung from Blair's shoulder and her hand rested on the handle of her Colt Python in its holster.

"Blair," Kahn said, and he was unable to keep the relief from his voice. "Where have you been? I called over an hour ago."

Blair shook her head. "The boss called me twenty minutes ago and I dropped everything."

Kahn sighed as he bit his lip. Mad, that little shit. "Thank you," he said. "I appreciate you coming out here. I'm sure you have better things to do."

She put a hand on his shoulder, rubbed it gently, and said, "Not really. What happened to your arm?"

"I slipped on a banana peel."

She didn't laugh and the duo stood in awkward silence for half a minute before Kahn climbed onto the ATV's jumpseat.

"Mr. Maddox would like to see you," Blair said.

Kahn sniffed and said nothing.

She smiled at him, and they locked eyes for a heartbeat, the ATV's headlights casting her long shadow down the trail.

Kahn smiled back. She was a beautiful woman, but... He didn't know if he'd ever be able to be with another woman. He no longer loved Evelyn, but he was broken, and every woman who came into his life reminded Kahn that he was no good for anyone.

Blair hopped onto the quad and cranked it up. "What's the deal? Are we heading back to the lodge? Or do you want me to take you to your truck?" she asked.

Kahn had no desire to speak with Maddox, nor was he under any obligation to do so. Instead, he would get himself bandaged up better and go find the deputy sheriff. He said, "Take me to my truck. Please."

She nodded, put the ATV in gear, and thumbed the throttle.

Kahn leaned forward and spoke into Blair's ear. "Won't you get in trouble with Maddox if you don't deliver me?"

She looked over her shoulder, smiled, and said, "I'll tell him you turned off your beacon and I couldn't find you."

4

In a prior life, The Red Robin had been a manor house. Set way back off the road and protected by forest, the two-story Victorian house was out of place in the sparse community of ranches and cabins. A staple of the area for generations, the place was old as dirt, and it hadn't been maintained very well over the years. The structure was patched with dirty plastic siding in places where mandatory repairs had been made, while the rest of the cedar shake facade was covered in peeling white paint. The window frames, weathered and worn, had taken on the gray hue of age, and the plain sign announcing the bar's name was faded and smudged with dirt.

Kahn pulled into the dirt parking lot, shut down the pickup's engine, and sat in the silence. His arm throbbed, but his stop at the hospital had provided him with sixteen stitches, painkillers, and a new dressing. It was 10:51 PM, and it had been a long day, but he wouldn't be able to put his head on a pillow until he spoke with Misty. The deputy sheriff had to make some decisions and needed all available information.

Misty called The Red Robin her second home, and Kahn breathed a sigh of relief when he saw her Jeep Compass. In the last hour, as he waited for a nurse and sat silently as she tended to his wounds, Kahn had time to think about the evening's events and order his thoughts. At the end of the day, the way he totaled things up, his new information added up to very little. So he'd seen the beast. Big deal. He'd seen it before, and he would see it again. But the good news was the stream, the beast drinking from it, and the opportunity to set a trap, lie in wait, and exploit the element of surprise.

The inside of the bar was in slightly better shape than the outside. Upon entering, Kahn was greeted by an empty podium with a sign taped to its front that read: Please don't wait to be seated. The faint chortle of Bob Dylan carried through the murmur of the drinkers, the scent of smoke thick in the air. The joint was crowded for almost eleven o'clock on a Tuesday night, and waitresses bustled about with trays of drinks and Tony was a blur of movement behind the bar.

A central staircase loomed straight ahead, and it went up to bedrooms that had been converted to storage and office space. To the right was the old living room, the back of which opened into a smaller room with a fireplace, and beyond that was an outside porch. These spaces were filled with tables and chairs. This was the side of The Red Robin where people went to eat and escape the noise of the bar. Most of the tables were empty.

To the left was the old dining room and beyond that the kitchen. Here table-like shelves lined the walls along with stools, and a bar ran down the center of the space, its head feeding into the kitchen. He had only been in the basement once, but Kahn knew that it was used for food storage, and customers occasionally hid out down there when the weather was too nasty to step out onto the back porch to catch cancer or get high.

Half the seats at the bar were available, and Misty sat alone between empty seats.

In another life, Kahn and Misty might have been an item. They would have 'hung out' as the kids say. But he was damaged goods, and she was old enough to be his mother and was at the end of her road. Soon she would head somewhere south to live out the rest of her days, leaving Kahn and the Ozarks behind. Her long gray hair was pulled back in a ponytail, and her sunburned face glistened and sparkled with a light sheen of makeup. Misty wasn't wearing her uniform, but her badge was displayed on her belt, and she wore her sidearm.

Kahn caught the deputy sheriff's attention and pointed at the glow of an exit sign that marked the hallway where the restrooms could be found. He made quick work of relieving himself, but as he stared into the mirror above the sink while washing his hands, the heat of worry and sorrow seeped through him. His brown hair was slick with the grease of the day, and though he'd cleaned up at the hospital, there were still smudges of dirt on his face. His brown eyes were red with fatigue, and the tips of his overlarge ears, which had led to the nickname Dumbo as a young boy, were crimson with heat. He had stripped off his hunting vest, and the hospital had given him a clean t-shirt that announced the hospital's fundraising drive, but he still looked homeless. He felt homeless. Kahn hadn't been home for two days, and he mentally thanked his ex-wife for buying the auto-feeder for Snoop—a wild coon cat who called Kahn's place home and always showed his whiskery face looking for food whenever Kahn wasn't around, as felines are wont to do.

His arm shrieked with pain as he used his damaged wing to open the bathroom door. A quarter-sized dot of blood marred the bandage, and the white gauze was already dirty.

"How you doing, partner?" Misty said.

Kahn grunted.

"That good? What can I get you?"

19

Though the flask he carried in his backpack proved otherwise, Kahn was trying to cut back on the devil juice. Still, there was a time for everything, and he needed a whiskey. "Jack up."

"Tony, can I get my friend here his usual?" Misty said. Her words weren't slurred, but they weren't rock steady.

The bartender nodded curtly and two minutes later a tumbler of bourbon appeared before Kahn.

"What's so important it couldn't wait until tomorrow?" Misty asked as she sipped her tequila and chased it with a swig of beer.

Kahn relayed the night's events, focusing on the attack and how he'd tracked the Howler to a watering spot.

"You saw it again?" she said, her tone free of emotion.

He nodded and said, "I know it's a legend, and all that, and it's rare to find someone who has seen the creature, but it's not like people in the Ozark Mountains have never heard of the Howler."

"As you know well, we're actually in the Boston Mountains, one of the three distinct plateaus that make up the Ozarks, and are often lumped together and called the Ozark Mountains," said Misty. She sipped her tequila and eyed him over the rim of her glass, a smile sliding over her features.

"Were you a professor before signing up with the cops?" Kahn asked, half-joking.

Misty chuckled. "No, just a know-it-all and I'm just getting started. Technically, this area isn't even true mountains. It's a deeply dissected plateau."

Kahn was an outdoorsman, and he had experienced most types of terrain, so he knew something of mountains and their origins. He said, "I know the mountains around here weren't pushed up by tectonic plates colliding or volcanic eruptions like the Rockies. Instead, the region was shaped by millions of years of erosion. The land got worn down, carved away by rivers and streams. What you see now is the result—deep cuts in the earth, forming valleys like Borderland Pass, which stretches across the game preserve. The river that originally carved out the valley dried up eons ago, but the terrain left behind became a natural boundary."

Misty smiled and leaned in conspiratorially. "Geologists call it a river valley, but there's a lot more to the story. The Caddo and Quapaw tribes used to pass through here, and some local historians even think the Mayans ventured this far north. All those old myths got tangled together, and that's how Borderland Pass got its name. Crossing the valley meant you were stepping into another tribe's territory—something that could cost you your life."

Kahn had heard all that before, but suddenly the old tales had taken on new significance. He said nothing as he took a pull of Jack.

Misty put her elbows on the bar and said, "The Ozark Howler is a sly creature. Legend says it can vanish in an instant, silent and unseen, as you've witnessed. It's an apex predator—one that doesn't belong here… in this world. It's from another time, when the world was wild, and it was a king among beasts."

Kahn sensed Misty was building to something, so he stayed quiet.

"They say the first settlers here fought the Howler. I've already mentioned the Mayans, but the Spanish conquistadors also came through this land. And the Native Americans—you know about them too. All of them tried to capture or kill the beast."

A burst of laughter pierced the murmur of the crowd, and Misty took the opportunity to sip her tequila and take a deep drink of beer.

"My mum used to tell me this story, a common tale told to children in these parts to keep them in line. It's the tale of the Ozark Howler and the great hunt. It dates back to the mid-1800s when this area of the country was still wild. A massive bear-cat with pointed ears, three-inch claws, fangs, horns, and yellow-rimmed eyes stalked the land. The story goes that the creature would come for kids who wandered out of bed—that part's nonsense. But what wasn't made up was the beast attacking livestock—cows, goats, and sometimes people.

"Supposedly, the Howler wiped out the animals of a wealthy landowner up near Searcy. Cows, sheep, pigs—all of them dead, throats ripped out, entrails strewn everywhere. The thing that really got to people was the waste. It wasn't hunting to eat—the beast was killing for sport. Back then, folks understood when an animal defended its territory or took livestock for food. The Native Americans knew this best. They used every part of an animal they killed. But the Howler's carnage was something else.

"So, the landowner gathered a group and put a bounty on the beast. He paid locals to comb the Ozarks for it."

Kahn's mind backtracked to his encounters with the creature—how it moved like a shadow, using the forest itself as a weapon.

"That hunt became the stuff of legend," Misty said. "I even found journal pages online—a first-person account from a farmhand named Freddie Weston, who joined the hunt. Those pages read like something out of an F. Paul Wilson novel. Blood, chaos, sorrow." Misty paused, rolling her shoulders as she searched Kahn's face for a reaction.

Kahn wasn't impressed. He'd heard similar stories applied to every so-called cryptid, right down to the Boogeyman.

"The first hunter they found was hanging upside down from a tree, caught in his own trap," Misty went on. "His face was clawed off, and his gut was split open, his insides spilling out. Weston described it as 'grizzly beyond what my mind could imagine.' Messed up stuff. Before giving up, the hunting party tracked the Howler across the Ozarks, which is how it got its name. The journal said the beast played with them, leading them on false trails. When they found the second hunter, the head of the group wanted to call off the search."

Kahn finished his drink and held up his empty glass.

As if it were a race, Misty polished off her tequila, downed the rest of her beer, and licked her lips.

"The second guy's head was crushed," Misty said. "They found a bloody rock nearby, and the man's fingers were chewed off, and his body was covered in stab wounds—probably from the Howler's claws or horns."

Kahn felt a chill creep down his spine, a knot of unease forming in his gut.

A new round arrived, and the duo drank.

Misty continued, "The main hunting party was four days deep into the Ozarks when they found the second dead hunter. Like I said, Weston thought the Howler was leading them on. It attacked their camp one night, slipping past the watch and dragging a man right out of his tent. Weston described the chaos in detail—men running, some wanting to chase the creature, others just wanting to survive. The man footing the bill wanted to turn back, but Weston joined a group that went after the Howler. The man taken was his friend, and he couldn't just leave him.

"The small party followed the trail for two days. Then they started finding pieces of Weston's buddy. A thumb, an ear, a hand, a leg. By the time they reached the corpse, all that was left was the torso—nothing but muscle, gristle, and bone where his head and limbs should've been."

Bob Dylan had given way to Johnny Cash who was wailing about having been everywhere.

"Crazy, right?" Misty said. "At first, I agreed with Weston and thought the beast was toying with them, but then I realized animals don't think like that. They follow their instincts, and sometimes that makes them seem smarter than they are. Anyway, Weston and the others ran. They didn't stop, didn't sleep. When they stumbled back into town, they discovered that the Howler had attacked again. The townsfolk blamed the hunters for stirring up trouble and shunned them. Can you believe that?"

Kahn could. Fear made people do strange things. He looked at Misty, the question burning on the tip of his tongue. "Why are you telling me this?"

She shrugged. "There's more, believe me. I thought… I don't know. I guess I want you to respect the Howler, whatever it is or you'll…"

Or he'd end up dead like those hunters all those years ago. Kahn nodded, lifted his Jack, and the duo clinked glasses.

"Listen," she said, Misty's voice taking on a new urgency. "I was going to call you in the AM, but since you're here… There's been some new developments."

Kahn lifted his eyebrows as he sipped bourbon.

"I spoke with one of the two hunters that were attacked last week," she said. "A Russell Kipper. He's a rich dude from Kansas City, and he gave his son a turkey hunt as a birthday present. Russell wouldn't give me his kid's contact information, and I let it slide. I asked Russell if he'd signed an NDA, and he said he hadn't. When I asked why, he said because, and I'm quoting now, 'I don't go after the dangerous stuff'. When I asked him what he meant, he clammed up."

Kahn nodded. He had a good idea what Russell had meant by 'dangerous stuff'. The only explanation he could think of was the man was referring to the Howler.

Misty watched him, letting him work things out before saying, "Yup. I think the Borderland Game Preserve might be offering Ozark Howler hunts on the down-low."

That idea had never occurred to Kahn.

"And that's not all," Misty said. "You didn't see the murder scene right after the incident, but I did. I took extensive video and pictures, and a general examination was performed to determine Greg Aldridge's preliminary cause of death."

Kahn said nothing.

"The crime scene bigheads who reviewed everything think the body was moved because of signs of lividity."

Kahn knew what that was but couldn't pull it from the memory banks. He stayed silent.

Misty continued, "After death, blood settles in the lowest parts of the body, causing purplish discoloration. If the body has been moved, lividity patterns will appear inconsistent with the body's current position. They also think the time of death provided by Slade is off because rigor mortis had passed, the body was bloated, and the skin was discolored and marbled with dark blood vessels. Not stuff you see with a body that's been dead for less than twenty-four hours, which is the timeline based on when I was called in."

"Why lie?"

She shrugged.

"What do you plan to do about it?" Kahn asked.

"In the morning I'm going to question Maddox, and I want you there with me."

Kahn smiled and finished his drink.

5

The Lodge at Borderland Game Preserve, Ozark Mountains, Arkansas, U.S.
10:16 AM CST, August 17th, 2022

The lodge was an imposing structure that blended into the forest that surrounded it. Built from a combination of timber and rough-hewn stone, the two-story building embodied a rustic elegance and a timeless grace. The slate roof glistened with moisture, sweeping eaves, and balconies overlooked the dense forest, and modern conveniences like lampposts and luggage carts were designed to appear dated, almost like in an amusement park. In a strange way, that's what the game preserve was. An amusement park for killing.

Kahn found Misty waiting and she got out of her squad car when he pulled in next to her.

"Morning," she said.

"We'll see." Kahn polished off his coffee, left the mug behind, and winced as he used his wounded arm to lift himself out of the pick-up.

Bird song carried over the gravel lot, and a river stone path led to the lodge's grand main entrance where Maddox and his number one man, Slade, waited.

"The security guard must've called ahead," Kahn said. There was a manned guard booth at the head of the long winding driveway that led to the lodge and hunting staging areas. Though there were many unofficial ways to enter the preserve, the road to the lodge was the game preserve's only thoroughfare.

As Kahn and Misty approached Maddox said, "Our meeting was at ten, right?"

Kahn sighed and rolled his eyes.

"Sorry to keep you waiting, Mr. Maddox," said the deputy sheriff, but Misty's face looked like she'd just eaten rotten fruit.

Maddox waved a hand. "You remember my lead guide and security chief, Tanner Slade."

"Of course," Misty said. She gave a curt smile.

Slade and Kahn made no sign.

"I've got coffee waiting for us in my conference room," Maddox said. "Shall we?"

The inside of the lodge was designed to evoke the atmosphere of a hunter's retreat while offering the luxury expected by its elite clientele. The entry hall had high vaulted ceilings, and thick log beams stretched overhead like the ribs of an ancient beast. A massive stone fireplace dominated the room, its hearth ablaze with a crackling fire that filled the space with the earthy scent of burning wood. Above the fireplace hung the preserved skull of a colossal stag, its antlers reaching outward like a crown.

Leather couches were arranged in nooks, and hand-carved oak tables held polished rifles and hunting memorabilia. Antlers and trophies lined the walls, and taxidermized bears, wolves, and mountain lions captured mid-prowl, their glassy eyes still fixed on some long-forgotten prey, stalked the room. The wooden floor, polished to a rich sheen, creaked slightly with each of Kahn's steps.

An elaborate hallway led deeper into the lodge, and the foursome walked past the dining hall, where oak tables of various sizes filled the room and wrought iron chandeliers loomed overhead, casting a dim, flickering glow. The scent of charred pork made Kahn's mouth water.

Maddox said, "Wild boar is on the menu tonight. Caught two days ago in the preserve."

Kahn harrumphed but said nothing.

"Is the lodge full?" asked the deputy sheriff.

"Almost." Maddox smiled like he was talking to shareholders. "Each of our fifty-eight private suites was designed to offer the utmost in comfort while still maintaining an untamed aesthetic," Maddox added. "Wooden furnishings, plush animal skins, and fur-lined bedding are standard, as are private balconies, where guests can take in the breathtaking views of the preserve, and the haunting beauty of the wilderness at night."

Kahn said nothing.

As if he was on autopilot and trying to sell a timeshare, Maddox kept going. "The lodge provides an array of amenities catering to the discerning hunter. We have a stable with well-trained horses and a full complement of all-terrain vehicles ready to take guests deeper into the preserve's more remote areas, while a range of hunting gear, from traditional bows to state-of-the-art rifles, are available for use. A skeet-shooting range and an archery course allow for some light competition between guests, but it's the promise of the hunt that draws them to Borderland Pass."

"I imagine there's been a lot of stories about the killed hunter and the attack whispered around the fire pit," Misty said.

"We're here," Maddox said as he opened a door labeled Executive Conference Room.

The rich bitter scent of fresh coffee greeted Kahn as he entered and took a seat. Like the rest of the lodge, the room was rustic, yet it held a modern charm. Polished wooden conference table and chairs, an elaborate wooden bar, and an LED screen encased in a wooden frame mounted on a wall.

Kahn poured coffee into a bone-colored clay mug and sipped. "Now that's good."

"It's a Columbian brand we bring in… special," Maddox said, and then a smile ran across his face.

An awkward silence descended, and Kahn cleared his throat.

Misty sipped loudly, then said, "Thank you for meeting with us. I know you're a busy man."

Maddox pursed his lips and angled his head, but said nothing.

The deputy sheriff took another sip, then said, "I spoke with Mr. Kipper."

A hawk shrieked outside, the shrill cry rising above the tinkle and ring leaking from the kitchen and the push and patter of the HVAC system.

Maddox's expression didn't change, but Slade's jaw tightened.

"He said he didn't sign an NDA," Misty said.

Maddox's eyebrows went up, but he stayed silent.

"Didn't you tell me that all guests signed an NDA? Greg Aldridge, the hunter who was murdered, signed one. Why not Kipper and his son?" said Misty, her mug frozen halfway to her mouth.

Maddox shook his head. "I didn't say ALL guests signed an NDA. Just the… serious hunters."

"Serious?" Kahn said.

"Come on, Mr. Kahn," Slade said. "I've heard all about you. You're one of the best out there, and you're telling me you don't know that not all hunts are of equal difficulty and danger?"

Kahn chuckled. "I don't know what you heard about me, but I can tell you I've never signed an NDA to go hunting."

"Legal protection for the lodge is required, Mr. Kahn. We offer a dangerous service," Maddox said.

"Indeed," Misty said. "But why not just a liability waiver? You use those also, right?"

Maddox grinned. "Of course."

"Then why an NDA?" Misty pressed.

"I've already explained this to you," Maddox said. "To protect the—"

"The lodge," Kahn said. "Yeah, we get it." He wasn't bound by the pleasantries of being a law enforcement officer. He was just a dumbass who was good at tracking scat. "But why the inconsistency?"

Maddox sighed. "Some of our guests prefer to experience more of a… thrill when hunting, so our guides take them places where they do advanced hunting which, surprise, surprise, is more dangerous, and requires techniques that the preserve doesn't want the world to know about."

Slade added, "If everyone knew our tricks, what would they need to come here for?"

"That's some pretty thin shit," Kahn said.

Maddox snorted and started to protest but Misty put up a hand. "Let's move on." She locked eyes with Slade and said, "Were you the one that moved Aldridge's body?"

Kahn rocked back slightly as he tried to control his surprise at Misty's directness.

Maddox's mouth fell open a crack, and he didn't speak, but the surprise on his face turned to worry as his cheeks reddened.

Slade did a better job at hiding his surprise and he managed, "What are you talking about?"

"There were clear signs of lividity," she said.

Maddox and Slade stayed silent.

"You know what that is, right?" Misty mocked. "After death, blood pools in the lowest parts of the body, causing purplish discoloration. Because the body was moved, the lividity patterns don't match the position where you claim to have discovered the body. And you told me you didn't touch the corpse. Didn't even roll it over. Right?"

Maddox sipped his coffee.

Slade stared at the hunter-green carpet.

"I also think Slade's estimated time of death is wrong," the deputy sheriff said. "Rigor mortis had passed, the body was bloated, and the skin was discolored and marbled with dark veins—signs of a body dead for more than twenty-four hours, not less, as Slade suggested when I was called in."

Maddox chuckled and looked at Slade, who looked like he'd lost ten pounds in the last five minutes. "That's an interesting take, but..." He shook his head. "I fail to see—if what you've said is true, how this information changes anything?"

Now it was Misty and Kahn's turn to stay silent. The guy had a point. Proving they'd lied or hidden certain facts didn't prove that Slade or the preserve had anything to do with Aldridge's death, but still... The murder scene had been messed with. That didn't appear to be in dispute, but the question that kept coming around was why?

A long silence filled with the stirrings of the kitchen staff and the distant hum of a vacuum hung over the table.

"Well, is there anything else we can help you with? Slade has to prepare for a deer hunt and camp cookout, and I've got duties to perform," Maddox said.

"Deer, huh?" Kahn said. "No dangerous stuff today?"

"Dangerous stuff?" Slade said.

Picking up on his cue, the deputy sheriff said, "Mr. Tanner said that's why he didn't have to sign an NDA. Because he wasn't going after the dangerous stuff. What was he referring to?"

"I don't rightly know," Maddox said.

"The Ozark Howler?" Kahn didn't know if it was smart to throw the cryptid's name out there, but what was done was done.

Maddox looked at Slade, and the men broke into a slow-growing laughter. "The Howler? Really? That's what this is all about?"

"You're kidding, right?" Slade said, but something in the tone of the man's voice told Kahn the guy was being disingenuous.

Kahn and Misty said nothing.

Maddox shook his head, a sly smirk spreading over his face. "The Ozark Howler isn't real, Mr. Kahn, and it's time you stopped pretending it is. Let's be honest: if a giant, horned beast with glowing yellow eyes had been roaming the Ozarks for centuries, we'd have more than campfire stories and blurry photos by now."

"There's no reliable sightings, no credible physical evidence—nothing!" Slade said, but it was easy to see that his outrage was manufactured. "Believers cling to folklore and exaggerated tales, but there's zero scientific backing for this so-called Howler. It's like chasing Bigfoot or the Loch Ness Monster; it's fun to imagine, but that doesn't make it real."

The pair was on a roll, and Misty and Kahn exchanged glances as Maddox continued.

"The Ozarks are remote, yes, but not so remote that a creature the purported size of the Howler could hide forever. Hunters, hikers, and trail cameras would've captured something more substantial by now. Instead, all we have are tall tales recycled from one generation to the next. These legends are rooted in fear and superstition, not facts."

"You protest a bit too strongly," Kahn said.

"Really?" Slade said. "People like you think every strange noise and shadow in the woods is evidence of the Howler when in reality, it's just a cougar, a bobcat, a bear, or even the wind. The Ozark Howler is nothing more than a myth—a spooky bedtime story to entertain tourists and frighten kids."

"So, you don't offer Ozark Howler hunts to your premium guests?" Misty said.

A laugh that sounded like a bark escaped Maddox's lips. "That might be the craziest thing I ever heard."

"Really? And so is covering up the details of Aldridge's death," Misty said.

Maddox shook his head.

"Because your guest was killed while on a Howler hunt, by a Howler," Kahn said. He could make wild accusations, but the deputy sheriff couldn't.

Maddox stood and looked at Slade, who surged to his feet. "I think we're done here. Is there anything else I can help you with today?" The lodge master's face was frozen in a tight smile, but if his eyes were guns Misty and Kahn would've been bullet-ridden.

"Not today," Misty said. She sipped her coffee and showed no sign of getting up.

Maddox nodded, and he and Slade headed for the door.

When Maddox's hand grasped the door handle, the deputy sheriff said, "Kahn is going to be setting up multiple stands and blinds out in the preserve. I'd like you to dedicate a few people to him, at least for the next few days. You are to instruct your guides to avoid the northeastern quadrant including the Borderland Pass area." She downed the rest of her coffee and pressed to her feet.

Maddox nodded as he said, "Of course."

As Kahn and Misty exited the conference room the deputy sheriff said, "If I find out you're lying to me this old lady is gonna burn you down."

Maddox rolled his eyes and Slade chuckled.

"Laugh it up, fuzzball," Misty said.

6

Six hours later, Kahn and two of the preserve's guides, Blair Stone, and a young alpha known as Buck, left staging area two and headed for the northeastern quadrant via ATVs. The morning mist had lifted, and the sharp tang of pine hung in the air, the gentle breeze stirring the tree canopy and the weeds and wildflowers that ran along the edge of the trail.

Misty had offered to come along, but like an aging sports hero, Kahn wanted to save the deputy sheriff for when he really needed her. She had spoken with the sheriff who made a few phone calls, and she was driving to Little Rock to meet with a State Special Investigator and share what she had discovered about Aldridge's murder.

Kahn was surprised Maddox had assigned Blair to him. The woman was known as a straight shooter, and she wasn't inclined to sing the company song, but still... It showed that Maddox was doing his best to appear as though he were doing everything possible to aid the hunt and the investigation. Buck, well, Kahn didn't know the man, but based on a small sample he didn't like the overconfident, inexperienced youngster. Regardless of motivations, Kahn was happy to have them both. They would serve as his backup, and there was nothing better than a little help when things went sideways, which they always did.

The spot where he'd seen the Howler drinking from the stream was still a few miles distant, but the trio split up. He sent Blair east, where she would circle around and set up her tree stand between the interstate and Kahn's location. Buck would set up to the west. His backup would be too far away to holler to, but close enough that they could be on the scene fast if he needed them. The deepest part of Borderland Pass cut through the preserve to the north, and if the beast fled that way there would be no chasing after it. If the beast went south, toward the lodge, Slade and his people would have to deal with it.

Neither hunting guide asked what they were hunting for because they'd been briefed by Maddox. The company line was the trio was pursuing a large bear exhibiting unusual behavior. Misty contacted the state troopers, and highway patrol officers watching the local section of I-49 would keep an eye out for any unusual animal activity along the interstate.

The Honda cackled as Kahn brought the ATV to a stop and killed the engine. Though he had a lot of gear to haul, he wanted to keep the hunting site as pure as possible, so he'd planned for a three-mile hike through the rough Ozark terrain. There was still a couple of hours of daylight left, which was more than enough time to get to his spot and set up his elevated blind.

He'd procured another Remington 700, and he slung it over his shoulder as he dismounted. A gear cart, not unlike a hand truck with beefed-up wheels, was attached to the load rack of the ATV. It held his pop-up blind and its aluminum stand, which weighed over a hundred pounds, along with the rest of his hunting gear, ammunition, and other supplies.

Once free of the ATV, Kahn snapped open the cart's extender arm and made sure everything was secure. He checked his Beretta in its holster, slipped on his pack, and hung his goggles over the ATV's handlebars as he pulled the key free of the ignition and dropped it in a pocket. He marked the location of the machine on his phone's GPS, stowed the device, and painted his face black using the ATV's side mirror.

Getting to the dell took longer than he'd anticipated. He couldn't find his original path, and trailblazing quietly took time. So it was that as the sun dipped below the tree line Kahn stared down into the hollow, the stream murmuring over stones, the scene unusually quiet as the day chorus packed up their instruments and the night symphony prepared for the evening performance.

A fawn drank from the stream, its narrow head bowed, its white tail like a torch in the growing dusk. The wind was out of the west, which was normal, so Kahn waited until the deer was finished drinking and had moved on before he worked his way around the dell to its eastern edge. There were animal trails crisscrossing through the waist-high weeds that clogged the edge of the stream's banks, and Kahn went about setting a few trigger warnings and traps.

He filled several cans he'd brought with pebbles from along the stream's edge and used them to construct three tripwire alarms using thin line that he strung across animal trails. If the Howler tripped the wire the sound of rattling stones in metal would announce its presence.

Kahn also installed two motion-activated trail cameras equipped with infrared sensors that would send alerts to Kahn's phone when motion was detected, offering both an early warning and visual confirmation of the Howler's approach.

There wasn't enough time to create a pit trap with spikes or a net trap, but Kahn had packed supplies to construct a log deadfall and snares.

He used a dead tree branch that was hanging precariously over a heavily trodden deer path to create a deadfall with a rope. If the Howler snagged the rope, the branch would get tugged from its perch onto the beast. Kahn estimated that the Howler weighed over a thousand pounds, so the snares were designed to entangle the creature so Kahn could move in for the kill. He strung plastic-coated cables along two paths and baited each with a small chunk of raw meat.

With that done he set about baiting the area with his Special Sauce. The concoction was an aged brew of blood, rotten chicken innards and meat that stewed in a sealed barrel for months before the liquid was siphoned off and placed in a squeeze bottle. A little bit of the stuff stank so badly that one drop in the lodge's kitchen would trigger a dreaded deep clean. Kahn emptied half his squeeze bottle, leaving the bait on the same trails where he'd set the traps and the trigger warnings.

Branches creaked and cracked as the wind argued and the orange glow of the setting sun peeled through the forest and cast daggers of light over the dell, the stream glistening like tiny diamonds floated on its surface. Kahn selected a bare patch surrounded by a thicket of brambles at a turn in the river where sediment and debris had accumulated, creating a small pond-like backwater that was filled with smallmouth bass. Fishing was one of the game preserve's lesser thrills, but angler excursions were offered weekly, especially during trout season.

Kahn unfolded the six-foot tripod tower base, which was made entirely of steel. Its powder-coated finish was designed to withstand the elements, and its adjustable legs allowed for stable placement, even on uneven or sloped ground.

He lowered the ladder, double-checked the contents of his pack, and climbed up to the platform. While standing atop the ladder, Kahn unfolded and set up the blind, which was nothing more than a five-foot by five-foot fabric square that provided woodland camouflage and protection from the elements. It had large, zippered windows, offering multiple vantage points for shooting or scouting while maintaining a low profile. The enclosed design also helped control Kahn's scent, and the height offered a strategic vantage point to observe wildlife and improved shooting accuracy.

Heart racing, Kahn dropped his pack and leaned the rifle against it as he pulled free the Beretta and placed it atop the backpack. He unfolded a camping stool and sat, but as soon as his ass hit canvas his stomach started rumbling, so he retrieved beef jerky and water. He made sure his radio was set on silent before setting it atop the pile of gear. The trio had agreed on radio silence unless there was an emergency, and texting would be used for updates and check-ins. That was possible thanks to the signal booster at the lodge.

Buck and Blair had hang-on tree stands, and as Kahn glanced at his watch, he figured the pair would be in position. He texted, "Status?" into the three-way group chat.

Blair responded in seconds. "In position. Nothing out of the ordinary so far."

Eleven minutes slipped away, and Kahn's stomach was beginning to stir when Buck responded with, "Nothing to report."

Dusk faded to darkness as the gurgle of water rushing over stones rose above the chorus of the night beasts and the faint hum of I-49. Sitting in a hunting blind, nature's music lulling him toward sleep as he stared out at the moonlit darkness used to be one of Kahn's favorite things to do. There used to be no questions, no people polluting his mind and scattering his thoughts, making him remember. But now... There was nothing in the blind but memories, and those memories just wouldn't let him be.

Kahn closed his eyes, Evelyn's screeching wail splitting his head.

The details of the coffee shop were no longer there, and Kahn and his wife sat alone at a corner table, the gray blurry walls surrounding them like the inside of a cloud. There was no one in the world except them.

"What does this mean?" Kahn had asked, but he'd known what the news meant. It meant the end of his life. The end of his family.

"It means..." Evelyn looked down at the table, tears welling in her eyes. "If you can't," she shook her head. "I don't know what to say."

"I'm sorry, Evelyn. I love you and Jenna more than anything. You know that. But I can't..."

"You're weak," she hissed, her eyes burning like cinders, her mouth disappearing into a thin red line.

The other customers hidden in the gray cloud surrounding the couple murmured and the air crackled with lightning-like energy.

Anger surged through Kahn. He was angry at the world, at God, and at his wife, but mostly the rage he felt was directed at himself. None of this was his fault, but did that matter? He needed to step up. He needed to be a man. Tough. Resilient. A provider. So far, he'd failed miserably.

"I guess I am," Kahn pushed out. He'd never thought of himself as weak, but his wife was right.

Evelyn got to her feet, slammed the rest of her wine, and picked up her purse.

Kahn grabbed her wrist. "Don't leave. Please. We need to—"

"What, Kahn? What do we need to do?" She was screaming, and her rage had torn away the gray backdrop hiding the coffee shop like a heatwave smothered clouds. Blank faces stared at him, and the pissing of milk being scalded was the only sound.

"Fix this," he said, his voice low and frail. "I can fix this."

"You can't fix anything, Kahn." She started to walk away.

"Wait!"

She turned one last time.

"I love you. And Jenna. What am I supposed to do?"

"You know damn well what you need to do, but you're too pathetic to do it," Evelyn said, her face wrenched in a twisted scowl. "What you can do is help me pay for things, but if you truly love Jenna, stay away."

"No!" Kahn vaulted to his feet and slammed the table.

"Yes," she said. "You had your chance and we're…" Evelyn shook her head. "We're permanently broken. Goodbye, Jake."

Kahn watched his wife leave, and she faded to nothing as the dirty clouds swirled and he sat alone in blackness. Distant memories of packing, leaving his life and shop behind, and disappearing into the forest blended with the darkness, an unnatural heat spreading through him as Kahn rubbed his eyes. He could barely see Evelyn's face anymore. It was as if she was being erased from his memory and he feared the same thing would happen with Jenna.

A rattle of pebbles hitting metal rang over the dell, and a shadow fell across the moonlit stream as the night creatures' singing fell three octaves.

7

Kahn pressed the rangefinder's scope to his eye as he trained it on the elongated shadow. He pressed a button that activated the unit's laser, and the rangefinder emitted a low pulse as the laser bounced off the ground behind the shadow and returned to the device. The distance was then calculated based on the time the laser took to return to the unit.

Seventy-two yards, with an estimated angle of elevation of thirty-eight percent. He put the device atop his pack, lifted the Remington, and adjusted the calibration of the rifle's scope to coincide with the rangefinder's results.

The shadow got longer, but vegetation hid the creature. Kahn's skin itched with anticipation as he peered through the rifle scope.

A gust of wind rattled the tree canopy, and the shadow disappeared as if it had never been there.

Kahn leaned back and dropped his aim but continued to peer through the rifle's scope at the glistening stream and dark shadowy underbrush that encroached to the river's edge. The evening beasts chortled and buzzed, and Kahn waited.

And waited.

And waited some more.

Midnight slipped away as the moon arced across the cloud-torn sky, pinpricks of stars bleeding through the haze. He was dozing, his eyelids drooping, his muscles aching, his stomach bitching for more food, when the sound of sniffing worked its way into the blind. At first, Kahn thought it was the wind, and all evidence supported that belief. Despite the trigger warning's announcement, none of the traps had been activated, and as he checked the surrounding area with the night vision goggles nothing bigger than a squirrel stirred.

But the breathing and huffing got louder and more aggressive. The sniffing became clearer, a low, rhythmic inhalation as if the air itself was humming with deliberate precision. Deep and guttural, the low rumble reverberated just beyond the edge of sight, stirring the stillness of the forest. Each sniff brought a soft, almost inaudible huff, and the underbrush to the east rustled ever so slightly as the rhythmic sound grew louder.

The sniffing paused as if the creature had homed in on something— its target or its curiosity piqued. When the sniffing resumed it was closer, its rhythm more insistent, the breaths heavier and laden with intent. Kahn felt the tension in the air as the sounds of the unseen animal shifted and drew closer. With every measured sniff Kahn felt like an invisible hunt was underway and he was the prey.

Kahn fumbled for his flashlight and made sure it was close at hand.

The sound of shuffling feet, followed by a growl filled the blind before pebbles ringing against metal broke the stillness.

He pressed the binoculars to his eyes and widened his search area as he slowly panned his head from north to south as he peered east.

A branch snapped, and there was a loud growl, followed by a whimper, and then everything went still except the undercurrent of the night music.

Kahn got to his feet, pulled on his pack, and grabbed the rifle.

The blind shook, and Kahn froze, his eyes fixed on the dark opening that led to the ladder, his nerves poking the underside of his skin.

A bark-howl followed by the Howler's telltale cackle-laugh echoed inside Kahn's head. The beast was close, and Kahn frantically searched, cycling between the binoculars and the rifle scope.

With a screech of metal, the blind shook again.

Kahn steadied himself, the chill of the evening air settling in his bones. The stand's metal base creaked slightly as he shifted his weight. Without warning, a deep, violent shudder ran through the structure, and the sudden jolt caused Kahn to stagger as the stand lurched sideways.

The world tilted as the stand toppled, the metal legs screaming with a sharp, grating screech. Kahn grabbed a tent pole, his hand tightening around the cold steel, his knuckles whitening as gravity took hold. The stand fell over, its base slamming into the earth with enough force to rattle his teeth. He was tossed sideways, his body tangled in the framework of the fallen structure and the fabric of the pop-up blind. The wind rushed from his lungs as the impact jolted him to the core. Metal groaned and twisted beneath him, the once-sturdy tripod now a crumpled heap. Pain flared in his wounded arm as he lay entwined in the blind's remains, the acrid taste of dirt and adrenaline sharp on his tongue.

Kahn was disoriented, his heart pounding in his ears, the unexpected violence of the fall leaving him momentarily stunned as he tried to catch his breath, the cool night settling in around him.

The sniffing resumed.

Strong and weatherproof, the tent blind, which could be set up on the ground or atop its stand, was crafted from polyester, but its thin material made it partially transparent and allowed light and faint shapes to pass through.

A massive hulking monstrosity loomed next to the destroyed blind. The beast stood on its hind legs, its front claws pawing the wreckage, searching as it growled and sniffed.

Kahn felt around for the rifle, couldn't find it, then reached for the Beretta only to find an empty holster. He'd placed the gun atop his backpack and now everything was scattered about the crumbled blind. If the Howler pounced, he was done for. Kahn stayed silent, his shallow breaths nothing but faint puffs. Then he remembered Blair and Buck. He padded his shirt, found his phone, and pulled it free.

With the Howler only feet away, the beast clawing at his hiding place, Kahn thumbed out an emergency message to his partners, ordering them to double-time it to his position.

His fingers moved silently across the phone's screen, barely making a sound, yet the beast fell silent as if it could sense even the faintest of his taps. The creature's stillness felt deliberate, like the beast was responding to the subtle vibrations of his actions and Kahn couldn't help but wonder if the Howler could detect more than just sound.

A paw raked the polyester, and three slices appeared in the fabric.

Kahn gasped, the breath stolen from his lungs. Panic surged through him, his heart pounding as he strained against the unforgiving wreckage. Just moments ago, he'd been sheltered from the dangers lurking in the woods. Now, he was helpless prey, ensnared in the remnants of his sanctuary.

As he searched for a weapon, a low growl reverberated through the air, sending the invisible ants marching down his spine. The dark shape of the Howler loomed above him, a monstrous shadow with piercing, glowing eyes that cut through the night. A wave of dread crashed over him. He had come to the Ozarks seeking refuge from the chaos of the outside world, hoping to find solace in its isolation. But now, he realized, he was facing a terrifying reality—he was about to die at the hands of a primal creature that few believed existed.

There was no time left. Kahn needed a weapon, and he remembered the knife strapped to his leg. He pulled the blade, its familiar weight a small comfort. He wouldn't go down without a fight. Taking a deep breath to steady himself, he prepared to cut through the fabric and free himself.

The creature's breathing was heavy and labored, the scent of wet fur and earth filling Kahn's nostrils. With an eerie silence, the beast pawed at the remnants of the tent, its claws tearing through the fabric as if it were paper. Kahn heard the rustling, the sound of nails scraping against metal, and his heart raced faster.

A violent tug ripped apart the tent's fabric, and the Howler's massive head burst forth, its eyes glowing yellow in the dim light. The creature's broad snout and gaping jaws exposed menacing teeth, ready to unleash terror. Beneath its shaggy fur, powerful muscles rippled with each movement, and a deep, guttural snarl erupted from the beast.

But the creature looked... different. Its horns were nubs, as if they were just growing in, and the dark monkey-like leathery skin around its eye sockets was smooth and free of life wrinkles. And was it smaller—a youngster?

Kahn felt a strange vibration course through his bones as if each one were resonating with an unseen force. The snarl ran through him like bad clams, unsettling and visceral. Adrenaline jolted him, heightening his senses and sharpening his focus as he coiled to strike.

With a primal scream, the beast lunged, jaws snapping closed.

Kahn rolled, narrowly avoiding the creature's attack. The knife glinted as he swung it, aiming for the beast's exposed flank. Steel met fur, and Kahn felt the resistance, the blade cutting through as he landed a shallow gash.

The Howler pulled back and raged in pain.

Kahn crab-walked backward, the torn tent rippling around him as he freed himself. Breathing heavily, he gripped the knife tighter, his eyes locked with the Howler's wild gaze. Blood dripped from the wound he had inflicted, painting the monster's fur crimson as the beast unleashed its fury.

Knowing it was his last chance, and that a good offense was better than a good defense, Kahn charged, knife out before him like a miniature lance. He ducked beneath a swipe from the Howler's massive paw, and struck at the creature with the blade, aiming for the beast's throat.

But the creature was quick, and it dodged as it attacked with its front paws.

The air crackled and Kahn felt the rush of wind as the claws missed him, but the force of the knife swing knocked him off balance. He stumbled, his foot caught on a rock, and he tumbled to the ground, the blade flying from his grasp.

Desperation took hold, the Howler bearing down on him as Kahn scrambled to retrieve the knife, his fingers brushing the cool metal. He grabbed the weapon just as the beast lunged again, jaws wide.

Some moments last a lifetime, and years can often feel like minutes, but Kahn had been in the timelessness of the crosshairs before, and muscle memory took control. He went limp and collapsed as he swung the knife upward in a desperate attempt to stab the Howler's midsection.

The Howler roared, jaws flexed open, snout pointed like an arrow, its eyes ablaze with fury as Kahn's strike missed and the beast sailed over him.

Kahn rolled, pressed to his feet, and dove behind the wreckage of the stand, but the fluttering canvas and the tangle of connected bent metal poles were all that separated Kahn from the beast.

All his knowledge about close-quarters encounters with large wild animals surged into his mind. The key was to avoid sudden movements. Loud noises or aggressive actions were risky; animals didn't respond well to them. More often than not, they would retreat when faced with aggression, but that wasn't guaranteed. Every move had to be calculated, every action deliberate. But calculated moves required thought and time, and in the absence of both raw instinct and emotion took control or death was the likely outcome.

The beast's yellow eyes stared at Kahn through the wreckage, its crackling breaths like the groan of a small engine. It lunged at him with its baseball mitt-sized paws extended. Sickle-shaped claws tore into the twisted metal that had been the blind's tripod base. Steel shrieked and mewed as it bent, and the entire pile of wreckage was pushed at Kahn like a tidal wave of garbage.

He spun on his toes and ran, the glowing stream cutting through the darkness before him. Wet sand sucked at his feet, the arguing of rending metal and the harsh growling of the Howler chasing after him.

River stones and vegetation made the edge of the stream slippery, and Kahn chose his steps carefully as he half skipped, half ran into the stream. The water was only a foot deep, but it felt like it rose to his waist, each frantic step twice as hard as the one before it.

The stream was thin, and Kahn splashed through the shallow water to the other side without falling. As he stumbled into the greenery on the opposite bank he spared a glance back.

Moonlight lit the scene in harsh black and white, the Howler silhouetted against the tree line to the east. The beast struggled with the remains of the stand, the bent metal poles catching on the creature's fur and tangling up the beast's appendages. With a mighty shriek, the Howler jumped straight in the air, flailing and twisting like a cat as it threw off the blind's wreckage and landed on all fours, its mouth open in a toothy grin, a low gurgle-cackling rising over the rumble of the river.

A thick line of evergreens loomed ahead, and panic surged through him. The guns, his gear, it was all behind him. But so were all his snares and tripwires. That was a good thing, but was it? He knew where they were, and he could use them as weapons.

Kahn made a hard left and tracked the eastern edge of the stream, his feet slipping on slick river stones as he pushed through waist-high weeds.

The Howler let loose a deafening roar as it charged into the stream, its massive form crashing through the water. Beneath its powerful stride, the ground trembled, echoing through the forest like the ominous growl of an approaching storm.

There was a gap in the vegetation, a narrow sandy section where the stream kicked west. Kahn cut right, leaped over running water, and plunged into the water reeds on the opposite bank.

8

The night air was thick with moisture and fear, and it pressed in on Kahn with the weight of something ancient and untamed, a primal gravity that suffocated his heart and fooled his senses. His breaths came in shallow gasps as he stumbled from the water reeds onto a narrow deer path that was scarcely more than a thin strip of dirt worn smooth by countless hooves and the passage of time. The trail twisted away from the stream into the dense vegetation beyond the sighing water reeds.

Kahn followed the path, his pace steady despite the roots and vines encroaching on the hardpacked dirt and pulling at his feet. A tall oak tree loomed ahead, towering above the undergrowth, and relief flooded through him as he recognized where he was.

Moonlight knifed through the thin clouds, painting the weeds a patchwork of silver and black. He knew where his traps were—basically, but in the dark, with the beast on his heels...

A twig snapped underfoot as he ran, Kahn's heart pounding in time with each thump of the Howler's paws as the beast closed in. Its rattling growl-hiss echoed through the night, growing louder with every step, driving Kahn forward in a desperate sprint.

The path curved sharply to the left as it narrowed and became barely wide enough for Kahn to navigate without snagging his jacket on the blackberry brambles that crowded the edge of the trail. The wind whispered and sighed, its voice calm but unsettling as it stirred the greenery with a ghostly cadence.

Kahn's boot caught on a root, and he nearly went down, but he skidded like he was riding a wave and managed to stay on his feet. His heart hammered in his chest, adrenaline surging as he pushed on, his muscles burning.

The trill and vibration of his phone drew his attention, and Kahn pulled the device and saw that he'd received a notification from one of his trail cameras. He chuckled to himself as he ran on, his gaze shifting to the camera strapped to a fallen tree that stretched like a wooden curb through the weeds.

He glanced back and shadows slithered and shifted, a flicker of something massive and black, too fast for his eyes to fully register. But it was there. And it was coming.

The path split in four directions and Kahn headed right. His deadfall trap wasn't far, and as he leaped over one of his snares, he turned up the juice, his legs pistoning as he ran faster than he had since high school when he competed in the hundred meters. His chest burned, but he ignored it along with the numerous flashing red lights on his mental dashboard that warned of an impending breakdown.

In the gloom with the moonlight cutting through the thin clouds, the tripwire looked like a strand of silver hair, and Kahn's gaze strayed upward to the branch poised to fall. He skipped over the line and slowed, adrenaline sending shards of pain to the tips of his fingers and toes.

Kahn smiled as the twang of the tripwire snapping cut through the huffing of the beast, the gurgle of the river, and the distant hum of the interstate.

The limb was tugged from its position, swung in a wide arc, and missed the Howler as it twisted mid-stride, hardly losing a step.

Kahn gritted his teeth as tree branches hanging over the trail clawed at his face and arms. He couldn't stop. Not now. The Howler's roar split the night behind him, closer than before, a sound so full of rage it made the maggots in Kahn's stomach churn.

All the traps were behind him now and the beast was too close for games. He needed his weapons—the knife just wouldn't cut it—he laughed silently at his mental wordplay, the crickets back at full blast and cheering the Howler on.

The beast was so close Kahn imagined he felt its breath on his neck, and panic drove him as he lunged off the path into a thicket of weeds.

A roar followed by a menacing gurgle-hiss rumbled through the darkness as weeds whipped Kahn's face and tore at his legs. He couldn't see the stream, but he surged toward the sound of water rippling over stones. With the creature behind him, if he could get back to the river, he could track it to the wreckage of the blind and his guns.

The rattle of stones bouncing around inside a can rose over the night orchestra, followed by the thwap of a rope going taut, and the yelp of an animal.

Kahn slowed as he looked back and didn't see the eyes of the beast. He stopped running, the stream a silver line before him in the darkness.

Screeching and wailing carried from the weeds, the unmistakable sound of an animal in its death throes. It sounded like a deer to Kahn, and judging by the panicked bleats and frantic thuds and huffs of struggle the animal had been caught in one of his snares.

A guttural growl, deep and feral, drowned out the deer's mewing. Kahn's breath hitched, and for a moment, he stood frozen, torn between running and going back—to do what? It was time to kill this thing, but to do that...

Kahn headed south along the stream. He'd gone in a half circle, and the wreckage of his hunting blind wasn't far.

A final screech, followed by a crack that sounded like a small tree breaking carried down the stream, though Kahn knew it was no tree. The night band stopped playing, and the sound of tearing meat, snapping bones, and the huff and wheeze of the Howler as it attacked Kahn's catch drowned out the ringing in his head.

When he reached the tangled mess of metal poles and torn fabric he paused, listening. The grotesque murmur of flesh being torn and eaten filled the night, but the Howler had stopped chasing him, and Kahn set about searching the wreckage for his weapons.

He pulled on the knot of poles and metal shrieked. Kahn froze as he stared into the darkness in the direction of the Howler.

The sounds of the Howler feasting stopped.

Sweat dripped down Kahn's forehead into his eyes despite the night chill.

A growl, part anger, and part curiosity echoed through the silvery gloom.

Kahn considered bolting again, but how far would he get? So far, he'd been lucky, but luck never lasts. Though it seemed like an hour, only five minutes had slipped away since he'd called for backup, and Blair and Buck were still a few minutes out. If he could find a gun...

Noise be damned, he dropped to his knees, searching around like a blind person desperately looking for his cane. He pawed through the wreckage, pulling away fabric and bending and jerking on metal. He saw his pack, but it was flipped over and everything he'd had atop it—his Beretta, had been thrown aside.

His fingers found metal and hope surged through him as he grasped it, only to discover it was his Maglite.

The crackle of bending and breaking vegetation carried from the swaying weeds.

Kahn's pulse quickened, and with no time left, he flicked on the flashlight, its beam like a white storm in the darkness. Seconds ticked away, Kahn expecting to be mauled at any moment, the light bouncing around as he searched. The edge of the flashlight's beam caught the gleam of the Beretta and Kahn went for it.

Metal poles poked at him as he pressed into the wreckage, crawling with the light in one hand, his other stretching out, the gun three feet from his grasp.

The grunting and huffing resumed, as did the horror of tearing meat and smacking jaws.

Kahn wiggled in deeper, stretching, his arm threaded through a knot of metal poles, his back aching. The tips of his fingers brushed the weapon, and he pulled at it, the gun sliding through the dirt. After a few more seconds of fiddling, his fingers massaging the gun to move it toward him, Kahn grasped the weapon and pulled back, metal shrieking and twisting.

He aimed the gun at the darkness that hid the Howler, and as he got to his feet, he checked the weapon and verified that it was ready to fire.

Another notification from his phone and Kahn pulled the device free. It was his second trail camera, and Kahn's gaze shifted toward the tall weeds that hid the beast and its meal, then he tapped his phone.

The small image showed a dark figure moving down a deer trail—Blair, her rifle at the ready, her eye pressed to the gun's sight.

Kahn's nerves settled to a dull roar with cold steel in his hand, and he went back to searching the wreckage. He pulled free his pack and was able to wedge the rifle free, though he broke its scope in the process.

A flashlight glowed in the west, its cloud of light leaking into the dell. Buck.

The breeze brought the smell of blood and the earthy, pungent mix of wet fur, sweat, and the musty odor of damp soil. There was an underlying hint of body oils and grime that was magnified by the dampness, and Kahn recognized the Howler's stink.

He killed and stowed the Maglite, pulled out the night vision binoculars, slipped on his pack, and slung the rifle over his shoulder. As he had prior, Kahn held the night vision binoculars in one hand and the Beretta in the other. The binoculars weren't much use when he was on the move, but there were deep patches of shadow everywhere, and night vision was the only way to keep from getting ambushed.

With help on the way, Kahn left the wreckage of the hunting blind behind for a second time as he inched back into the tall weeds, tracking the sound of the Howler as it feasted.

A gunshot rang out, followed by an angry roar.

Kahn picked up his pace, brushing aside weeds, gun up, his head on a swivel. His boots crunched over vines and fallen leaves, but it was the smell that hit him—a pungent rot, thick and wet, like a wound festering in the sun. He slowed, his grip tightening on the Beretta, his senses coming into focus. The sound of buzzing flies joined the chorus of crickets, and as he broke free of the tall weeds his stomach lurched.

What was left of the deer hung awkwardly from a snare trap, its body contorted at an unnatural angle. Its neck, stretched taut by the crude wire, had nearly been severed, the skin peeled back to reveal muscle, tendon, and bone. Its fur was matted with dark blood, and the deer's flanks had been ripped open, the delicate skin shredded by claws or teeth. Ribs jutted out like splintered wood, snapped clean through, exposing the pulpy remains of organs. Chunks of meat hung from the bones, half-chewed, with patches of fur torn away. Blood soaked into the ground beneath it, turning the earth into a muddy, rust-colored mess.

The Howler was nowhere to be seen, and as Blair stepped from the weeds, Kahn said, "I guess you missed it."

"Are you alright?" she asked as she looked around, searching for the Howler.

"I'll live, but it took down my stand." She started to say something but Kahn held up a hand. "Which way did it go?"

She pointed south.

Kahn stowed the binoculars, retrieved his flashlight, and turned it on as he inched closer to the deer corpse.

Blair made a crude sound of disgust.

The gashes that scored the ground around the deer's carcass were so deep that roots and dirt were thrown about like something had dug in with a feral rage. Kahn could almost hear the low growl of a predator in his mind, jaws gnashing as it tore through flesh, its hunger wild and insatiable. The snare trap hadn't killed the deer quickly—it had been left to suffer, hanging there, a struggling feast for the Howler.

Kahn traced the trail of blood splatter with the flashlight, seeing the way it fanned out, sprayed in arcs where the deer had kicked in its final throes. But the real horror was the face—or what used to be a face. The deer's head, still twisted in the wire, had been chewed almost beyond recognition. Its eyes were gone, plucked out, leaving dark, oozing sockets, and the jaw was half-shattered, with chunks of its tongue hanging from the open maw like tattered cloth.

Buck burst onto the scene, swinging his weapon around like he was playing soldier. "Everyone steady?" he asked.

That was the question. Kahn opened his mouth to say the Howler had attacked him and knocked him out of his stand like a baby bird falling from its nest, but then he remembered Buck, and maybe even Blair, would think he was nuts. He said, "Something knocked over my stand and mauled a deer caught in one of my traps."

"So why are we standing around? Which way—"

Kahn surged into motion, ignoring the arrogant ass as he tracked the beast south. He heard Blair and Buck behind him, and he slowed and put up a hand. Patches darker than shadows hid behind every plant, and moonlight gave every object a shimmering silver glow that distorted its size and depth. His stomach protested, his thoughts going to his daughter as he pushed through thick weeds, heart hammering.

A hundred yards off at the center of a large patch of weeds a huge wedge of rock stuck from the ground like a rotten tooth, and atop it, backlit by the glow of the moon, was an Ozark Howler.

Kahn pressed his eyes to the binoculars.

The Howler was a grotesque fusion of predator and nightmare from another time, its head, like that of a great bear-cat, was massive and its features were twisted and exaggerated—its snout elongated, its teeth jagged and oversized in spots and undersized in others, as if some were coming in for the first time. And those eyes—two glowing orbs of fire that burned with intelligence through the glowing white light and vibrant greens of the night vision.

A branch snapped and Kahn looked over his shoulder.

"Sorry," mouthed Blair.

The creature's ears twitched, and it growled, low and menacing, as its yellow eyes found the trio.

9

To the south, the stream curved sharply eastward, its gentle flow cutting through weeds and water reeds. The bend led to a patch of tall weeds, which gradually disappeared into the shadows of a towering evergreen forest, the darkness beneath the trees deep and impenetrable. The wind died away, the tattered clouds settled, and thick streams of moonlight leaked through and painted the landscape in harsh black and white. Kahn looked through the binoculars again.

The patch of chest-high weeds ahead swayed gently, whispering as they brushed together, the wind rippling through them. Their tips shimmered in the night vision binocular's artificial glow, a surreal, electric green against the shadows. The weeds swelled in irregular clusters, some forming dense knots of vegetation, others spread thin. Dew clung to their surfaces, shining like liquid emeralds. The ground was rough and uneven, with mounds and scattered stones breaking up the terrain. Larger rocks encircled a massive boulder, atop which the Howler sat, watching from its high perch.

In the distance, the thick wall of the evergreen forest loomed, a mass of darker, deeper green beyond the weeds. The trees were huge, their branches locked in a silent battle. Pine needles spun and eddied, creating an eerie texture in Kahn's night vision, their sharp edges blurred by the distance. The trees swayed ever so slightly in rhythm with the wind, releasing the occasional flurry of needles. Beneath the canopy, the forest was swallowed by blackness.

It felt like there was something in the woods watching. The Ozarks breathed, alive with hidden movement, but concealed under a blanket of thick, untouchable greenery.

Kahn adjusted the night vision, and the world around him washed in a new series of ghostly green hues. His breath went still when his gaze locked onto the Ozark Howler silhouetted against the pale moonlight.

The creature was not yet fully grown, its horns just starting to grow in, and Kahn's past suspicions were verified. Its black fur was mottled with streaks of dark gray, and its body was lithe and sinewy, its muscles still developing. The Howler crouched with feline grace, its long legs poised as if ready to spring, its thick tail swaying. Two golden eyes burned through the night and sharp crescent-shaped fangs, half of what their fully grown length would be, protruded from its open maw.

This wasn't the mythical terror from the stories—at least, not yet. But even in its youth, the beast radiated a raw, primal energy that spoke to the monster it would become.

A growl rumbled over the weeds and Kahn let the binoculars fall to his chest where they dangled on their neck strap. With the fancy scope gone, Kahn aimed his rifle the old-school way as he prepared it to fire.

Blair sniffed and Buck coughed gently.

The shot was at the outer edge of Kahn's guarantee-zone, with a scope, and Kahn's finger hovered over the trigger. "Steady," he said, his voice barely more than a breath.

"I can make the shot," Buck whispered.

Blair sniffed again but said nothing.

The Howler moved—just a fraction, but enough to send a ripple of tension through the trio. It raised its head, sniffing the air, its massive chest expanding.

Kahn's mind raced. He wanted this over. Now. "On my mark," he whispered. "We aim for the head, all three of us. It'll bolt after that if it can, so make your first shot count."

Blair stepped up and positioned herself on Kahn's right, and Buck took the left flank, weapons up and ready to fire.

The Howler tilted its head slightly, its ears perking up as if it understood what Kahn had said and knew the plan. A growl rolled from the beast's throat, a threat, a warning.

Kahn steadied himself, his heartbeat slowing as his finger moved and touched the trigger. He experienced a moment of regret, as he always did before he took a life. Killing another living thing is a violation of the natural order, a rupture in the delicate balance that sustains life. In the animal kingdom, survival hinged on instinct and necessity, but when humans killed for reasons beyond survival—out of fear, greed, or power—it became a crime against nature.

For Kahn, the act of killing reverberated beyond the immediate loss, even though it was his job. The natural world thrived on balance, and when a life is taken without reverence or necessity, it's not just the creature that perishes.

But the Howler wasn't a cryptid to be feared because of legends and balance—it was feared because it survived and thrived in the darkness, blending with the mountains that birthed it, killing indiscriminately. Maybe not indiscriminately. The woods were the Howler's turf and regardless of how long humans had prowled the Ozarks, it was the beast's home.

"Now!" Kahn said, and three rifles fired almost in unison.

The crack of gunpowder expanding and the zip and whiz of bullets cutting the air echoed through the stillness.

For a heartbeat, everything went silent except the distant hum of I-49, the smell of gunpowder hanging in the air.

The Howler flinched, its head jerking back, but it didn't fall.

It roared a bone-chilling scream that tore through the night, urging birds into panicked flight. The Howler sprang from the rock, a swift blur of fur, claws, and teeth that vanished into the tall weeds. Its movement was so fast and fluid that it melted into the shadows, leaving only rustling weeds in its wake.

"I can't see it!" said Blair, her voice a tension level below panic. She was an experienced hunter, but there was a world of difference between hunting turkey, deer, and elk, compared to a relic from another era designed to be an apex predator among apex predators.

Weeds bent and snapped, and snarls mixed with labored breathing carried through the foliage.

"We need to take cover or we're—" said Buck, but he was cut off as the Ozark Howler burst from the vegetation, a missile of aggression, hatred, and primal power.

Kahn dove to the side.

The Howler crashed to the ground, its massive frame landing on all fours where Kahn had stood a moment before, dirt and dead leaves exploding into the air.

Buck scrambled back and fired a wild shot that knifed through the greenery.

Blair held her ground, her face a mask of determination. She fired and hit the Howler on its side, but the beast barely noticed.

The Howler's head turned, its fiery eyes locking on Blair.

"Oh, shit," she muttered, ducking as the beast lunged at her.

Kahn rolled to his feet.

The Howler bounded into Blair, swiping at her with claws that could tear through metal as it took her to the ground.

Blair bucked and heaved, trying to free herself, but she wasn't fast enough, and the beast was too strong and too big. The Howler's claws caught her across the stomach, ripping through her hunting vest and shirt. Blood sprayed in the moonlight as she cried out, her arms flailing in a final effort to free herself.

Buck fired and the bullet punched into the Howler's flank.

The creature jerked onto its hind legs and staggered, but didn't fall. It was relentless, driven by some force Kahn couldn't understand. The beast snarled, spinning to face Buck, its eyes burning with fury.

Blair was on the ground, clutching her chest, a dark rivulet of blood leaking from her mouth as her innards spilled onto the ground, her face pale but alive.

Kahn wanted to help her, but there was nothing he could do except get help, and he couldn't do that without first killing the Howler. He dropped his rifle and drew the Beretta, which was better for close-quarter work, and it had a full magazine of 9 MM parabellums.

The Howler cackled as it charged Buck.

Buck barely had time to aim his gun before the creature was on him.

With a thud that echoed over the chaos, the Howler slammed into Buck with the force of a freight train. He hit the ground hard, and he wheezed as the wind was knocked from his lungs and his gun skidded out of reach.

The Howler loomed over Buck, its jaws wide, saliva dripping from its jagged teeth onto the hunter's young face.

"Not today," Buck growled as he pulled his knife from his belt.

The Howler's head, its primary weapon, lunged forward, jaws wide, teeth glinting in the moonlight.

Kahn aimed the Beretta, fired, and kept on firing, the cloud of fury and loss filling him with anger.

Buck slashed upward, his blade sinking into the Howler's neck, the monster's open jaws a foot from his face.

The beast shrieked as it reared back, yellow eyes bulging as blood leaked from its wounds.

Kahn screamed in fury as the Beretta clicked empty, but he kept pulling the trigger, the snap of the hammer hitting metal rising above the whimpering Howler.

Buck stabbed his knife into the ground, got to his feet, and retrieved his gun.

The creature staggered, its movements slowing. It growled as its fiery eyes dimmed, and fell in a heap. As the beast took its final breaths its massive body inflated and deflated as it rolled about, flattening weeds.

"Finish it!" Kahn shouted.

Buck fired at point-blank range and double-tapped the beast between the eyes. The back of its head exploded, painting the surrounding greenery with blood that looked black in the moonlight.

The Howler let out one final, ear-splitting peal of rage, its body twitching as the last of its life drained away.

For a moment, there was only silence.

Blair was splayed out on the ground, her breathing ragged and wet, blood spilling from her mouth and from the gaping wound in her midsection.

Kahn rushed to her side, his heart pounding as he dropped to his knees, hands trembling as he tore open her hunting vest.

The Howler had slashed deep into her abdomen, its claws carving through skin and muscle. Blood, slick and dark, pooled beneath her in the dirt, and her intestines were exposed, glistening in the silvery gloom, the edges of her flesh ragged and torn as if she had been opened from the inside out. The smell of iron and raw meat mixed with damp earth choked the air.

"Blair, stay with me," Kahn said, desperately pressing his hands against the wound, trying to hold her insides together, but the blood was too much, slipping through his fingers in hot, sticky bursts. Her skin was pale and clammy, her breathing shallow and labored, each inhale a struggle.

Blair's eyes fluttered, glassy and unfocused as if she couldn't see Kahn. She coughed, and blood sprayed from her mouth, her lips quivering as she tried to speak, but only a weak, gurgling sound escaped her lips.

Kahn tightened his grip, his hands soaked crimson, his voice frantic. "Don't you dare die on me, Blair! Just hang on!"

But she was slipping away. Her body convulsed and twitched with the last remnants of life. Kahn's heart wrenched as he watched her pupils dilate, her gaze fixed on some distant place beyond the pain, beyond him. He screamed her name again, but she was gone, her body limp.

Kahn gagged.

Blair's intestines sagged through the slashes in her abdomen, and the coppery scent of blood filled his nostrils as he knelt, trembling, covered in her blood. The forest closed in around them, Blair's lifeless body a grim testament to the dead beast lying ten feet away.

"I've called for help," Buck said, but it was far too late. All the man's bravado had drained away and he looked like he'd lost a hundred pounds in the last five minutes. He still held his gun at the ready, but his eyes were glassy with tears, and his gaze constantly strayed to his dead teammate.

Kahn wiped his face with the back of his hand as he staggered over to the Howler, intending to kick the carcass until his foot hurt. Instead, he just stared, lost in the unique beast he and his partners had killed.

In death, there was no doubt that the Howler wasn't fully grown. Kahn figured it was one or two years old. Many of its teeth weren't fully formed or were broken, it had no battle scars, no mange wreathed its head, and its horns only protruded an inch from the beast's sloped forehead.

Youngling or not, the preserve had its pelt, and Kahn's contract was completed, though the price had been high. He didn't know if Blair was married or had children—he didn't think so, but still... He glanced at the woman's fallen body and his stomach burned with shame and anger. He should have been better. Faster.

Kahn stood next to the creature, panting, his heart racing.

It was over.

Or so he thought.

In the distance, a cackling-howl carried from the trees, harsh and violent.

And then another.

10

The Lodge at Borderland Game Preserve, Ozark Mountains, Arkansas, U.S.

8:47 AM CST, August 18th, 2022

As defined by the modern proclivities of the time, a Shit Show was a spectacle of pure chaos, where everything that can go wrong does so in the most catastrophic way imaginable. Kahn likened it to watching a train derail in slow motion, yet with an almost comical level of absurdity. Control, logic, and order had all left the building, leaving behind a tangled mess of confusion, mistakes, and flaring tempers.

Kahn had been to many Shit Shows, some of his making, and some to which he'd received gratis tickets. As he watched Maddox give orders and scramble to contain the damage, he knew the lodge manager was only making things worse, like trying to put out a grease fire with water.

Conference Room A was filled, but mostly with observers. Maddox and the sheriff were tangled up with the staties, and everyone was arguing and trying to lay blame as they debated where the strange animal corpse—their words, not Kahn's—was going to be put on ice.

Kahn's gaze strayed to the door every few moments in anticipation of the arrival of the feds, or the state investigators who would swoop in and take the Howler and then pretend the beast didn't exist. Blair's death would be chalked up to the ever-convenient "unknown wild animal" and that would be the end of that, at least for Kahn.

He was a spectator at the show along with Misty, Buck, Slade, and others he didn't know. Sections of I-49 were probably a white line nightmare because half the on-duty troopers had been standing around waiting for the briefing, which in the end amounted to "if you see something, say something."

Kahn had decided to keep his suspicions about the preserve selling Howler hunts in his back pocket for another time. He'd given it lots of thought as he stood around waiting for the transport back to the lodge the prior night, and he'd stewed as he lay in his bed staring at the ceiling. He didn't have any solid proof, and all the locals had heard tales of the Howler, and his credibility would take a hit. Misty agreed, although she hated withholding information in an active investigation. It reeked of a mark on her record.

The night had been a long one, though Snoop made an appearance and even came inside where he'd curled up on a chair. Kahn had fallen into a shallow sleep, and when his alarm went off, his muscles aching from the prior day's overexertion, he'd been anything but eager to listen to Maddox's bullshit.

An announcement was made that all information provided at the meeting was confidential, but Kahn knew that meant less than a promise from a politician. Cops and guides would tell husbands and wives, who would tell family and friends, and by week's end, the tale of the Ozark Howler and the terror it caused in Borderland Pass would be added to the long list of Howler legends.

With nothing really settled, and no real plan, the meeting broke up and Maddox and the sheriff wandered over to where Misty and Kahn sat sipping coffee. If there was one thing Kahn liked about the preserve it was its exotic blend.

"I guess that's it then?" Misty asked the sheriff.

Sheriff Olave wasn't old, or young. He was a middle-aged lawman with a mortgage, four kids, and a wife with a proclivity for living above her means. The man was always angry, never smiled, and though he was fair, if his boots got splattered with even the slightest bit of feces the person responsible would pay. He pulled up his gun belt and said, "For now. We'll keep an eye out, as will the various trooper units."

"And the Ho... carcass?" asked Kahn.

"Let's go take a look at the thing," the sheriff said. "I haven't seen it yet."

Maddox got Slade's attention, and the guide joined the group. The lodge director said, "Slade, can you take the sheriff and his people out to staging area B and show them the animal?"

Slade nodded.

Maddox turned his attention to the sheriff. "It's hanging in a horse stall." He looked around conspiratorially. "I'd hurry if I were you," he added with a sly smile.

Kahn said nothing. Maddox also thought the beast was going to be spirited away soon, and what could be better for him? With the problem gone, he could tell everyone the creature had been killed and go back to business as usual.

The group exited out the back of the lodge and followed a winding path through a manicured forest, signage pointing to the various staging areas. As they walked, Kahn said, "There was no mention of Blair's service. Who spoke with her family?"

Misty coughed her "shut up" cough.

The sheriff cleared his throat. "The body will be picked-apart by the basement vultures in Little Rock, and then I reckon she'll be buried. No information has been provided by the family to date."

Well, how clinical, Kahn wanted to say, but instead asked, "And the family?"

"She's from up north," Slade said. "No husband or kids, and she didn't have a boyfriend—or girlfriend, which was a surprise. She was ho—a nice lady."

Nobody said anything and the faint call of a hawk echoed through the trees, the day orchestra a dull roar.

"As to your other question, Maddox called her parents," Slade said.

In the end that's all anyone amounted to, a phone call and a mound of dirt.

The weathered barn at staging area B was a blend of rustic charm and rugged functionality. Its thick, dark-stained timber walls rose solidly from the ground, and its roof, pitched steeply to shed rain and snow, was covered with slate-gray shingles streaked with moss and lichen. Large wooden double doors, reinforced with black iron bands, dominated the front, flanked by narrow windows of frosted glass that filtered light into the interior. At the roof's pinnacle, a weathervane in the shape of a galloping horse creaked as it spun lazily in the breeze.

Slade opened a regular-sized door next to the double doors and held it open for the sheriff and the rest of the party.

Old-fashioned lanterns hung from exposed rafters, casting a warm, flickering glow, and the air carried the earthy scent of hay and horses. Saddle racks lined the far wall, showcasing an array of well-oiled leather tack. The floor was compacted dirt softened by scattered straw, and the entire space was sectioned off into spacious wooden compartments, each lined with thick timber beams. These immaculate stalls featured sturdy gates and gleaming brass nameplates engraved with the name of the horse that called it home.

Kahn knew each horse was bred specifically for hunting, and the beasts stood proudly within their enclosures, their glossy coats shining in the soft light. A loft above the stalls stored bales of hay, its edges guarded by a wooden railing.

Slade led the group down the center aisle as horses whinnied and crunched hay. There was no staff mucking the stalls or feeding the beasts. The barn was secured, and only authorized personnel were allowed inside. Cameras peered down from the rafters, and each stall was secured with a magnetic lock.

At the midpoint of the barn, the main aisle reached a crossroads where two smaller aisles branched off to the right and left. The central row continued straight ahead, leading to the double doors at the far end of the structure.

"This way," Slade said as he made a right.

Kahn and the others followed like ducklings.

Slade paused in front of a stall with its door open. A black curtain hung across the entrance, obscuring the view of the inside. Slade grabbed the curtain, but before pulling it open, he looked at the group like a magician preparing to yank the sheet off his grandest illusion.

As the curtain slid open the sheriff made the sign of the cross and said, "Now what in the hell?"

The young howler hung from a hook at the end of a rope tied to the wooden beam above the stall. Dark lines of dried blood ran over the beast's dark fur from multiple bullet holes. The deep slash from Buck's blade had severed tendons and muscle, and the beast's head hung at an unnatural angle. To Kahn, the Howler appeared smaller in death, its ruffled and matted fur nearly concealing the newly formed horns that would have become spikes.

Sheriff Olave covered his nose, trying to block the stench of decay as he stepped forward and bent over. He leaned close, staring into the corpse's gaping maw.

Menacing teeth pushed from receding pink gums, and the Howler's pointed ears were pressed flat to its skull. A haze covered the beast's yellow eyes, which were open and staring into the next world with a defiance that unnerved Kahn.

A dried puddle of blood stained the hay below the creature, its long legs hanging almost to the floor. With its muscles slack, the Howler's claws were exposed, and Kahn's stomach turned when he saw the blood on them. Most likely Blair's blood.

"Do you still think it's a rabid bear?" Kahn asked, anger burning his stomach.

Misty sighed and Slade snickered.

The big lawman turned to Kahn and said, "What would you call it?"

Kahn had no pig in this race. He'd been hired by the sheriff to help the lodge catch a killer that had been terrorizing the preserve. That task was done, and he didn't owe anybody anything. Except, that wasn't true. He owed Misty, Blair… and maybe even Buck.

"I'd call it an Ozark Howler," Kahn said. He was done tiptoeing around. Two people were dead, and two others had been attacked.

The sheriff didn't laugh, or get angry, he just stared at Kahn, his mouth hanging open.

"It's not a grown one, as you can see," Kahn continued. "But the horns…" He stepped past the sheriff and pointed at the nubs sticking through the black fur. "This means it's a male."

"Well…" the sheriff said. "I'm no scientist, or conspiracy theorist, or cryptid hunter. Clearly, the thing is some type of mutant, but that's above my pay grade, and you don't even have a grade."

With that, Kahn's sails fluttered, windless, and the conversation died. The sheriff had a point. He wasn't the asshole police, and he wasn't responsible for the safety of anyone other than himself, and his daughter.

Maddox appeared at the crossroads with a man in a suit. Behind them, there were four technicians wearing biohazard suits and wheeling a large gurney.

"Sheriff Olave?" said the suit as he approached. The man offered no hand, no ID.

The sheriff sighed hard and loud before saying, "Yeah."

"I'm State Special Investigator Candle. I'm here for the corpse."

Kahn wanted to scream and tell the man the hell he was, but he bit his tongue. As the sheriff had eloquently pointed out, he had no standing. Again, he had to ask himself why he cared. He knew that Ozark Howlers existed—he'd seen and heard them, and helped kill one, but he didn't care if anyone believed him. It did surprise him, however, that in all the discussions and strategizing, nobody asked or expressed concerns about the possibility of more… mutants.

The sheriff waved an arm, indicating that the state people should proceed.

Kahn watched as the four technicians in white worked like a ballet troupe that had danced together their entire lives. Two of the techs held the gurney steady beneath the Howler's corpse as the other two delicately maneuvered the dead beast onto the gurney and released it from the hook. The rip of a zipper being closed gave way to the rumblings of an air pump as the techs unfolded and straightened plastic and a coffin-like containment tent inflated around the corpse.

The entire operation took four minutes, and when they were done the technicians wheeled the Howler away without a word.

"You'll get a report when the autopsy is complete," Investigator Candle said.

The sheriff snickered, but the rest of the group stayed silent.

When the Howler and its entourage were gone, the sheriff said, "Well that's it then."

"Yes, it is," Maddox said. "And thank you, Sheriff."

Kahn figured he was done, but how often was he right?

The group filed out of the barn, dispersing in different directions as Kahn, Misty, and the sheriff made their way toward the parking lot.

Only two law enforcement vehicles remained in the lot: the sheriff's and Misty's. "Stop by the main office, Kahn," the sheriff said as he dropped into his squad car. "Your check is at the main desk." He slammed the door, started the car's engine, and drove off, leaving Misty and Kahn standing in a cloud of dust and grit.

"Hello," came a faint whisper.

Kahn and Misty exchanged glances of confusion.

A man in a work uniform stood on a pathway that cut through the hedge surrounding the lot. He was motioning with his finger for Kahn and Misty to join him.

Kahn hiked his shoulders, and the pair went to the man.

The guy led the pair away to a spot on the path out of sight from anyone watching from the lodge.

Despite his rat-like face and weaselly body, the man spoke with a steady and upbeat voice, his demeanor surprisingly cheerful. "I'm sorry to bother you but..." He looked over his shoulder as if expecting Maddox to be standing there. "I just thought you should know..."

Kahn and Misty waited.

"Maddox, Slade... and others," the guy said as he looked at the ground.

"What's your name?" Misty asked.

The guy looked up, defiance painted over his features as he said, "That's not important. What is important is that the Howler was in the preserve because Maddox wanted it here."

"What are you saying?" Misty asked.

"I'm saying Slade and some of his guys drove the beast west to this side of the highway, so the assho—customers, could get a thrill."

"Over I-49?"

"Beneath it," the guy said. "Where the train tracks run under the road, just beyond the truck stop."

"Why didn't you bring this up when the bigwigs were here?" Misty said.

Kahn felt the heat of guilt boil in his stomach. He and Misty had also kept secrets.

"Look, my name isn't Paul, and this is between you all."

"That's not enough... Paul," Kahn said.

"Look, I lied to get this job," the man said. "I'm an ex-con and Maddox doesn't know. I've got kids, man, bills..."

Birds chirped and leaves rustled in the trees.

"I have to get back to work," the guy said and disappeared down the path.

"What do you make of that?" Misty asked. "I don't think there w—"

The sharp, anguished cry of a woman shattered the peace, tearing through the day with a nerve-tormenting edge.

11

Misty sprang into motion as she drew her sidearm.

Kahn followed her, and the pair raced across the parking lot to a trailhead where paths that led to the lodge and the rest of the facilities converged.

A shout, and then a single gunshot, followed by the crack of a bullet splintering wood.

The duo ran toward the sound, peeling left and following the narrow path that led to the lodge's staff entrance.

An alarm sounded, and a wobbling, dull wail rose and fell in volume like it was experiencing power surges.

Kahn's heart pounded in his chest, his eyes locked on Misty's back as she ran. Then his brain registered the gun in her hand, and he felt for the Beretta on his hip, but it wasn't there. He was unarmed because he'd come to a meeting with cops who had plenty of guns. Kahn didn't have so much as a pocketknife. He considered going back to his car but quickly decided against it as he heard Misty's thumping footsteps which reminded him that he, at least for now, was one of two.

Misty and Kahn moved cautiously but fast down the trail as it wound through dense shrubs, the scent of pine and damp earth hanging in the air as it mingled with the ominous silence. As the pair approached the bend where the underbrush thickened, Misty stopped short.

A person lay crumpled on the path.

Kahn's breath caught as he stopped next to Misty. The pair exchanged a brief knowing glance, and without a word advanced, Misty with her gun up and ready.

When the duo got closer, the smell hit them—a sickening, metallic stench of blood mixed with something else, something foul and decayed. Misty gagged, covering her nose with the sleeve of her jacket.

Kahn pressed forward, grim determination filling him with a surreal heat. His worst fears were realized when he reached the downed worker.

It was a woman, what was left of her. Her body was torn and shredded so deep in places that bone glistened through the ragged remains of her uniform. The kitchen worker's apron, once white, was now soaked crimson, and her torso had been ravaged, her abdomen ripped wide open. The Howler had gutted her with brutal efficiency, and dark blood pooled beneath her, soaking into the path as the early bird flies buzzed around the open wounds, drawn to the carnage.

Her face was barely recognizable. Half of it had been slashed away, leaving an empty, gaping socket where her right eye had once been. The other eye remained wide open, glazed over in death, staring up at the blue sky. Claw marks stretched from her face and down her right side to her waist, the jagged wounds revealing torn tendons, exposed muscle, and a section of large intestine. The corpse was missing a foot, a hand, and several rib bones were absent.

Misty stumbled back, her breath coming in shallow gasps, her face awash with horror. She pressed her fist to her mouth, her eyes wet with tears and wide as quarters.

Kahn crouched beside the body, his eyes tracing the unmistakable signs of the vicious attack. There were bloody paw prints around the corpse, large ones, too large for any predator except an Ozark Howler. He reached out and touched the torn fabric of the woman's apron, guilt seeping through him, though he didn't know the woman and had nothing to do with her death.

"This wasn't just an attack," Kahn muttered, shaking his head. "It was revenge for its child."

Misty nodded, unable to tear her gaze away from the corpse.

Kahn stood and looked down the path toward the lodge. Nothing moved, but the bloody footprints trailed in that direction.

The sound of pounding feet carried down the trail and Slade appeared. He held a shotgun, and his face was twisted with rage. When he arrived, Slade took in the carnage, and in a genuine sign of emotion, he shook his head and said, "Isabel was a nice lady. Cooked my venison meatballs special for me."

Slade bit his lip and turned on Kahn and Misty. "What the hell happened..." He shook his head. "Why didn't you do anything?"

"We just got here," Misty said.

"Like you," Kahn added.

"Where's your gun, Kahn?" Slade asked.

Kahn glanced sheepishly back down the path toward the parking lot.

Slade tossed Kahn his Benelli M4.

Kahn caught the weapon and said, "Thanks."

"You're welcome," Slade said as he drew his Colt Anaconda.

With the pleasantries completed, the trio followed the bloody paw prints, Slade leading.

The blood trail led off the path and the trio followed it into the thick underbrush. Their footsteps crunched on the thick carpet of leaves and pine needles, each step muffled by the tangled foliage. Stray daggers of sunlight fought through the tree canopy, casting an eerie glow over the bloodstained earth. The scent of decay was thick, metallic, and nauseating.

A pop, like eggs frying. Not a gunshot, but something wet.

Slade held up his hand, signaling for the others to stop.

A flattened eyeball surrounded by blood and goo lay before Slade. The eye was unmistakably brown. Same color as the murdered staff member's remaining eye.

Further on the trio found a severed hand in the dirt. The fingers were curled, frozen in the last agonizing moments of life. The wrist had been torn clean from the arm, ragged muscle and sinew dangling like frayed rope.

Slade swore under his breath.

"Jesus," Misty muttered, her voice a whisper. She was no stranger to death, but this...

Kahn's jaw clenched as he stood over the grotesque scene, eyes tracking the trail of blood that intersected with the path that led to the lodge's rear patio.

"Keep moving," Slade said, his voice tight.

The trio pressed on, following the crimson trail through the trees. When they reached the path more body pieces drew the trio on.

A chunk of flesh, still attached to part of a rib, lay discarded like a butcher's scrap. The bone was gnawed on and tooth marks were visible. The trio also discovered a clump of dark, matted hair caught on a low-hanging branch, still attached to a shard of bloody scalp.

Kahn covered his mouth, trying to keep his breakfast from making a curtain call.

The hunters followed the bloody trail, and more body parts littered the path—a foot still in its black sneaker, a chunk of muscle, each a brutal reminder of the creature's hunger. The morning felt alive with tension as if the Howler was watching, waiting for them to step too close.

A sharp, piercing crack echoed down the path, followed by the rapid tinkling of fracturing glass.

The trio came to a halt as if they had one mind.

A chaotic tinkling, followed by high-pitched ringing, like gigantic wind chimes caught in a storm drove out the sounds of the day chorus. Larger pieces of glass crashed to the ground with dull, heavy explosive bursts that left behind a lingering hiss as the last shards settled and silence crept in.

With the faint echo of shattering glass still ringing in Kahn's ears, the partners sprang back into motion, driven by the need to locate the source of the sound.

As Kahn reached the end of the path, three guests ran past him in a chaotic rush, yelling and screaming in panic.

One of the large windows that looked out on the main porch was broken, shards of glass hanging from its frame like broken teeth. The terrace was a disaster area. Tables were overturned, eggs and bacon littered the ground, and blood splatters marred the blue stone patio.

A waiter was down, clutching his side where the beast had slashed him.

Kahn paused at the man's side and said, "Hang on. We'll get you help."

The guy nodded, but his eyes were glassy, and he was losing a lot of blood.

Kahn watched through the broken window as a wave of splintered wood exploded through the entry hall as the Ozark Howler tore through the lodge. With a guttural growl, the Howler swung its thick, muscled forearm, swiping its five-inch sickle-shaped claws across one of the hand-carved oak tables, the solid wood scratching like fine china. The rifles displayed on the table clattered to the floor, their sleek finishes marred with blood. Metal clanged and spun across the stone floor as the creature moved through the space like a storm.

Kahn spotted the staff through the large windows as they scrambled to escape and dove for cover behind the reception desk. Even though the lodge catered to hunters, the staff weren't strapped.

The Benelli was heavy in Kahn's hand. He wanted to fire on the beast and blow it back to hell. Thing was, though he didn't know what type of shells where in the gun, he did know that a shotgun was an imprecise weapon, and there was too much stone and too many people in harm's way.

A fire crackled in the massive fireplace that dominated the room, and the preserved stag skull mounted above the hearth was the Howler's next victim. With a powerful leap, the beast swiped at the skull, shattering the mounted antlers with a crunch that carried through the room as the fragments of the stag's crown tumbled to the floor.

It was then Kahn noticed the Howler had no horns—a female. Though he had no way of knowing for sure, he was certain the beast was the dead Howler's mother. What else could elicit such a barbaric and spirited attack?

Razor-sharp teeth gnashing, the Howler whipped its body around, slamming into the fireplace. Stones cracked, clouds of dust and ash filling the air. Mortar crumbled, and the entire structure shifted as if it might collapse. The fire hissed and sputtered as logs were dislodged and tumbled onto the floor, sparks flying.

Flames licked polished wood as the beast tore into the couches with savage glee, its claws raking the supple leather, and shredded fabric and feathers joined the thickening smoke that clogged the air.

As the Howler fled the lounge, its claws ripped over a taxidermized bear, its glassy eyes fixed in eternal aggression as it was knocked over. The antlers that lined the western side of the room cracked and shattered as the beast zigzagged and bounced off the wall, its massive body colliding with another heavy oak table as it threw itself onward.

Slade fired, the Anaconda bucking slightly in his hands.

With an agility and speed that defied its size, the Howler leaped over the reception desk and clawed at the people hiding behind it as Slade's shots punched into wood. The Howler slashed the receptionist and tossed her aside like trash, the woman's cry fading to nothing as did her life. With a giggle-growl that turned Kahn's stomach, the beast leaped onto a desk chair, reducing it to a heap of twisted wood and leather before bolting for the cover of a hallway that led deeper into the lodge.

Slade was the first to move, followed by Misty, and the pair jogged along the edge of the building until they reached the lodge's patio entrance.

Kahn considered climbing through the broken window, but many of the glass shards sticking from its frame were bigger than butcher knives, and he wasn't interested in getting filleted.

The beast let out a bellowing roar as it fled, the sound bouncing off the broken walls.

Slade and Misty threaded through the fire and chaos, guns up as they searched the smoke for the beast, but it was gone.

Kahn eased into the lodge, smoke curling from a deer skin rug that had caught fire, flames licking the wooden floor and rustic walls. The thick smell of burning fabric and wood filled the air, stinging Kahn's eyes as he considered retreating. He saw a fire extinguisher mounted to the wall. The world would go on without The Lodge at Borderland Pass Game Preserve, but there were still people in the lodge.

He slung the Benelli over his shoulder and grabbed the fire extinguisher. The weight of the red cylinder felt solid in his hands, its metal surface cold despite the growing heat. Kahn yanked out the safety pin, the thin metal piece clattering to the ground as he advanced on the spreading flames.

"Aim low," Kahn muttered to himself, recalling the basic instructions.

The flames crackled and popped as they devoured the floor and the rug, hungry for more fuel. Kahn leveled the nozzle at the base of the fire, where the flames were fiercest, and squeezed the handle. A jet of white blasted from the extinguisher with a sharp hiss.

As he sprayed the extinguisher's dry chemical—monoammonium phosphate, if he remembered correctly—it smothered the fire under a thick cloud of white. Kahn moved with precision, sweeping the extinguisher from side to side as his arms complained and his stomach bitched.

The flames recoiled as the powder coated them, turning from vibrant orange to a dull, ashy gray.

Sweat beaded on Kahn's forehead, though whether it was from the effort or the heat, he wasn't sure. He squinted through the haze as he aimed the nozzle and systematically doused the remaining embers.

The fire was out, but some spots were still smoldering. Kahn's arm ached from the tension of holding the extinguisher, but he didn't take a break. He scanned the room again, checking for any signs of rekindling, and dousing embers. When he was satisfied, Kahn released the extinguisher's handle, cutting off the flow of powder. He stepped back, his muscles knotting as the adrenaline fled, his eyes stinging, head ringing.

"Kahn!" came a screaming female voice.

It was Misty.

12

The lodge's lounge was a charred ruin. Broken furniture, shattered antlers, and the remains of destroyed trophies littered the floor. The once-elegant hunter's respite looked like a war zone, the place ravaged. Where there had once been order, the Howler had left only chaos.

Slade sprinted after the creature, Misty right behind him, the pair determined not to lose sight of their target. The duo vanished into the passageway where the creature had made its escape, the pounding of the beast's paws striding over wood leaking into the lounge.

Kahn dropped the fire extinguisher and let the Benelli fall into his hands.

People crawled out from hiding spots as Kahn ran to the receptionist's aid, but the woman was gone. The Howler had slashed her neck cleaner than any human murderer could have, and blood leaked rhythmically from one of her carotid arteries.

He chased after Misty and Slade, heart pounding, smoke stinging his eyes.

The hallway was a chaotic jumble of thick smoke, moving shadows, slamming doors, and gunshots. Medieval-like wall sconces that held LED flickering candles cast soft light on the commotion as Kahn's head settled to a dull roar, the thick, chalky smoke caked in his nose. His hands were black, and his exposed arms and clothes were covered in deep gray ash. Larger specks of black soot clung to his clothes and here and there embers burned like pinpricks of potential trouble.

Kahn brushed himself off, checked the Benelli, and continued through the smoke which was thinning as he moved away from the lounge.

A sharp staccato burst of gunshots froze Kahn in place as bullets tore into wood and pinged off metal. Screaming and screeching, both human and inhuman, carried through the tumult, followed by cracking wood and tearing metal.

When Kahn caught up to Misty and Slade, they were braced on opposite sides of an open doorway. The door itself had been busted open, and beyond a wide hallway led to an equipment room, which was an antechamber of the kitchen.

Guests appeared in the hallway in both directions, some holding weapons, some drinks, and others stood unmoving, gaping in astonishment.

"Go back to your rooms and lock your doors," said Slade.

Clientele that stayed at the lodge were, for the most part, one-percenters, and they weren't used to being addressed in such a manner, so none of them moved. A couple of the arrogant dip-wads even lifted their chins in defiance.

"Now!" screeched Slade as he raised his weapon.

That sent the guests scrambling back to where they'd come from. Slade turned to Kahn and said, "I'm going in first. I want to—"

Kahn ignored the man, pressed the Benelli's stock to his shoulder, and surged through the broken door, the shards of which were still hanging from elaborate metal hinges. Smoke from the fire had filtered into the hallway, and a thick haze hung five feet from the floor, partially obscuring Kahn's line of sight. The beast was huge and there was no way it was hiding, but still…

Slade gripped Kahn's shoulder and rushed by him, his pistol up in a doublehanded grip, his head swinging back-and-forth. He took cover behind a large stack of boxes labeled paper goods.

Kahn thought that was a poor choice, so he veered left and took-up position behind a stack of one-gallon tins of imported olive oil. Worst came to worst, at least olive oil was good for the skin, and if he was killed, he'd leave behind a good-looking and nice-smelling corpse.

The storage area had a set of double doors that were still swinging on their saloon hinges. There was a loading area and a rollup metal door that was closed and locked. The air was filled with the scent of burnt wood, but beneath it the oily decay-laden body odor of the beast made the place stink like a butcher's dumpster.

Slade motioned toward the double doors and the trio advanced, moving through pallets and shelves of dry goods, food stuffs, and equipment waiting to be cycled into the kitchen.

When he reached the doors, Slade pressed his face to the opening between them.

Kahn looked over his shoulder through one of the windows that adorned each door. He'd worked in a kitchen once when he was in high school, and Kahn had seen more than one dinner hit the floor because the wait staff wasn't paying close enough attention to the comings and goings.

The kitchen was rugged, yet pristine, designed to feed over two hundred people three times a day. Polished stainless steel dominated nearly every surface, and prep tables ran in rows down the center. Mounted along the walls steel cabinets gleamed, their reflective surfaces bearing subtle scratches and faint, brushed lines from years of use.

Kahn used the cabinets to search the room, but he didn't see the Howler. Faint red paw prints ran between a row of tables and disappeared into the smoke-shrouded rear of the room where there was another swinging double door. The kitchen staff had fled.

A massive walk-in cooler stood like a steel fortress in a corner, its heavy door equipped with a thick, insulated handle. It was undisturbed. Not far from it, there was a walk-in freezer, slightly frosted over, and the Howler had also passed it by.

Slade moved forward, probing the smoke as it dipped and eddied.

Misty dropped in next to Kahn, but said nothing, her gaze locked on Slade as she peered through the door's window. Words weren't needed. Kahn knew Misty wasn't going to take any unnecessary risks that could derail her retirement, and if that meant the beast got away, so be it. Though it burned his stomach, Kahn had to admit he felt the same.

"Clear!" Slade yelled.

Kahn and Misty surged into motion, nudging through the swinging doors and passing work tables strewn with bread, eggs, and a variety of vegetables at various stages of preparation. Knives sat on cutting boards and abandoned coffee mugs steamed. The floor of gray, non-slip tiles was spotless save for the occasional partial bloody paw print. Bright LED lights glared down from above, and sturdy wooden stools with steel legs stood around the work tables.

A series of heavy-duty gas ranges and industrial ovens lined the walls and brushed-steel range hoods extended into the ceiling, their powerful fans quietly humming as they sucked in smoke.

Kahn and Misty caught up to Slade and the guide whispered, "I think it went out those doors on the opposite end. It was probably chasing the staff. Cover me."

Slade eased by an expansive grill, complete with a wide iron griddle plate. The griddle's surface was blackened and seasoned, and bacon sizzled and burnt scrambled eggs smoked. Slade turned off the griddle and moved around a heavy, brick-lined smoker, its dark door open, revealing a charred interior. The smell of hickory and mesquite lingered beneath the stench of burnt wood, but the smell wasn't unpleasant.

As Slade entered the dishwashing area, he took a moment and used the many stainless-steel reflective surfaces to check the area around him. There was no sign of the Howler, not so much as a growl.

Kahn wanted to run forward and burst through the doors, gun singing, but he knew that might be exactly what the Howler wanted. He'd seen what the beast could do when it lay in wait. Cautiousness was king, even if it was frustrating as hell.

The dishwashing area gleamed with cleanliness, even with the smoke and the morning mess uncleaned. A deep, triple-basin sink gleamed under powerful lights, its water was still running. Slade turned it off.

The peal of a man screaming ripped through the kitchen.

Slade said, "Let's move. Double-time it." He headed for the doors at the opposite end of the kitchen.

Kahn and Misty chased after him, passing through the final section of the kitchen where all the real work took place. The pair ran through prep stations, the lights mounted under the stainless-steel work tables illuminating rows of sharpened knives, butcher's cleavers, and a full arsenal of spatulas, tongs, ladles, and thermometers lined up on magnetic strips.

Slade disappeared through the double doors, the sound of yelling, gunshots, and the howls of the beast carrying into the kitchen.

Kahn and Misty paused at the threshold of the dining hall, the doors swinging before them. He didn't know what Misty was thinking, but if her thoughts were anything like his, she was angry at herself for putting her life at risk for a bunch of rich posers who called themselves hunters.

The pair gave themselves a heartbeat, then nodded at one another before bursting through the doors together, guns up and ready.

Guests streamed for the exits, some reaching for weapons but realizing this was no controlled game hunt and instead focusing on exiting in a less than orderly fashion. The Ozark Howler was perched atop a table, its yellow eyes scanning the room, its thick fur matted with dried blood. The beast's maw hung open, revealing rows of dagger-like teeth, each stained a dull yellow and slick with saliva. Thick nostrils flared as the Howler inhaled and a menacing growl built in its throat.

An old guy stood in a corner, his revolver in his hand as he took shots at the beast, but it was too fast and too agile.

With a snarl, the beast launched from the tabletop, bobbing and weaving as it charged the old guy.

The man's gun clicked empty, and he looked right, then left, and then appeared to accept his fate as the beast's curved talons tore into the man, ripping through flesh and bone with an ease that was both horrifying and surreal. Blood sprayed the wall, flecking the dark wood and drenching the floor.

Kahn would hear the man's scream in his dreams for a long time.

Slade moved as he fired. He held a Sig Sauer in one hand, and a radio in the other as he tried to aim at the beast, but it was like trying to hit swirling smoke.

Most of the diners had escaped, but a few stragglers were backed up at the exits. A waiter cowered under a table, hands clamped over his mouth as if to stifle his breathing.

The Howler's nostrils flared, its honey-colored eyes locking onto the waiter. In two shifty strides, the creature overturned the table, sending plates and silverware clattering across the floor. The waiter scrambled backward, trying to escape, but the beast disappeared behind the upturned table and the waiter's scream was abruptly choked off.

"Fire!" screamed Slade and the trio opened up.

Kahn's arms shook as the Benelli thundered, two fast shots that peppered the overturned table the beast hid behind.

The table splintered and broke as Misty and Slade added to the damage, the steady shots ripping into the wood and splintering its edges.

Wood shattered and cracked as the Howler used the remains of the overturned table for leverage and launched itself into the air, a shifting missile of blurred fur.

The trio stopped firing.

A rumbling growl echoed through the hall as the beast landed on all fours, its gaze finding the last pocket of survivors. It moved toward them, blood dripping through its crimson teeth, its powerful body coiling and preparing to strike again.

Kahn had seen enough, and so had Slade, because both men burst into motion at the same moment, anger taking control, the red fog of hatred and death clouding Kahn's vision.

"Kahn, wait!" Misty yelled.

But Kahn was gone, and he fired the semi-automatic shotgun as he ran, a battle cry he hadn't ordered shrieking from his mouth, his throat burning from the effort and the smoke. Vibration shook his body, pain knotting his arms and wrists. Pellets sprayed from the gun, peppering the furniture and the floor as the empty shell kicked free of the firing chamber.

Slade wasn't having much better luck, even though he was closer, and the Sig Sauer was a much more precise weapon and held more bullets.

Hunting was supposed to be a clash of instincts, a rhythm of patient pursuit. A creature like the Howler, with its sharp, ghost-like movements, demanded patience—more patience than Kahn cared to give, but as it is with many things what Kahn cared to give didn't matter. The Benelli was empty, and he had no shells to reload.

The creature veered sharply right, then left, launching itself over a table and charging through a cluster of chairs, scattering them like miniature bowling pins. Its powerful surge drove it straight toward the entrance to the bar, a blur of force and agility.

Slade stopped firing as Misty ran toward the cluster of survivors. The volley of gunshots might not have hit the beast, but it deterred its attack just enough to change its path of devastation, and that saved the lives of several guests.

Kahn didn't feel too great about that, though. He'd helped kill the Howler's kid, and if he hadn't done that the creature probably wouldn't have attacked the lodge. To that the rational side of his brain reminded him he wasn't the one that drove the Howlers to this side of the highway in the first place.

Slade put a hand on Kahn's shoulder and said, "Come on. This isn't over. Not by a long road."

"No bullets," Kahn sputtered. "And I'm ready to go down." He laughed, not because what he said was funny, but because he thought it was pathetic.

Slade looked around, saw a plate of abandoned pancakes, and snapped it up. "Here, eat these on the run," he said as he pressed the plate into Kahn's hand. "And we'll get you a loaded gun."

Kahn nodded.

The Howler cast one final, baleful glare across the dining hall before retreating into the bar, leaving behind a slaughterhouse.

13

The bar was empty, and everything was still, the shrieks of escaping guests fading as the ringing in Kahn's head made focusing difficult. Abandoned drinks sat untouched on the bar and scattered across empty tables, their chairs pushed back, and half-eaten snacks and forgotten purses hung over chair backs, left behind and waiting for their owners to return. Besides the entrance from the dining hall that Kahn and his companions had used, the room had three additional exits. Each led to different parts of the complex, offering alternate routes in and out.

Grand double doors stood open, revealing a hallway that led deeper into the lodge. Across the room, the door that opened onto the cocktail portico remained shut, while the door behind the bar swung rhythmically on its saloon-style hinges, marking the entrance to a storeroom.

Slade and Misty moved across the space, guns up as they searched.

The muffled sounds of yelling and screaming penetrated the bar, but Kahn heard no growling, pattering feet, or any of the telltale sounds of the beast.

A group of armed people that looked like a mix of staff and guests crept up the main hallway. They approached the open doors with caution.

Through the large windows on the outer wall, Kahn saw armed men forming up, waiting for the beast to burst through the exit into daylight. Shadows danced into the bar through the windows, and everyone appeared ready to shoot at the slightest provocation. The group was a powder keg of nervous energy, frustration, and anger, and it would only take an appearance by the beast to set it all off. The question was, with everyone in so tight, how many people would be hit by friendly fire?

All these images and thoughts barely had time to register in Kahn's muddled mind, before Slade yelled, "Behind the bar." As he bolted across the room Slade spoke into his radio, mostly reporting what appeared obvious; the Howler had gone through the entrance behind the bar, otherwise, the folks manning the other exits would have lit the beast up by now.

Kahn caught his breath as he jogged across the deserted room. This would all be over soon, and he didn't need to be in the middle of it. He slowed to a walk as he envisioned what was behind the door. The storage room most likely gave way to an exterior exit, where the Howler would meet a cadre of hunters, staff, and guides eager to put down the beast that had destroyed their sanctuary.

Slade leaped over the bar and took a moment to take a pull off a bottle of tequila sitting atop the polished black oak. Motivations aside, Kahn knew he could count on Slade to kill the beast if given the opportunity. With the Howler dead, and a second carcass to hand over to the staties, many of the questions that Slade would be asked would become irrelevant. But again, for the thousandth time, he had to ask why he cared and remind himself that he wasn't the asshole police. He wasn't any kind of law at all, nor had he ever been.

With the smooth grace of an experienced hunter, Slade raised his gun as he gently pushed open the swinging door. He moved quickly, each movement calculated and precise. In that moment Kahn saw the shadow soldier in Slade, and all the man's actions and tales took on new grains of truth.

Misty stood before the bar, gun in a doublehanded grip as she covered Slade.

Slade pushed through the door.

Time seemed to stand still as Kahn drew in a deep breath, head thumping, eyes still stinging from the smoke.

Misty shifted on her feet, her aim dipping slightly as she adjusted her stance.

A thunderous bark-growl carried from the storeroom, and Slade exploded through the door he'd just gone through, hit the bar with a skin-crawling crack, and fell to the floor like a bag of potatoes.

Misty fired, but her bullets smacked into the swinging door.

Slade's moaning spurred Kahn into motion and he staggered forward, unsure what to do next. When he reached Misty's side he could see over the bar, and to his surprise the hunting guide slash security chief was moving as he clutched his arm.

Kahn scrambled around the bar and Slade had enough fortitude left to offer Kahn his Sig Sauer.

There was really no choice, and Kahn abandoned the first weapon Slade had loaned him—the Benelli M4—and accepted the Sig-9.

Slade gritted his teeth, wincing as he forced out, "Kill it, Kahn. Kill it!"

The group of armed men coming from the interior of the lodge flowed into the bar, led by Maddox and Buck. Maddox looked like he'd just gone shopping at a Bass Pro Shop, but Buck was his normal rumpled self. Both men carried rifles and had sidearms on their hips.

Maddox strode forward with the air of a man who thought he knew more than he actually did. His eyes ranged around, and when he didn't see any of his people he asked, "Where's Slade?"

"Over here," Slade said as Kahn and Misty helped him to his feet. His right arm hung like a broken wing, but he looked otherwise unharmed.

"What the hell happened to you? Where is it?" Maddox said.

Slade bit his lip, anger rolling off him in hot waves.

Kahn understood. Maddox hadn't even had the courtesy to ask his number one if he was alright.

Slade pointed toward the doorway that led to the storeroom.

"What are we waiting for then?" Buck said. Then noticing Slade was unarmed, he added, "Where's your gun?"

Yelling and several gunshots drew everyone's attention to the large windows that looked out onto a terrace where cocktails could be enjoyed while communing with nature. Bushes, decorative grasses, and flowers filled the beds that lined the natural stone patio, and behind it, a thin forest of evergreens filled the horizon.

Misty saw it first and a dribble of a scream escaped her lips.

An Ozark Howler was moving through the vegetation, its huge fur-covered form unmistakable. Kahn got a good look at the beast as it flashed momentarily across an opening in the greenery.

The group on the patio fired, and the crack and pop of the gunshots leaked into the bar. Kahn should have felt the tension drain from him, but instead, his nerves picked up the pace and tap-danced on his spine. Sweat dripped down his face, and his gaze strayed to the door behind the bar.

Maddox raised his weapon and glared at Slade.

"It must've gone out the back and come around," Slade said.

"Can you help? Or do you need a doctor?" Maddox asked.

More gunshots erupted outside, but Kahn could no longer see what was happening.

"Let's move," Maddox said, and he, Buck, and the crowd trailing after them moved toward the rear exit.

"Hey," Slade said. "I need a weapon."

Maddox didn't stop moving as he spoke. "With one arm what good will you be?" He didn't pause for a response. "Someone give him a handgun," he finished, but he didn't look back to see if his orders were obeyed.

A guest dressed in hunting casual clothes stepped forward and held his position as the rest of the mob followed Maddox. The guy looked like he'd rather be any place else, and as he handed over his Glock his face smoothed with relief.

Maddox and his followers exited the bar, and the rumble of the boss demanding a report carried into the room.

Slade accepted the weapon with a nod and surged after his boss, pain tearing at his face.

Kahn said, "Slade, wait."

"What?"

Kahn pointed at the door that led to the storeroom.

Slade shook his head and pointed at the windows. "You've got eyes, don't you Kahn?"

"I do," Kahn said in a voice so calm and cool he surprised himself. "Do you? Have eyes, I mean."

Slade licked his lips, anger and pain creasing his face, his broken arm hanging at his side.

"I got a decent look," Kahn said. "At that creature." He pointed at the windows. "That Howler had a fully grown set of horns."

Slade sighed.

Kahn waited, letting the man work it out.

Ten seconds slipped away, and Kahn's patience was almost gone when understanding bloomed on Slade's face. He pointed in the direction of the storeroom. "That one doesn't have horns."

"Right," Kahn said. "That's Mom."

"And that's probably Dad outside," Misty said.

"How can this be?" Slade sounded like a little kid who hadn't gotten what he wanted for Christmas. "The distances." He shook his head. "How could they have come so far so fast? There were..." His voice trailed off and he looked at the floor.

Kahn said nothing. Slade had caught himself. Yeah, the beasts were a long way from where you and your boss drove the creatures under the highway so you could create an attraction for your rich guests. Kahn's stomach boiled, but he reigned in his anger. He said, "Come on, Slade. You know this preserve like the back of your hand. A bear can travel how far in a day?"

Slade reinflated, his chest rising as he nodded. "You're right. A large bear, like a grizzly or a black bear, can travel around fifteen to thirty miles per day through wooded, uneven terrain, depending on the bear's purpose. A bear will move slower if it's foraging, patrolling its territory, or searching for mates."

"I've seen some of the tagged bears move much faster than that," Misty said.

"Agreed," Kahn said. "If motivated, a bear can travel up to fifty miles a day. The preserve is 4762 acres." Kahn paused as he did the math in his head, which was still ringing dully. "That's 600ish square miles, which means we have to assume the Howlers can traverse the preserve easily if t—"

A loud grunt followed the sound of boxes falling, and then the crash and pop of bottles shattering leaked into the bar from the storeroom.

"I've had just about enough of this bitch," Slade said. He worked his way behind the bar again, one arm hanging at his side, the loaner Glock raised. When he saw the open bottle of tequila still sitting on the bar, he put the Glock in the crux of his arm, lifted the bottle, and took a long pull. When he was done, he put the bottle back down, gripped the Glock in his good hand, and said, "For the pain."

The guest who had given up his weapon backed up, his eyes darting toward the windows.

Another loud series of grunting and sniffing, but this time there was no crash of boxes, no breaking glass. The door behind the bar swung open a crack, and a large black nose poked through the opening.

Kahn and Misty dropped like they were dead, using the bar for cover.

Slade screamed a deep, full-throated wail that ended with his voice cracking as his newly acquired Glock barked.

When the shots stopped Kahn peeked over the lip of the bar and saw that Slade and the beast were gone, the door leading to the storeroom swinging wildly.

Kahn pressed to his feet and helped Misty up. "I'm going after him," Kahn said.

Whatever Misty saw in Kahn's face made her hold her tongue and she nodded. When Kahn pulled away, she surged to her feet and said, "I'll go out back and cover the exits as best I can."

Kahn nodded reluctantly. He had no right to tell the deputy sheriff to do anything, but the image of Misty sitting on a beach in retirement was fading, and he needed to bring it back into focus. "Misty, be careful. This…" He motioned around him at the expanse of the lodge. "Isn't worth your life. It's not worth a mosquito's life."

She nodded, and the words drained the fight from her eyes.

Kahn watched Misty thread through the tables toward the rear exit as he went around the bar. He had the strange uncomfortable feeling that he was never going to see her again, but he shook it off and eased through the swinging door after Slade.

The storeroom was dark, save for a single light over a workstation piercing the grayness. There were no windows, and the lights were off. Kahn reached out to flip the switch but thought better of it. Surely the lights were motion activated, which meant Slade didn't want the lights on, though he couldn't come up with a good reason why. Sure, it would hamper the Howler's sight, but it would also hurt Slade's ability to track the creature. Kahn didn't know much for certain, but he was sure the Howler had better eyesight than people, especially in the dark.

The door swung gently as Kahn got low, his borrowed Sig Sauer aimed into the gloom.

"Lights!" It was Slade. "Now! Turn on the lights!"

Kahn flicked on the lights.

The storeroom was bathed in harsh LED light and a screech followed by the commotion of falling boxes and breaking bottles filled the room.

A growl rose above the calamity as Slade moved out from behind a stacked wall of beer kegs.

The Howler's shadow fell on the far wall, the dark shape melting over shelves of stored booze. Kahn figured the creature was stunned by the bright light because it moved slowly on all fours, shuffling along as it grunted and growled, but the creature sounded more frustrated and confused than angry.

The creak of a door opening carried through the room, and Misty called out, "Kahn? Slade?"

From behind a stack of supplies, darkness bled into the air—a shadow so dense it swallowed all light around it. The sight sent a cold tremor through Kahn, his muscles tensing, his heart beating like a war drum signaling the hunt.

14

The Ozark Howler broke for daylight, a knot of muscle and teeth moving like the wind through a stack of boxes, cutting across a corner of the room and angling towards the rear exit where Misty waited. Boxes stumbled, glass shattered, and metal shrieked as cans dropped to the ground and popped, the beast so large it was unable to move in the tight space without knocking things over.

Kahn saw Slade in his peripheral vision. The guy moving like a ghost, right arm dangling, left arm up and out straight, the Glock ready to fire. Dust and shredded cardboard floated in the air, and the layer of fire smoke had been replaced with gun smoke.

Misty fired three times in fast succession before her gun fell still.

He knew it was Misty that had fired because of the sounds her revolver made; the deep crack of the hammer, the whoosh of the bullets leaving the barrel. When her gun went dry, Kahn tried to envision her utility belt; did she carry a speedloader? Normally he'd say no, but today...

Every nerve in Kahn's body and most of his brain centers were urging him to stay put. To not move an inch. One of the beasts was outside, the other was heading for the exit and had left him behind. He didn't know how many bullets there were in the Sig Sauer, so he stalled.

Kahn quickly popped out the gun's magazine and thumbed out seven bullets. There was one in the chamber so that made eight. He stuffed everything back together and searched for Slade and Misty, but he still couldn't see them. After the initial volley of gunshots and screaming things had gone still.

He had to see what was going on. What was the harm in taking a peek? That didn't mean he needed to get involved, right? He slipped from cover and threaded between two stacks of cardboard boxes filled with recycled beer bottles waiting to go to their second lives.

Sunlight angled through the door at the end of the main aisle. The doorframe was cracked and broken, and a tuft of black hair clung to a bent nail like a forlorn rabbit's foot.

Slade appeared out of the shadows as he emerged from a row of supplies waiting to be unloaded.

Gone as if woven into the wind, the Howler had slipped away, leaving an echo of terror hanging in the heavy stillness.

"Where's Misty?" Kahn said when he arrived at Slade's side. In that moment that was all he cared about.

Slade pointed at the open door.

"The Howler?"

Slade nodded as he pushed forward, gun up. For the first time, Kahn noticed the lines creasing the guide's face, the dark bags beneath his eyes, and his reddened cheeks. Kahn wasn't the only one running out of gas.

Gunshots leaked into the room, and it was as if they had hit Slade in the butt. The man doubled his pace, legs cycling as he burst through the open door into sunlight.

Kahn followed, and as he exited the storeroom and entered a small fenced-in maintenance area filled with dumpsters and recycling bins, he called out, "Misty?"

A smear of blood stained the concrete slab that defined the area, and the enclosure's entry was broken open, the gates bent back on their hinges. There were no other signs of the Howler.

Another series of gunshots rang out, but they were too far away for the shots to be related to his chase.

"Misty!" Slade shrieked.

"In here," came the echo of Misty's voice from inside a dumpster.

Kahn rushed to the dirty-green metal box and lifted its cover, and as he did so relief washed through him.

Misty lay in a pile of trash, her empty gun in her hand, her ponytail broken open, her long gray hair spilling over her chest and shoulders. Her eyes were wide with fear, but when she saw Kahn, her features softened, and she reached out a hand.

Kahn helped the deputy sheriff climb out of the dumpster. She'd never looked so old to Kahn, but she was alive, as was the dream of visiting her at her retirement home down south.

The wind gusted and sighed, and Slade asked, "Did you see which way it went?"

Misty shook her head no. "When I saw it coming for me, I hid."

"Are you alright?" Kahn asked.

She nodded.

"Did you see Maddox and the others?" Slade said.

"They were gone when I went out the bar exit. I figure—"

More gunshots, followed by a roar and yelling carried over the fence into the waste area.

Slade asked, "Did you hit it?"

Misty nodded slowly. "I think so."

A branch snapped and together the trio's heads turned as they tracked the noise.

Slade led the way, his pace hurried as he bolted through the busted gates.

Muscles tensing, his senses heightened by the chase, Kahn ran after him, his head thumping as he tried to keep his mind in the hunt. He'd been hunting long enough to know that letting his guard down, even for a moment, could mean death.

Misty kept close, her breaths coming in tight, controlled puffs as she followed.

A driveway for trucks ran from the maintenance area into the trees, and several paths spidered off in various directions. A hedge of rhododendrons boxed in the trail that ran east, and an entire section of the large bushes with deep green oval leaves were flattened, leaving no doubts which way the Howler had gone. Claw marks gouged the ground around the destroyed shrubbery, and the area was disturbed by the beast surging over the soft loam.

Slade held up his gun, signaling for the trio to stop. He knelt and pointed the weapon at a smear of blood on a low-hanging branch. "Looks like it's wounded," he muttered, barely audible over the forest's music. "That means it's not just angry, but desperate." He sighed. "Desperate animals will take anything down if they think it'll buy them a second longer."

Misty shifted on her feet, her face pale but determined. "Then let's not give it a second."

The three plunged into the trees, guided by the eerie, intermittent growl that echoed ahead. They were the hunters, but the woods seemed to close in around them, trapping them with their quarry.

A snarl pierced the silence, closer than Kahn had anticipated. The sound rippled through the trees like a serrated blade, agitating the nerves just beneath his skin.

Slade came to a sudden stop, and before Kahn could ask why, he saw the reason.

Ahead, crouched beneath the spreading boughs of a large blue spruce tree, two golden orbs peered out from the shadows. Though he couldn't be certain, Kahn didn't think the beast had horns.

Reading his mind, Misty said, "I think that's Mom."

Kahn saw the anger in those eyes, and it chilled him. He raised his gun, signaling for Slade to move in from the other side.

Then several things happened at once, time spinning forward so fast that individual motions were lost in a blur, and yet each second seemed to last minutes.

The Howler launched from the shadows, a massive knot of fur and fangs, its roar echoing through the forest.

Kahn and Slade fired.

The beast dodged, too quickly, slipping in and out of the shadows and disappearing in a blur.

It was toying with them, testing them, and drawing them on. That thought was late in coming because a knot of fur and teeth burst from the foliage, front paws out, claws extended, spike horns dulled with dried blood.

Misty shouted, but she didn't fire. Kahn figured she was out of ammunition, or maybe the trio was packed too tight. Instead, she hurled her knife.

The blade spun through the air, hit the Howler's shoulder, handle first, and fell to the ground.

Kahn dropped to the forest floor as Dad charged Slade, massive claws outstretched.

Slade threw his empty gun at the beast as he pulled his knife.

The Howler stood on its hind legs, its gaping maw hanging eight feet above the ground, saliva dripping on the pine needle carpet as the creature eyed Slade.

Kahn fired, but only one bullet took flight before the dull click of the hammer striking an empty firing chamber told him the gun was empty.

As the beast came at Slade, he dodged to the side and lashed out with his blade, his broken arm hanging limp. It was a scene straight out of a comic book; the inferior, tiny human facing down an apex predator that made Slade look like an ant by comparison.

Horror dawned on Kahn as he watched the guide face down the beast, his blade the only thing standing between him and death.

Misty picked up a stone and threw it at the creature—but it was focused on Slade, driven by primal rage.

Panic leaked through Kahn. The trio was out of bullets, and the prospect of fighting the Howler hand-to-claw was a losing battle. He listened for approaching voices, but the day chorus had gone still and only the wind whispered of death and destruction.

The Howler attacked.

Slade did his best to ward off the onslaught, but he was outmatched, undersized, and he had no viable weapon.

Claws raked across Slade's chest, tearing flesh and scarring bone. His scream echoed through the forest, a sound of pain and defiance as he staggered back, trying to hold his ground even as blood soaked through the ragged tears in his chest.

Kahn was frozen, unable to do anything, horror rooting him to the ground as he watched the Howler descend on Slade, its claws tearing at him, jaws open and ready for the opportunity to go in for the kill. It was obvious that the fight was draining from Slade. He was moving slowly and awkwardly, his blood splattering the forest crimson.

"Slade!" Kahn surged forward as his voice broke.

Misty grabbed his shirt and yanked him back, her face streaked with tears. "We have to go!" she shouted, her voice sharp but choked.

The Howler's head darted forward, jaws snapping as Slade tried one last time to fight the beast off. But one good arm and a blade weren't enough, and as the seconds dripped away so did Slade's life. He stopped dodging, his fingers uncurled from the knife handle, and the blade dropped to the ground.

With a growl of rage, the beast punched Slade with its right front paw, its claws piercing the guide's chest like he'd been poked with a giant fork.

Slade gurgled as blood seeped from his mouth and his eyes rolled back in his head.

The Howler held Slade there, the dead man dangling from its claws like a marionette.

Kahn was happy to see Slade was dead because what happened next would have brought agony beyond imagination.

Before pulling its claws free, the Howler bit Slade's head, teeth grinding into bone as the beast tried to crush the dead man's skull.

But Slade was just as hardheaded in death as he was in life, and the Howler gave up. The beast released Slade's head, pulled its claws free, took a step back, and admired its work as the corpse fell to the ground in a heap.

Anger welled in Kahn, but he was nothing, a bug, and he could no more hurt the Howler than he could work his way back into his family's lives.

A scream and the sound of voices approaching.

The Howler threw back its head, the charcoal-sized nose at the end of its long snout sniffing the air. Then it turned tail and disappeared into the trees.

Misty crawled to Slade, but there was nothing to do except close the man's eyes. The deputy sheriff twisted into the sitting position and let her head fall into her hands as she fought back tears.

Kahn's muscles tightened as the adrenaline fled, pain knotting his neck. The ringing in his head dulled, but as he stared at Slade's crumpled body sorrow washed over him. Yes, the man had contributed to his own death when he brought Ozark Howlers onto the game preserve, and Slade had never been known as warm and fuzzy, but still… As was all too common in the world these days, the punishment didn't seem to fit the crime.

The forest grew silent, an oppressive calm settling in the wake of Slade's death. A foul stench carried over the scene, and Kahn realized that Slade's bowels had given way as the Howler killed him. Nobody should die in their own shit. Nobody. It took a great deal for Kahn to care about something. It hadn't always been that way, but life has a way of building calluses so thick those protected by its embrace fail to see anything outside their small world.

He was invested now, whether he wanted to be or not. His life had been a series of unplanned and unwanted events that had led to places he never wanted to go, but none of that mattered. All that mattered now was the Howlers.

Kahn helped Misty to her feet. She was shaky and she gripped Kahn's arm as he said, "Are you O.K.?"

Misty let go of Kahn, her hands shaking, her face pale. "He…he saved you," she said, her voice barely a whisper.

Kahn nodded as he clenched his fists, his mind spinning with grief and guilt. But the Howler… Howlers were still out there. "We'll finish this," Kahn said, his voice resolute. He met Misty's gaze, his grief hardening into determination.

Misty smiled a crooked, painful smile, then said, "How are we going to find them now?"

"I know where they're going," Kahn said.

15

Borderland Pass, I-49, Ozark Mountains, Arkansas, U.S.
3:12 PM CST, August 19th, 2022

Twenty-four hours slipped away as Kahn and Misty recuperated from their ordeal and prepared for their Howler hunt. Kahn made sure Snoop had plenty of food, and Misty took a few days off from work. She was going on a hunt with a friend, though she'd brought her badge and her service weapon, and when push came to shove, a cop was a cop, on duty or off.

Traffic on I-49 was light, most folks having already made their daily commute to school or work. The partners traveled north, the narrow strip of forest to their left acting as a barrier between the northbound and southbound lanes. Delivery trucks and slow-moving vehicles driven by retired folks dominated the right lane, and Misty had to slow to a frustratingly leisurely pace to nudge her way in so she could pull onto the shoulder.

The wind roared as I-49 knifed through the western edge of the Ozark Mountains. Sharp sunlight angled across the highway, the thump of the vehicle passing over expansion joints creating an upbeat tempo that quickened Kahn's pulse. Shadows danced under the white oaks and shortleaf pines that packed the sides of the road, the underbrush thick, the gray forms of the rolling mountains beyond still shrouded in thin early morning mist.

Kahn stared out the window, searching the side of the road. He couldn't help but think back to the massive multicar pile-up the prior year. A couple of miles up the road there was still a black stain on the concrete where the fire had burned for days. He couldn't remember how many were killed or unaccounted for, but he knew deep down that the Howlers had something to do with the accident, though it was no more than a gut feeling that he didn't fully understand.

The highway shoulder abruptly fell away, and a smooth concrete slope cut through the overgrowth of weeds. A barren strip of land knifed through the forest to the east, and it contained the railroad tracks and power lines. The manmade scar extended into the distance as it climbed into the hills.

Misty pulled to the side of the road and continued off the shoulder until the car was as close to the forest as possible, but not close enough to trap Kahn, who had just enough space to wriggle out the passenger door.

Waves of heat rolled down the interstate, and the air reeked of gasoline, oil, and rubber. Cars whipped by in waves, the ever-present blend of low rumbles and high-pitched whines filling the car like a relentless tide. Each passing vehicle added to a symphony of overlapping hums and throaty engines, with growling trucks punctuating the mix. The sound ebbed and flowed, rising to a crescendo as vehicles neared, then fading into a duller hum as they sped away, yet never falling silent.

"Are you ready for this?" Misty asked.

Misty had been with him when the lodge employee spilled the beans about how Maddox, Slade, and others drove the Howlers through the underpass into the preserve. Without evidence, there wasn't much anyone could do. Even if Kahn found proof like a broken gate or footprints, how could he tie them to Maddox?

Then there was the fact that Slade's death hadn't moved the needle much. He'd been unmarried, had signed an NDA, and nobody was pushing for an investigation. He'd been killed while defending the lodge against a rabid animal. Kahn couldn't blame the bigwigs in Little Rock. There was nothing to gain by joining the conspiracy theorists and acknowledging the existence of the Ozark Howler.

He said, "I'm as ready as I'm ever going to be." Kahn believed that with their child dead, and revenge taken, the male and female Howlers would try to get back to their territory where they would go through the birthing process again.

Cars and trucks streamed by as the partners exited the vehicle and pulled their gear. Misty placed her hunting license, her Sheriff's Department parking pass, and a note with her photo and badge number on the dashboard, explaining the situation. After double-checking that her gear was in order, she locked her vehicle and said, "Last thing we need is my ride getting towed."

It wasn't a far walk and when they reached the cut in the land they climbed down a concrete culvert and worked their way to the train tracks, the dark maw of the underpass looming before them.

The train tracks cut through rugged, forested hills, a stretch where Borderland Pass broke to accommodate the highway. A bridge those driving on the interstate barely noticed arched over the train tracks and power lines, supported by massive concrete pillars mottled with streaks of dark grime and rust. The bridge's underside was a rough expanse of gray, crisscrossed with seams and bolts, discolored by water stains that ran down the smooth surfaces in crooked, rusty lines.

Shadows hung beneath the road, cotton-like spider webs filled every right angle, and the dim light that fought its way into the cave-like space supported little vegetation other than weeds. Deeper in the tunnel faded to blackness as it plunged beneath the thin forest that separated the northern lanes from the southbound.

Train tracks ran down the center of the underpass, two sets of twin silver streaks that gleamed faintly as they trailed into darkness. Near the tracks, thick bundles of power lines ran along rusted metal poles, each support leaning slightly as though pushed by years of Ozark wind. The power lines were taut and hummed faintly as they stretched parallel to the tracks before they, too, disappeared into blackness.

The ground around the entrance to the underpass was a mix of hardened dirt, patches of grass, and scattered litter: crushed cans, broken glass, and scraps of torn paper blown in from passing cars. Small, resilient plants poked up through the gravel and sand, their leaves dusty and splayed wide under the sparse light. Here and there, graffiti marred the pillars and nearby rocks, faded but visible, with scrawls and symbols Kahn didn't recognize. There were no paw prints or any other signs that indicated Howlers had been through the underpass recently.

Weeds and tall grasses crept to the rocky edges of the tracks as if reclaiming their territory. Beyond them dense evergreens towered over the land, their long shadows stretching over the railroad tracks. There were no fences on this side of the road and there were several locations for Misty to set up her stand.

Kahn helped her choose a tree and stood by as the sixty-plus deputy sheriff slung her rifle over her shoulder, climbed the tree, deployed her stand, and pulled up her gear. When she was set, she slipped on her headset and did a radio check.

"Do you copy, Kahn?" came Misty's voice over Kahn's earbud.

"Copy," Kahn said. Then he headed west and threaded through the underpass, the concrete vibrating as the road hummed above.

The mountain valley known as Borderland Pass narrowed to the north, the train tracks running along its northern edge, and the southern portion cut across the northeast quadrant of Borderland Game Preserve.

Kahn trekked down the center of the tracks, and when he entered the dark tunnel between lanes, he pulled his sidearm. Small beady eyes stared at him in the darkness—field mice and other small rodents, and their dickering and the scrapes of their feet tickled Kahn's nerves and he pulled his flashlight.

The train tracks curved slightly as they left the underpass and disappeared into the underbrush, snaking their way along the landscape before vanishing around the bend of a hill.

When he broke free of the underpass on the western side of the interstate, a six-foot chain-link fence ran along the outer edges of the tracks to his left marking the northern border of the preserve. A double gate wide enough to accommodate large vehicles was secured with a heavy-duty chain and lock.

To Kahn the lock looked new, the gates newly repaired, and there were boot prints in the dirt, but all that proved nothing. He couldn't visualize the staties confiscating Maddox's footwear to perform a tread analysis.

He dropped his pack, leaned his rifle against it, and dug out bolt cutters and a bottle of his Special Sauce.

After checking for trail cameras and finding none, Kahn made fast work of the chain with the bolt cutters and after a few minutes of work, he had the double gates open. The opening was the perfect size—not so small as to be missed by the Howlers, but large enough to avoid spooking the beasts.

The Special Sauce was a dark, rancid liquified blend of aged blood and decaying meat,

and an oven-like breeze blasted Kahn as he walked the tree line, using the squeeze bottle to bait the area.

His thoughts drifted to Misty as he worked. They'd debated baiting the eastern side of the highway, but they hadn't seen the point in it.

Like the land that ran away from the underpass on the eastern side of the interstate, the western stretch was clogged with weeds that bled into the blue stone shoulder that flanked the train tracks. The forest's edge was filled with tall evergreens, and Kahn chose one that was equidistant from the underpass and the open gates so he would have a complete view. Misty was his failsafe, but there was no way he was letting the Howlers get past him.

There were many strong branches, so Kahn was able to climb forty feet into the tree without incident. It had been a while since he'd been up this high, and he was no fan of heights. He tied himself off for safety and set about unfolding his tree stand and bracketing it around the trunk. When he was done, he sat in the stand's chair and pulled up his pack which was attached to a rope connected to his belt via a carabiner.

He slipped the Remington from his shoulder, its new scope calibrated and ready for use. Kahn sat on the stand's sliver of a seat, leaned the gun across his lap, and drew out his thermos of coffee, but didn't open it. Instead, he put the container down on the stand's platform at his feet, raised the rifle, and put the scope to his eye.

Tree branches swayed, and leaves rustled. Could he be this lucky? Kahn flicked off the safety, made a slight adjustment to the scope, and let out a slow breath.

A buck strode from the trees, lifted its nose, and sniffed. It was a four-pointer, and the beast's gaze swept the railroad tracks as if sensing Kahn's presence.

But that wasn't possible. He was hidden, the wind was out of the west, the stink of the interstate was everywhere, and he'd sprayed himself with scent eliminator that contained enzymes and natural compounds that broke down scent molecules, including his sweat, skin oils, and bacteria that coated him like a second skin.

Kahn's concerns proved unfounded as the deer wandered along the fence line, slipped through the open gates, and passed directly beneath him. Moments later, it vanished into the darkness of the underpass.

He updated Misty and settled in, the excitement replaced with tedious observation.

Hunting for anything was a waiting game. Every second stretched and lingered, drawn thin by the thump and whiz of tires rolling over the highway. Kahn slowed his breathing as time unraveled, drawn out by the tension in his chest, each heartbeat an impatient thump against the silence.

The scent of damp earth and decaying vegetation seeped from the woods, and the wind whispered tales of the Howlers. Kahn knew they were out there, hidden beyond the tangle of branches, close enough that his stomach churned with anticipation. But waiting is a dance with time, a silent exchange where patience tests resolve, and every breath feels like a promise to the hunt.

A train rumbled, hissed, and creaked as it passed through the underpass. If the Howlers had been nearby, they were surely keeping out of sight unless they were looking to ride a rail out west. Daylight drained away and shadows stretched and shifted under the tree canopy to the west, creating moving shapes that teased Kahn's overactive mind. His hand tightened on his rifle as he focused and became aware of every creak, every whisper, despite the constant background hum of the highway.

The forest held its breath, and the rustling underbrush and the forest band faded, leaving a charged silence in the air. Kahn shifted his position, and the tree stand creaked as he laid his rifle across his legs. He cracked his neck and took a pull of coffee. Staying alert was of utmost importance because when on the hunt waiting wasn't passive. It was a poised, deliberate act, a silent ritual where he became part of the landscape.

As Kahn tuned in to his surroundings and let the peace of complete observation take control, he felt more relaxed than he had in a long time. The relief didn't last long, and as Slade's mauled body and his daughter's tear-streaked face filled his thoughts the ever-present triplets of shame, guilt, and doubt tried to tear away his resolve.

Kahn didn't expect to see the beasts until dusk, but he was dealing with a beast he knew very little about, so he bucked up and drank more coffee. Many normal animals, including large hunters like cats, wolves, and even bears, were most active during dawn and dusk. These times offered lower light and cooler temperatures, making it easier for the beasts to move without overheating and providing cover for ambushing prey. The keyword was normal. He knew better than most that nothing about Howlers was normal.

He rolled his shoulders back, sniffed the gas fume-laden air, and waited.

16

Dusk crept through the tall evergreens, the last rays of the setting sun angling through the forest. Headlights blossomed along the interstate, starting as a gentle glow and growing in intensity as dusk faded and gave way to night. The night symphony was warming up, but they were background music to the buzz, rumble, and thump of the interstate. Kahn had never realized how much the sound bothered him, and it was destroying his hunting peace.

A few deer, some squirrels, and an occasional chickenhawk or wren made an appearance, but he heard no howls or hisses or growls, nothing at all to indicate that the Howlers were anywhere near.

In the thickening darkness, Kahn could barely keep his eyes open. The last four days had been a whirlwind, and even when he tried to sleep, Kahn only managed NREM, that netherworld between waking and slumber, and slow-sleep, the deep rest, wouldn't come. Weariness pulled at his eyelids. Kahn leaned back, flexing his hunting patience as he lifted the rifle and stared through the scope just to have something to do.

The Howlers didn't show that night or the next.

Kahn and Misty followed the same routine as the first day and got the same results. No paw prints, no disturbed vegetation, and no trail tracking through the open gates.

It was close to midnight on the third night, 12:18 AM, and Kahn was peering through night vision binoculars when he saw four golden orbs hanging five feet above the ground. The eyes bobbed and shifted as they approached from the south.

Kahn's breath caught in his throat like a fishbone, and he called Misty.

"On my way," she whispered over the comm.

Sweat dripped down Kahn's back into the crack of his butt as he watched the Howlers prowl the forest along the fence line, staying within the trees. Kahn had no shot because of all the obstructions, and he couldn't hear the beasts sniffing, but he could tell by the way their shadows moved that they had their heads low to the ground. Kahn had applied a fair amount of Special Sauce along the fence, going extra heavy by the gates, and he had no doubts that was the scent the beasts were tracking.

It took the creatures a few minutes to find the open gates, and the beasts vanished from view three times as they trekked through the trees at the edge of the forest.

Whether it was some primal instinct, a memory of being herded through the gates, or some other mysterious reason, the Howlers crouched on all fours in the woods just beyond the open gates, their chests pressed to the pine needle-covered ground. The mates waited there, watching, displaying superior patience because they too were hunters.

Kahn's nerves danced and argued with his stomach and neck muscles for the next ten minutes as the Ozark Howlers remained still, the occasional disappearance of their golden eyes as the creatures blinked the only movement he could track. The breeze fell away, and not even the undergrowth stirred with the steady breathing of the highway.

When Misty slipped from the protective cocoon of the underpass Kahn had the urge to call out to her, but of course, that was laughable. The slightest sound: the click of a boot, the cocking of a weapon, a sniff or sneeze—they would all be like alarms to the Howlers, who were most likely accustomed to the sounds of the interstate like Kahn and could filter out unneeded noise until there was nothing left but fine grains of sound.

Kahn returned his attention to the forest, the bright white and glowing green of the night vision disorienting. Misty knew what to do. He was certain of that, and he needed to let her do her thing while he watched her back. Kahn switched from the binoculars to the rifle's eye scope.

The beasts were gone.

He pulled away from the scope. The Howlers had disappeared like ghosts... again. Kahn didn't like the fact that the beasts were continually getting the better of him. Normally when he had prey in his sight, literally in the crosshairs, he rarely failed to return with the pelt, but these creatures seemed to know what he planned to do before he did it.

Kahn switched back to the binoculars and scanned the woods.

Misty had invested in night vision glasses, so she was able to hold her weapon correctly as she moved stealthily through the darkness. She eased along the fence, using it as protection on her left as she made her way toward the open gates.

A set of glowing eyes bounced up and down eight feet from the ground as a Howler bounded from the woods and catapulted into the section of fence next to Misty. The metal poles bent, and the chain link flexed and popped, but the fence held.

Misty threw herself to her right, staggering as she danced through weeds before landing at the edge of the blue stone shoulder that ran along the railroad tracks. She swung her rifle around and fired, but she was lying on her side, propped up by an elbow, and the shot whizzed past the beast where it fought with the metal fence.

With one of the beasts pawing at Misty through the chain link, Kahn searched for the second Howler but didn't see it until the beast was through the open gates and barreling toward the underpass.

For the moment Misty was O.K., so Kahn turned his attention to the Howler running for the underpass. He put the scope to his eye and tried to get the beast in the crosshairs, but it was impossible. The beast was moving too fast, weaving in and out of weeds, jumping and diving and twisting, making itself an impossible target.

Kahn fired anyway, and his shots ricocheted off stones, plunked into railroad ties, and dinged off rails, sparks flying.

Misty screamed and more shots rang out, but the beast that attacked the fence was already moving, sliding like smoke towards the open gates and through them, following its mate.

Kahn's rifle clicked empty, and he went to work reloading it as he watched Misty.

The deputy sheriff picked herself up and dusted herself off.

Kahn could load the rifle blindfolded but his nerves were jumping, and he was keeping more than half an eye on Misty. He dropped a bullet, and it hit the tree stand's deck, bounced twice, and toppled over the edge, the brass glinting in the gloom as it plummeted to the ground. He fished out two more bullets, stuffed one into the internal magazine, filling it, and slipped one into the firing chamber before jacking the bolt closed.

Using the rifle scope was pointless. Things on the ground were moving too fast for him. The moonlight painted monstrous shadows, making them glow around the edges, disguising movement and elongating distance.

Misty had abandoned her rifle, and she was running along the fence, her sidearm in her hand, but it was silent.

The lead Howler was almost to the underpass, and Kahn saw the worst case scenario developing. If the beasts got across I-49, finding them would become exponentially more difficult in the vast emptiness of the Ozarks beyond Borderland Pass.

Kahn aimed the best he could and fired four fast shots that peppered the train tracks and the blue stone that served as their foundation. Sparks scattered like fireflies, and when the gun clicked empty Kahn drew his Beretta. In his rush to help Misty, Kahn surged to his feet, the tree stand beneath him creaking and popping as he steadied himself, yanking on his safety line.

Darkness boiled up to meet him as Kahn stared down at the dark forms of the Howlers. The lead beast had fifty yards to go before it reached the safety of the underpass. The beast's black fur merged with the night, beast and environment blending better than a human hunter ever could.

The second Howler had made up some ground, and Misty fired at the creature as it galloped, using the tall weeds on the northern side of the tracks as cover.

Tension knotted Kahn's shoulders and neck. Things were going sideways, fast. He had to do something to stop the beasts from reaching the underpass. He picked a spot twenty feet in front of the lead beast and opened up, the 9 MM spitting bullets that riddled the ground before the Howler.

With a growl and huff of exertion that rose above the competing sounds of the interstate, the Howler changed direction and bounded up the concrete slope that led out of the underpass and up onto the southbound lanes of I-49.

Kahn's skin crawled, his nerves poking at his skin, the knot in his stomach turning to ice.

Following the lead of its mate, the second Howler changed course as it zigzagged and slithered through the tall weeds and onto the concrete slope. There, the beast paused and looked back in defiance, its shadow elongated by the moonlight.

Misty stopped running to reload as Kahn thumbed the magazine out of his Beretta, pulled a fresh one from his backpack, slammed it into the gun, and chambered a round, but he held his fire. The beasts were out of the 9 MM's range, even though he was a crack shot.

Down on the ground, Misty gave chase.

"Shit," Kahn said as he holstered his weapon and shifted his feet a little too fast.

The tree stand's bracket slipped, tree bark stripping away as the stand dropped two feet, but it might as well have been a mile. As the stand caught and steadied, Kahn overreacted and pulled on the safety line too hard. The line went taut, yanked him off balance, and he slipped, reached out wildly, and kicked his pack, which toppled off the small platform along with his empty rifle and his dignity.

Kahn steadied himself. All wasn't lost, he needed to get to the ground, but not by flying.

Leaving the stand where it was, Kahn clicked out of the safety line and climbed from branch to branch, darkness pressing in on him as he descended.

Misty fired, the shots a singular sound in the chaos of his twirling thoughts, and Kahn spared a glance in the deputy sheriff's direction. He could hardly see Misty as she worked her way up the side of the overpass. The Howlers were nowhere to be seen, and Kahn's stomach went nuclear.

One of the Howlers let loose with its unique cackle-like shriek, the call filled with rage.

The next sign of trouble was a sharp screech, the unmistakable bite of rubber against the road, high-pitched and desperate. It rose like a siren above the night symphony and the rush of the highway, cutting through the arguing wind that rattled the evergreen branches. The screech elongated, stretching and snapping.

Kahn's heart pounded as he climbed.

A booming air-shaking thud followed by metal wailing carried from the interstate—two vehicles colliding. Plastic cracked, glass shattered, and steel crumpled with a sickening crunch that rattled Kahn's bones.

Another impact, this time a lower, resonant boom as plastic popped and fractured.

The deep bass of a semi's horn blaring, followed by an explosion. Crunching and the grinding of metal on pavement as rubber moaned and tires popped, each second stretching as the sounds of the crash stepped on one another and grew.

There was a metallic groan as one vehicle introduced itself to another, releasing a tortured, almost organic cry of resistance as glass shattered in bursts like a cascade of breaking icicles, tinkling and bursting in violent succession.

Kahn was almost down the tree, and his thoughts drifted to what he was going to do when he got there. Chase after Misty? Or cut through the underpass and hope to impede the Howlers as they tried to cross the highway and drive them back? Good luck with that. Misty was his priority, and as the air filled with more screeches, a chorus of brakes locking, and the desperate yelp of tires skidding against the road, he knew what he had to do.

A guttural, tearing sound ripped through the forest—a bumper or fender torn free. Horns blared in discordant succession, some sharp, violent staccato bursts, others long and mournful, trapped in the blaring noise of panic.

Kahn jumped the last ten feet to the ground, and he landed on his feet but crumbled next to his pack, his knees aching, pain lancing his legs.

The wind picked up, carrying the astringent scent of burning rubber and hot metal. Distant voices, frantic and laced with terror, cut through the mechanical violence, merging into an urgent murmur of screams, shouts, and gasps.

A tire exploded, echoing like a gunshot, followed by another, and another, a chain reaction as tires succumbed to the weight of wreckage.

Kahn's blood pounded through his veins, his head ringing, his muscles protesting as he pulled his gun and threw himself forward.

A primal roar of rage, followed by another.

Through the chaos came the shrill cries of a woman that rose above the tumult, her pleading blending into the panicked tapestry of sound.

An eerie aftershock filled the air, punctuated by metal settling, glass tinkling, and the ongoing wail of broken horns.

Kahn ran by the dark maw of the underpass and hit the concrete slope at a full run, his feet slipping as he scrambled up to the interstate. His thoughts drifted to the pile-up the year before, and he had the fleeting thought that maybe I-49, or Borderland Pass, was cursed.

17

The section of I-49 that knifed through Borderland Pass was packed with destroyed vehicles. Apocalyptic devastation stretched into shadowy flame-dappled blackness, filling the road and its shoulder with a chaotic mess of SUVs, cars, and tractor-trailers. The sounds of human suffering and panic carried on the wind, headlight beams cutting through the darkness, forming large bright clouds in the smoke.

Kahn climbed from beneath the underpass and staggered onto the shoulder of the interstate.

People struggled to break free of burning cars as headlights flickered through the chaos. The shoulders along the southbound lanes were jammed, and at first count, Kahn figured there were thirty cars piled up. Nothing when compared to the prior year, but still a Shit Show of epic magnitude.

Kahn felt the urge to rush into the destruction and start helping because that's what people did when the going got tough. He'd seen it countless times; enemies became allies during a crisis, at least for the moment, and Kahn was happy to see people helping others.

An old man assisted a mother with a young child as she leaned against her destroyed car, cradling the unhurt infant in her arms as the man shielded her. Somewhere a dog barked, and between the squashed cars wounds were being tended to, water was being passed around, and more than one person was documenting the accident via cellphone as several people called for help.

A young woman filming the chaos panned around toward Kahn, and she paused, smoke billowing around her as she lowered her phone and frowned.

It was then Kahn remembered the gun in his hand, and he yelled, "I'm a cop." A chill crept through his bones. Thankfully she didn't catch that lie on camera, but his fib satisfied the woman, and she went back to work being the Coppola of the accident as Kahn tucked the Beretta away.

The "I'm a cop" lie made him search for Misty.

She was working her way between a crushed white pickup and a Honda Civic that was accordioned so badly its color was hard to discern. There were other people, some injured, some not, but all appeared stunned and wobbly.

The Ozark Howler's bark-like laugh echoed over the smoke-clogged interstate, reverberating through the wreckage as it sprang onto the hood of the white pickup Misty hid behind. Its yellow eyes gleamed with a fierceness that unnerved Kahn, the golden orbs cutting through the thick, sooty gloom. The creature let out another chilling howl—a strange blend of wolf's snarl, elk's bugle, and the wild cackle of a hyena, and each exhale shot smoky jets of condensation from its dog-like snout.

The staggering rays of dying headlights illuminated a sea of metal, an infinite number of surfaces perfect for causing a ricochet. Kahn pulled his gun but didn't fire, the risk of getting more blood on his hands was too great.

Coarse, shadow-streaked fur clung to the Howler's gritty, soot-covered body, and muscles bulged beneath layers of grime and shadow. The beast's massive head swiveled, jaws snapping closed, eyes sweeping the scene like searchlights.

A jolt of anticipation, excitement, and fear raced through Kahn, twisting his stomach, a persistent stab of pain knifing the base of his spine.

In a sinuous, serpentine motion, the creature shifted, shook its head, and rose onto its hind legs. Illuminated by the blaze of headlights and growing flames, it towered over the devastation, but as the beast bared its teeth Kahn saw no horns.

The truck's hood flexed and popped as the Howler climbed onto the pickup's roof and what was left of the windshield shattered into tiny square shards of glass.

As the pickup's roof caved in, metal squealing, Misty moved, easing along the pickup's wreckage and wedging herself into a protective fold in the crunched Honda.

Kahn searched for the male Howler, but there was too much confusion and smoke. A man was running around with a fire extinguisher, spraying every flame no matter how small. Black smoke mixed with the white, the gray noxious clouds swirling into the sky.

The distant wail of sirens carried over the devastation.

Misty popped up and squeezed off two shots as the female Howler jumped into the pickup's load bed.

One shot punched into the pickup's rear window, and it shattered with an explosive crackle. The second bullet caught the Howler in the leg, and it wailed as it reared up, front paws lashing out as it vaulted from the pickup's bed, the truck bouncing as its springs whined.

Misty dropped, rolled, and disappeared into the wreckage.

The Howler landed with one foot on the crumpled Honda and one foot on the remains of the pickup, its long arms fishing between the two destroyed vehicles, claws searching for flesh.

A wail of agony snapped Kahn from his paralysis, and he darted forward, slipping around a Corvette that had managed to stay unscathed, and a Chevy Tahoe that had been rear-ended. The drivers of the vehicles stared out at Kahn as he maneuvered through the carnage, and he came up short when he reached a small station wagon that was little more than a chunk of compressed metal and plastic.

The car's interior was a crumpled mess, the steering column shoved backward along with the entire mangled front end. Despite the airbag deploying, it hadn't offered much protection for the young woman trapped inside. Her blonde hair clung in matted clumps to her blood-streaked face, which was smeared with a layer of red so thick it was hard to make out her features. She was wedged tightly between the broken steering wheel and her seat, which had snapped from its mounts and reclined backward at a twisted, unnatural angle, leaving her pinned.

A jagged wound stretched across the woman's chest, raw and gaping. Torn organs were exposed, some forced through her ribcage around the steering wheel, as if the car itself had become part of her broken form.

Any hope of saving her was far too late—if she wasn't already gone, she was on the verge of leaving this world.

Kahn looked away as he wedged past the wreckage.

The Howler jumped, the two cars beneath it shifting as metal flexed and bent, plastic cracked, and the thump of the crinkled Honda's frame hitting the interstate rang over the knots of twisted metal. It dropped onto all fours and launched itself atop a mangled van, pivoted, and jumped down to the road, landing next to an overturned truck.

Kahn froze.

Misty crawled out from her hiding place, brushing shards of glass from her clothes. She sprang into motion, weaving between the mangled cars as she chased after the Howler, her focus unwavering despite the wreckage.

Another painful cry strummed the cords of Kahn's nerves, but this time Kahn saw the source of the sound.

A Tesla lay on its side in a tangle of mangled plastic and broken glass, its headlights cutting through the destruction clogging the interstate. Inside a middle-aged woman's face was reflected in the cracked windshield, streaked with blood from a gash above her brow, her dark skin glistening with sweat. The sour stench of leaking fuel and burning rubber filled the air, and through the toxic haze, he watched the woman as she struggled with her seatbelt.

The male Howler prowled alongside the Tesla, its shoulders rippling with raw, unnatural power, twisted horns shooting from its head like spikes of dark wood. Mottled with mud and streaked with blood, the creature's fur blended into the night.

A small explosion popped behind Kahn and he looked back to find Misty approaching.

The female Howler moved swiftly, leaping from one car to the next as she raced toward the slender line of trees that separated the southbound lanes from the northbound. Each powerful jump brought her closer to the narrow strip of forest, her path a blur of leaps and bounds as she navigated the wrecked vehicles.

Kahn held his breath and turned his attention back to the woman trapped in the cocoon of crumpled metal and plastic that the male Howler had taken an interest in. Accident victims streamed away from the creature, yelling and screaming in fear and panic as they threaded through the crushed vehicles seeking safety, but there was no place on the interstate safe from claws.

The Howler's eyes glowed a sickly yellow as it hunched closer, resting one massive paw against the Tesla's crumpled hood. It tilted its head, and for a fleeting moment, Kahn almost thought it was studying the woman, savoring her fear. Then the creature lunged, its claws scraping metal, leaving deep gouges.

Misty arrived beside Kahn, her breathing a series of puffs and wheezes. The deputy sheriff was almost done. "Are... you..." Her gaze followed Kahn's and when she saw the woman trapped in the Tesla, the Howler antagonizing her, Misty squeezed by Kahn and beelined toward danger.

Kahn wanted to scream, to tell his friend that it wasn't worth it, that giving her life would be meaningless. Tell that to the woman in the Tesla, came the rational voice in his head that had been relegated to the deepest shadows in the farthest corner of his mind. Survival, revenge, and murder filled Kahn's thoughts, and with a reluctance born of weariness, doubt, and insecurity he trailed after Misty.

Sirens pulsed through the tense air, and blue and red emergency lights spun through the smoky haze, casting strobe-like flashes that pierced the darkness with sharp, darting beams. The shadows around Kahn brightened as help approached, easing the tightness in his chest. But despite the relief creeping in, the Howler's cry tore away what little hope he'd found.

The woman in the Tesla stared up at the Howler, her face frozen in horror as the beast bore down on her. Her hands flew to her mouth, her seatbelt pinning her back as she struggled, kicking the dashboard, trying to push herself away.

With a screech of metal, the beast reared back, its horns ramming the car with powerful shoves, and shards of metal flew like deadly confetti. Kahn winced as he watched the woman twist, her body contorting to avoid the monster as it thrust its head through the broken windshield.

Misty screamed as she fired, but it was useless, there were too many obstructions.

The creature roared as the woman tried to shield herself, but the Howler pressed on, jaws snapping, its muzzle darting forward, jaws clamping down on the woman's shoulder.

A sickening crack, followed by a pop, reverberated through the wreckage, and blood splattered the inside of the car as the Howler wriggled its snout.

Kahn was wedged between two crushed cars. There was nothing he could do for the woman, and as her final death wail rattled his nerves and poked his guilt a deep sorrow and fresh guilt consumed him.

Misty didn't stop her assault, and when her gun clicked empty, she hid behind the remains of a box truck and Kahn hoped she had no ammo left.

It was then Kahn saw the man peering out from the forest on the eastern side of the road. No hum of motion leaked through the thin forest from the northbound lanes, and Kahn figured traffic had come to a complete standstill, bottlenecked by rubbernecking because of the accident. With no flow of cars, a thick cloud of light seeped through the trees, backlighting the man where he lay prone on his stomach in the underbrush.

The man had a crew cut, wore forest camouflage fatigues, and had a rifle on a bipod set up on a rock before him. The rifle was aimed at the Howler.

A gurgle crept into Kahn's mouth, acid stinging his throat. The man's senses were sharp, because his radar homed in on Kahn, his gaze steady. Kahn recognized the guy. He'd seen his face before. Recalling his morning's breakfast occasionally eluded him, and if the news was good—forget about it. But tragic things. True nightmares. They stuck with him and for some reason so had this guy's face. From the news a few years back? Kahn saw the ruddy face framed over a news anchor's right shoulder, and he was close to pulling the memory loose when Misty screamed.

Misty did have bullets, and she fired her reloaded gun as she screeched with fury. Bullets pelted metal, plastic, and rubber as the male Howler sprang away.

The man in the weeds at the edge of the interstate fired, the sharp crack of his high-powered rifle echoing over the northbound lanes of I-49.

Kahn saw what was going to happen next but was helpless to prevent it.

A knot of twisting fur, teeth, and claws exploded over the vehicle Misty was using for cover. She angled her aim upward, but before she could steady herself, one of the beast's huge paws swung through the narrow gap between destroyed cars and struck her hard. The impact threw off her shot as she struggled to regain control of her weapon.

As Misty fell a claw snagged her midsection, and she wailed as she slammed into a twisted fender and fell to the road.

Another shot rang out from the tree line, and as Kahn threaded through the wreckage, heading toward Misty's crumpled body, a spark ricocheted off twisted metal next to the Howler.

A mournful wail, like an aggrieved parent calling a child home for supper carried from the forest at the center of the interstate.

The male Howler turned its back on Misty and leapfrogged across destroyed vehicles like it was skipping on stones as it crossed a river.

When Kahn arrived at Misty's side, she was splayed out on the oil-soaked road, legs twisted at odd angles, her eyes open and staring into the smoke-filled sky. He thought she was dead, and sorrow leaked through him, but as he dropped to his knees and took her in his arms, getting her blood on his hands, she choked to life, her eyes fluttering as she spit up blood.

The male Howler roared, and Kahn looked up just in time to see the beast disappear into the forest. He ranged his gaze across the tree line and found that the rifleman was gone.

Emergency workers threaded through the chaos, helping those most in need, and the thumping of approaching helicopters brought some hope.

Misty's wound was bad, and her breathing was shallow and inconsistent, but she was alive. An airlift to Grave Memorial, a crack surgeon, and some superhero nurses, and she'd have some scars to punctuate her stories when she was sitting in a bar down south, her only worry what she was having for lunch. Kahn had to hold on to that because she was all he had to hold onto.

Her eyes fluttered closed.

Kahn shook her and said, "Hold on, Misty. Hold on."

18

Grace Memorial Hospital, Ozark, Arkansas, U.S.
1:12 PM CST, August 23rd, 2022

Tuesdays were slow visiting days. On Mondays, the guilt of weekend non-visitation was handled and the work week's responsibilities wrapped visiting obligations in the comforting cocoon of procrastination, which left hump day and its closest mates a respite for hospital staff that was perpetually trying to catch up. A cool breeze pushed into the waiting area where three solitary people sat waiting for fate to come calling, the sharp scent of coffee from the cafe settling over the smell of cleaning fluids fighting the indelible rot of sickness. Misty was being evaluated and Kahn was waiting for the sheriff and others to arrive so the doctor could give an update on her condition to everyone who needed to know.

The worst day of Kahn's life hadn't taken place in this hospital, but it was one like it, and weren't they all the same? Places where people came to die and those closest to them gave up small pieces of themselves as they watched. Miracles did happen within the sterile rooms where doctors and nurses tried to work their magic and play God, but Kahn had never experienced one. Hospitals brought only bad memories—his grandfather lying in bed with a knot the size of a softball protruding from the side of his head. Then his mother, and then…

Kahn rubbed his eyes, the memories coming hard and fast now, Evelyn's tear-streaked face materializing out of his mental fog.

It was late and the waiting room was empty, the lights dimmed like a funeral parlor. Evelyn sat next to Kahn, his wife sitting on her hands as she gently rocked back and forth, tears running down her face. Slick black bags hung beneath eyes that looked like they might leak blood, and her hair was a disheveled knot held in place by a hairband operating at the outer limits of its elasticity. Thin strands of hair spidered across her face, and her clothes were wrinkled. She wore a button-up blue shirt, and her slacks were a variation of purple that looked the color of an eggplant. The fashion choices concerned Kahn. Evelyn was always put together, even if she was only going to the market, and to see her now drained the hope from him like a frigid day drained body heat.

Dr. Kumar had emerged from the swinging doors like Dracula, lab coat whipping, dark hair slicked back, silver clipboard in his hand like a shield. The doctor's eyes swept over the waiting room, found Kahn and his wife, and motioned for them to join him.

"Let's sit where it's private... and more comfortable." The doc smiled his neat little smile, the one that made Kahn want to smack the guy. It was the middle of the night, his daughter was in a hospital bed, and he could find no reason to smile.

Kumar led the couple down a sterile hallway, LED lights blaring down. When he reached a closed door labeled Patient Services, the doctor opened it and ushered the worried parents inside.

Kahn knew it wasn't Kumar's office right off because there were no personal effects. No stacks of files or reports. It was a consultation room. A confessional where secrets and news were told and hope was exchanged and bartered for.

"Please take a seat," the doctor said, his tone and facial expressions shifting to dour reality now that he was in his confessional.

Evelyn took Kahn's hand, a rare act, and the couple sat close, legs pressed together, the tension flowing between them creating an intense heat Kahn hadn't felt in a long time.

"I'm afraid I have bad news," Dr. Kumar said, and all the air was sucked from the room.

Kahn couldn't breathe, and as he struggled to remember how to take a breath, the doctor went on.

"When you brought Jenna in, she was complaining of initial symptoms that could be associated with many illnesses. Her swollen lymph nodes—the lumps in her neck, armpits, and groin. Your daughter indicated that she didn't notice these lumps at first, but they got bigger over time. Then there's the persistent, unexplained fever that hasn't responded to the usual treatments, and the night sweating. It's very concerning that she's waking up drenched in sweat, even in a cool room. Her weight loss is another red flag, as is the constant fatigue, which has been leaving her unable to perform school activities. And none of this has improved with rest."

Dr. Kumar sighed.

Kahn was in shock, and when he glanced at his wife, he saw she was staring at the floor.

"What focused my testing was her abdominal pain and her loss of appetite. The lymph nodes in her abdomen are enlarged, and she's been experiencing shortness of breath and coughing, which usually occurs if there's pressure on the lungs or chest from swollen lymph nodes in the region."

Somewhere a woman screamed, and Dr. Kumar smiled tightly, then frowned.

"So... what does this all mean?" Evelyn had asked.

"I think she has non-Hodgkin lymphoma," the doctor answered solemnly.

"Cancer?" Kahn said, his voice cracking.

The doctor nodded. "I've conducted a range of tests, including a thorough physical examination. I verified her enlarged lymph nodes and checked her liver and spleen, which appear to be O.K. at the moment. I've run blood tests, including a complete blood count and tests for kidney and liver function. This will help assess overall health and look for signs of infection or other abnormalities. We've done a CT scan, and a PET scan is next. That will tell us exactly what we're dealing with—the size, location, and spread of lymph node involvement." Here Kumar paused and looked down at his desk, and Kahn knew the guy was gathering his courage for what came next. "Her chest X-ray showed that her lymph nodes around her lungs are inflamed. We'll do a biopsy of an enlarged lymph node, but... I'm not expecting to find anything that will change the diagnosis."

Kahn felt like he'd been smacked in the head with a sledgehammer. Sweat dripped down his face as the walls closed in, the doctor's voice becoming muddled and faint.

"An expert pathologist will review the biopsy sample to determine the type of lymphoma. In some cases, a bone marrow biopsy is also necessary to see if the lymphoma has spread to the bone marrow. Other specialized tests, such as immunohistochemistry, flow cytometry, or genetic tests on the biopsy sample can identify specific markers on the lymphoma cells, providing insight into the type and aggressiveness of the disease."

A cloud of dread engulfed Kahn. The thick mud of anguish seeped into his mouth and eyes and every pore. He felt his face heat up, and his stomach jumped with pain as every nerve danced and twisted.

"Is there..." Evelyn wept.

"Depending on the type, stage, and aggressiveness of the lymphoma there are things we can do," Dr. Kumar offered. "Commonly, her treatment plan would include a combination of chemotherapy, radiation therapy, immunotherapy, and possibly stem cell transplantation. Chemotherapy, which will most likely be the primary treatment, involves a regimen of drugs designed to target and kill the cancer cells throughout her body. In the case of aggressive lymphoma, intensive chemotherapy might be necessary, and this would be done in cycles over several months. The drugs are administered orally or intravenously, and due to their strength, they may cause side effects like hair loss, fatigue, nausea, and a weakened immune system."

A groan escaped Kahn's lips and Evelyn's hand tightened on his leg.

"My team would monitor her response and adjust dosages to balance efficacy with the risk of side effects. Radiation therapy might also be recommended. This approach involves directing high-energy rays at affected lymph nodes to destroy cancer cells while minimizing exposure to surrounding tissues. The treatment usually involves multiple sessions and, although generally well tolerated, can result in localized skin changes, fatigue, and, less commonly, longer-term effects depending on the radiation's location."

Kahn and Evelyn said nothing. What was there to say? His daughter was dying, and though the doctor didn't get into the statistics, Kahn knew surviving any cancer was a low-success gambit.

In a rare display of humanity, the doctor said, "There is hope. Let me and my team find out exactly what type of lymphoma we're dealing with here."

"So... she might live?" Evelyn said, but the tone of her voice held little hope.

Live? What the hell did that mean if his daughter would waste away to nothing and die before her twentieth birthday?

"The survival rate for non-Hodgkin lymphoma in teenage patients generally varies depending on factors like the specific type of NHL, the stage at diagnosis, and how well the lymphoma responds to treatment." Kumar licked his lips as he studied Kahn and Evelyn as if trying to decide if he should go further. He nodded and continued, "For adolescents with NHL, the overall five-year survival rate is relatively high, typically ranging from 80% to 90%. Some subtypes of NHL have higher survival rates than others."

Kahn's head slumped and his chin hit his chest. Five years. What the hell was five years? She was thirteen.

The doctor went on, but Kahn barely heard the man.

"For example, aggressive subtypes like large B-cell lymphoma have a five-year survival rate of around 85–90% when diagnosed at an early stage and treated promptly. This is one of the most common types of NHL in teens and responds well to intensive chemotherapy." He went on about Burkitt lymphoma, anaplastic large-cell lymphoma, and peripheral t-cell lymphomas. Kahn tuned it all out, thoughts of how he was going to pay for Jenna's treatments with his shitty medical benefits eating at him like his own personal disease.

The life he knew was over, and guilt leaked through him. His life. His daughter had just been sentenced to death, and he was worrying about himself. He was trash, and he didn't see how he could ever recover.

"Kahn. Kahn! You awake?" Sheriff Olave's harsh voice snapped Kahn from his misery, and he looked up. Whatever the sheriff saw in Kahn's face made his expression soften and he said, "You O.K.?"

Kahn nodded.

The sheriff looked at his watch and said, "Have you seen the doc today?"

Kahn shook his head no.

"Alright then," Olave said as he sat, the plastic chair screeching under the strain. He was in full uniform, sans campaign hat, and his aviator sunglasses hung from a chest pocket next to his gleaming star.

The pair sat in silence for several minutes before the sheriff chuckled and said, "She should've been sheriff, you know. She's been on the force way longer than me, she's local, played the deputy game perfectly, and had a nice clean record, even if it was undistinguished. I went to her before I agreed to run. Not to ask her permission or for her support, but to get her advice. Do you know what she said?"

Kahn had a good idea, and in most instances, he would've said so, but Olave was the sheriff, and cops were cops, and egos were egos, so he said nothing.

"She looked me dead in the eye, and said 'Only a moron would want to be sheriff.'" Olave snickered again.

Kahn laughed also, but when the merriment died away, the hospital reasserting its somber control, the pair didn't talk, the waiting room a silent pressure cooker waiting to explode.

There was a flat panel on a wall, its volume off as it displayed an ariel view of smoke pouring off the multi-car pile-up on the interstate.

As the uncomfortable silence stretched out, the sheriff pointed up at the TV. "When are they going to stop showing this?"

"Probably not until the next one," Kahn said.

Olave huffed. "That was some Shit Show last year. I'm still dealing with paperwork."

"I can imagine." Kahn had been deep in the Ozarks hunting and hadn't heard about the massive pile-up in Borderland Pass until he returned home. "Misty talks about it all the time. She calls it her war days."

"You got some information last night from the doc, right? How's she doing?"

"Same," Kahn said. "She's hanging on by the thinnest of threads. Her internal injuries are bad, but as you know those were buttoned up." Now he looked at his watch. "We'll know in a few minutes." His mind drifted back to that nondescript office where his world had been shattered.

"Don't worry." The sheriff clapped Kahn on the back. "She's a tough old bird and she'll pull through." Olave sounded like he was trying to convince himself.

With that, the air left the balloon, and the conversation died again. The pair sat, the rumble of the hospital bubbling around them, Kahn's eyelids drooping as sleep beckoned.

The zip of the hospital's entrance doors sliding open carried over the lobby and into the waiting area.

Kahn looked up to find an old man wearing a red flannel shirt and jeans using a walker to inch into the room. Though he didn't recognize the man because he'd never met him, Kahn knew Misty had a brother, and figured the bent and broken old guy had to be him. Kahn searched his memory for the man's name but couldn't find it.

Sheriff Olave pushed up from his seat and said, "Misty's brother, Harry. He's all she's got. Mom and Dad are dead, and their relatives, what few they've got, pulled up stakes and headed west years ago." The sheriff strode across the lobby with Kahn in tow and introductions were made and the sheriff helped the old guy to a seat.

"Nice to meet you both and put faces to the names," Harry said, his voice frail and broken. "My sister has told me so much about you both."

"All good I'm sure," Kahn said.

The old guy smiled. "For sure. Any change since last night?"

Kahn and the sheriff shook their heads in unison as if they'd practiced the motion.

The sheriff's eyes strayed to something behind Kahn. "What the hell is this now?"

Maddox and Buck strode through the sliding doors into the waiting room.

19

Maddox was dressed to the nines. He wore a blue suit, red tie, and polished loafers, and he carried a black leather file folder. His air of superiority and unwarranted confidence was unmistakable. The arrogant ass walked with a bounce in his step, chin held high, shoulders squared, posture rigid as his eyes fixed on Sheriff Olave and Kahn as though he intended to dress them down.

Buck looked ready to hunt. A pistol was strapped to his leg along with a knife, and he wore forest camo and a Memphis Grizzlies cap. His face was stubble-ridden salt and pepper, and his red eyes were narrow from lack of sleep and a dose of liquid courage. Unlike Maddox's pristine shoes, Buck's boots were caked with mud and Kahn heard the audible sigh and hiss of the cleaner as she hauled her mop and bucket across the lobby to clean the dirty boot prints the hunter left on the worn linoleum.

The sheriff hitched up his gun belt, straightened his tie, and went to meet the newcomers.

Kahn followed, more curious than anything else. Misty had been injured on the interstate, and Maddox and the game preserve had nothing to do with her current situation. Well, not nothing. She had been helping Kahn, who was contracted by the sheriff's office to hunt in the game preserve.

"How can I help you, Mr. Maddox?" said the sheriff in the voice that got him elected.

Kahn almost snickered. The voice was calm, steady, and nearly comforting, a far cry from his normal rough and tough tone that told anyone who heard it to obey his commands.

Maddox's gaze shifted to Kahn, who stood beside the sheriff but remained a step behind the lawman. "I'm here because…" Though it didn't seem possible, Maddox straightened further as he reigned in his insufferable arrogance. "How is Misty?"

"Alive," the sheriff said. "You could have called for that information. What's up? Why are you here?"

"I'm doing what one must when phone calls aren't returned," Maddox said.

"You called me?" The sheriff made a show of pulling his phone.

"No. Him." Maddox pointed at Kahn.

A thin smile leaked over the sheriff's face.

"Someone cut our chain securing the gates at the preserve's northern boundary along the railroad tracks," Maddox said. "Do you know anything about that?"

Kahn only stared, thinking, calculating. He didn't owe this guy anything, and anger stirred in the pit of his stomach, rage awakening.

Maddox turned to the sheriff. "The scene up on the highway was caused by him." He pointed at Kahn.

"Really?" Sheriff Olave said. "Do tell."

"He was screwing around up by the highway. Hunting for his bullshit mythical beast that will explain all his failures and hard luck."

Kahn stepped forward, struggling to keep his anger in check. "It had nothing to do with you and Slade driving the How—the mutants into the preserve on purpose? You know, so you could make your rich clients sign NDAs and promise the hunt of a lifetime. Be the first, and have the best story, but no pictures permitted. Where did you find such desperate losers that would pay for such a travesty?"

The sheriff pivoted until he was facing Kahn. "You've got proof of all that?"

"I'm telling you that's what happened," Kahn said, the nugget of heat in his stomach spreading like wildfire.

"Did you cut the chain or not?" Maddox pressed.

"No."

"Liar."

In a sudden, explosive movement, Kahn lunged forward, fists clenched.

Maddox stepped back and braced himself, widening his stance in anticipation of a blow.

Sheriff Olave stepped between them. "Y'all can't do this in here." His eyes darted toward the sliding exit doors.

"Care to take this outside?" Kahn said. If he didn't get out of the hospital he was going to explode.

The sheriff and Buck trailed Maddox and Kahn as they exited through the sliding doors onto the broad walkway that led to the parking lot.

Never one to punch first, Kahn flexed his hands and rolled his shoulders as he waited.

Maddox incorrectly perceived Kahn's hesitation as weakness, and he lashed out, a knuckle-cracking hook aimed at Kahn's jaw.

Kahn sidestepped, but the blow nicked his cheekbone, sending a shock of pain racing through him that blurred his vision for a heartbeat. He eased back, regained his balance, and threw a quick, sharp jab that caught Maddox in the ribs.

The lodge crony grunted but hardly faltered, his movements fluid as he advanced.

Onlookers approached and backed away at the sheriff's urging, but some stayed and stared transfixed at the fight like little kids in the schoolyard.

Maddox swung again, this time a brutal uppercut.

Kahn blocked the blow, the force vibrating through his forearm.

An elbow crashed into Kahn's ribs and Maddox spun, driving the wind out of him. Kahn wheezed, one hand clutching his side, as he tried to draw in air, his fury blazing out of control.

Like an uncoiling spring, Kahn threw himself forward, a boiling knot of anger. His shoulder rammed into Maddox's chest, and both men tumbled to the concrete.

"Need help, boss?" said Buck.

"The hell you will," Sheriff Olave countered.

Both men rolled and used each other's leverage to push themselves to their feet.

Maddox was off balance and Kahn delivered a quick jab to Maddox's stomach as the man pulled away, creating just enough distance to throw a powerful cross. The punch connected with Kahn's jaw as he pulled back, and pain spidered through his head as he steadied himself. Then he smiled, the anger draining away and leaving only cool hatred. Kahn spat blood and said, "Last chance to quit."

"Piss off!"

The pair charged each other like bulls and collided, a violent meeting of fists and elbows. Kahn's knuckles found Maddox's cheekbone, and Maddox's knee struck Kahn's thigh. The pain was numbing, the kind that burned for a moment and then dulled as adrenaline took over. Kahn barely registered the throbbing as he blocked another hit, his forearm bruising under Maddox's powerful punches.

Kahn feinted left, and as Maddox shifted to block, Kahn drove his knee up into the guy's stomach.

Maddox's face twisted, his breath coming in harsh gasps, but he didn't go down. He swayed, momentarily vulnerable.

Kahn gripped Maddox's shoulder and delivered a colossal uppercut that knocked the lodge manager from his feet.

Snarling and cursing, Maddox pushed himself up to a knee, then stood, breathing hard, his gaze murderous.

Security guards arrived, their voices shouting for the two men to stop, but the sheriff intervened, and the guards stood down.

The two fighters circled each other, and with a final surge of energy, Kahn lunged and tackled Maddox to the ground, pinning him with his forearm pressed hard against Maddox's throat.

Maddox struggled beneath him, growling, his hands clawing at Kahn's arm, but his strength was fading.

Kahn leaned in, his voice low and controlled. "This ends now. You want more?"

Maddox bucked and heaved as he hooked his arm around Kahn's neck and dragged him into a graceless grapple.

The pair wrestled, fighting for control, each man straining against the other's weight and force. Kahn's knee found Maddox's thigh, a blow that loosened the man's grip just enough for Kahn to wriggle free and get to his feet.

Maddox tried to get up.

Kahn punched the man twice in the chops, two fast, but powerful blows that dislodged a tooth.

Maddox hit the ground with a sniff, a curse, and a snort of blood.

"What the hell is going on here?" yelled Dr. Lester.

Maddox scrambled to his feet, breathing hard, blood dripping from his mouth.

Kahn wiped blood from the corner of his mouth, tasting copper as he smiled at Maddox.

"Just having a little disagreement, is all," the sheriff said.

Dr. Lester eyed the lawman like he was a bug that should know better, which of course the sheriff should. She said, "Inside. Now. And knock the mud off you. My staff have better things to do than to clean up after pigs." With that, she went through the sliding doors into the hospital lobby.

The good doctor, a slender middle-aged woman with dark hair and stress lines cutting across her mocha-colored face that conveyed her experience far outweighed her years, refused to allow her staff to clean Maddox and Kahn's wounds, saying, "That's why mommas are on this Earth. To take care of children."

So it was that Kahn dabbed at his face with alcohol wipes as he, along with the sheriff and Misty's brother sat in a patient services room slightly larger than the one that ended life as Kahn had known it. The doctor sat behind a desk, her audience of three sitting before her.

Dr. Lester leaned forward, her ponytail flopping over her shoulder as she sighed in that mournful way that must be taught in medical schools, then said, "Misty's injuries are extensive and deeply concerning. When the animal struck her, its paw delivered a blow so forceful it hurled her body and twisted her frame as she collided with a vehicle. The sheer power of that hit alone was enough to cause significant trauma."

Kahn sniffed, but the others remained silent.

"Then there was the coughing up blood and the internal injuries," the doctor continued. "Upon initial examination, Misty's chest showed signs of substantial bruising and swelling, consistent with blunt force trauma. The ribs on her left side are cracked, some fractured entirely. Fractured ribs lead to intense, unrelenting pain with each breath making it difficult for her to get enough oxygen. We've got her on an oxygen mix and her breathing, although stabilized, remains irregular and shallow, a sign that her lungs have been compromised and she's unable to expand them fully. The force from the attack likely caused damage to her spleen and liver as well, both of which are highly vascular and I believe they are bleeding.

"The blood she spat up after the incident concerns me greatly. Coughing up blood after such a trauma indicates pulmonary or thoracic damage. In Misty's case, the likely scenario is either a punctured lung or severe damage to her bronchi, which are sensitive passageways that can easily rupture under force. While the bleeding appears to have slowed, I'll need to conduct further tests to determine whether any clots or internal bleeds are still active or if we're looking at a slower, more progressive hemorrhage.

"Externally, she has numerous abrasions and lacerations, particularly on her arms and face where the force of her fall scraped her skin against the rough road surface. We've cleaned and dressed these wounds to avoid infection, but the healing process will be lengthy. Her arms show signs of severe bruising, likely from instinctively attempting to shield herself from the impact. Her left shoulder is dislocated, a painful injury we've managed to set back in place, but it will take time before she has full use of that arm again. Muscle strain and torn ligaments are also probable, and she'll need physical therapy to restore her range of motion fully."

Air moved through the single HVAC vent, the sheriff tapped his foot, and the hum of the hospital's lifeblood filled the room.

Kahn was in shock. He knew it was going to be bad, but...

"Misty's head trauma is another area of concern. Although her skull didn't sustain any fractures, she did experience a sharp impact that caused a concussion. Her symptoms include confusion, dizziness, and light sensitivity, and she has had periods of drifting in and out of consciousness since the attack. For now, we'll keep her room dim and subject her to minimal sensory stimulation. Concussions vary in severity, and it's hard to predict the recovery timeline, but symptoms may linger for weeks. As part of her care, we'll monitor for any signs of swelling in the brain, which could lead to more severe neurological damage.

"In terms of her prognosis. None of her injuries are immediately life-threatening, however, they are collectively severe and require vigilant monitoring. Over the next few days, we'll observe her lung function and monitor for any changes in her breathing pattern, as even slight fluctuations could signal complications like pneumonia, which is a common risk after chest trauma. Given her fractured ribs and the dislocated shoulder, her physical recovery will be slow, and she will need assistance with even basic movements for the next few weeks. Pain management will be key, as her body heals from the internal bruising and damaged tissue, and we'll need to keep her as comfortable as possible while ensuring that she's gradually reintroduced to physical activity."

"So she's going to be in here for a bit?" the sheriff half asked half stated.

The doctor nodded. "Weeks, and mentally and emotionally, her recovery will likely be challenging. Attacks of this nature can leave lasting psychological scars, so counseling and support will be vital to help her process the trauma. The impact of this experience on her mind cannot be underestimated; the fear and physical agony she endured may surface as anxiety, flashbacks, or insomnia. As her physical wounds heal, we'll address any post-traumatic stress symptoms."

Kahn didn't think Misty would ever go back to work.

As if reading his mind, Sheriff Olave grunted.

"But there is plenty of good news," Dr. Lester said. "If all goes well, Misty should regain full functionality over time, though there's a chance some injuries could have lasting effects. The dislocation, for example, may make her shoulder more prone to instability in the future and her respiratory function may be slightly weakened if the lung trauma heals with scarring, which can restrict lung capacity. However, her outlook remains positive. The main priority right now is keeping her stable and preventing complications."

"She got lucky," Harry said.

"I would say so," said the doctor as she pressed to her feet, signaling her lecture was at its end.

Kahn and the sheriff helped Harry to his car. Once Misty's brother had left, Sheriff Olave and Kahn said their goodbyes and promised to stay in touch.

As he walked to his car, Kahn saw someone watching from the shadows of the hospital's emergency exit. He paused, staring at the dark patch beneath the exit's overhang.

A man stepped from the shadows into the light. The guy's crew cut was tight, nothing more than stubble, and his ruddy face was familiar, yet unknown. Kahn strode toward the man, not knowing what he was going to say or do when he reached him.

It was the guy from the interstate—he was sure of that, but how did he know the man?

When Kahn was ten feet from the stranger, the guy said, "Don't fret, Kahn. I'm not here to trip you up."

"Who are you and what do you want?" Kahn said.

The guy looked around as if the world was eavesdropping. "My name is Ray Destrie."

Something in the tone of the guy's voice told Kahn he was lying. He said, "I saw you up on the interstate. Shooting at the Howler. Why were you there?"

"We don't have time for that now," Ray said, looking over his shoulder again.

"I'm not going to le—"

"Do you want to find the Howlers, or not?" Ray asked.

Kahn said nothing.

"I can show you where to find them."

20

Borderland Pass, I-49, Ozark Mountains, Arkansas, U.S.
8:12 AM CST, August 24th, 2022

Kahn picked up the man who called himself Ray at Betty's Diner and the duo sat in silence as Kahn drove to the interstate. The guy smelled a little ripe, but otherwise, he was clean and put together. He wore hunting garb and toted a pack, but Kahn saw no gun, though he'd bet good money that the man had one on him.

Morning rush was over, and traffic was light. Several wrecked cars were still stacked on the shoulder of the highway, and when Kahn drove across the overpass he slowed and moved into the right lane.

"Here," Ray said.

Kahn pulled to the side of the road and off the shoulder into tall weeds. He shut off the engine, the whoosh and pop of the interstate and the tapping of the hot engine the only sounds.

Other than a vague promise made at the hospital the prior day, Kahn knew nothing about his new partner. Ray Destrie had made the offer to help and told Kahn to pick him up at Betty's the next morning. That was that. No background information. No nothing.

Kahn wasn't in the mental space for rational thought, but as he forced himself to eat dinner the prior night, he had strained his brain for how he knew Ray but crashed before he could search the internet. His dreams were troubled, and when he woke Ray's origin story was the furthest thing from Kahn's mind.

As the pair got out of the car Ray asked, "Any new information on your friend?"

"No," Kahn answered. "But no news is good news, though." He retrieved the Remington and his pack, and a Beretta was in a holster on his hip. "Where are we heading?"

Ray looked at the weeds, gazing at the rolling hills beyond.

"Are you OK?" Kahn asked.

Ray's stare strayed north along the interstate as he said, "Yeah, I'm fine. Bad memory is all." The guy rolled his shoulders, cracked his neck, and added, "There's a dirt road up a ways that leads into the hills. About a mile in there's a long, overgrown driveway. That's where we're headed."

Kahn nodded, trussed his pack, and slung his rifle over his shoulder.

Ray led as the two men walked north along the interstate, leaving the overpass and Kahn's vehicle behind. Crushed and burnt-out vehicles lined the shoulder, and the highway itself was stained with oil, antifreeze, melted plastic, and the concrete was charred by fire.

Further north on the interstate were the scars of the prior year's accident. Kahn wanted to get the guy talking so he asked, "What are the odds of two bad pileups within a mile of each other?"

Ray snickered and said, "Borderland Pass. Not the luckiest spot in the world."

"So, what were you doing here?" Kahn said. The fastest way between two points is a straight line, and he wasn't in the mood for curves. Misty was in the hospital, there was a trail of dead and injured people behind him, and Kahn's life had narrowed to the singular focus of finding and killing the Howlers.

Ray harrumphed. "Just in the wrong place at the wrong time is all."

Heat spread through Kahn, that uncomfortable feeling that told him Ray was lying again.

The duo reached an apron of blue stone that connected with I-49's shoulder. Ray crunched over the stones and made a right onto a dirt road that was nothing more than two hardpan ruts separated by tall grass. The pair threaded down the righthand path, the rolling green hills rising before them.

"I was in that accident, you know. Last year," Ray said. "That's how I heard about the Howlers."

Cold licked the tips of Kahn's fingers and toes despite the growing heat. A thin layer of mist hung over the path, mingling with the grass and swirling in the gentle breeze that brought the scent of honeysuckle and pine. Kahn didn't know what to think. A couple of days ago the guy was on scene shooting at the Howler, and now he was claiming to have been part of the prior year's accident? "How?" Kahn forced out.

"Bad luck, I guess," Ray said. "Not only are some folks unlucky enough to get hit by lightning, but there's also a bunch of people so unlucky they were struck twice."

"What did the Howler have to do with the crash last year?" Kahn had suspected the beast's involvement, and he was eager for proof.

"I was heading north... you know all about the pile-up, right?"

Kahn nodded. Over a hundred cars, chaos, fires that burned for days, missing people—basically the king of Shit Shows.

"Well, that night after the emergency crews finally arrived, we were all brought to a hotel—those of us with no place local to go and no means to continue on our journey. I was there for over a week, and one night—the night before I left, I was in the bar, and I heard this guy telling his story."

Kahn said nothing.

"He said he saw something—he called it a massive shadow three times the size of the biggest bear he'd ever seen. He said whatever this thing was caused the accident, and that he saw the creature with his own eyes. Said it was an Ozark Howler.

"Part beast, part nightmare—that's what he called it. Said he saw its hulking shadow among the trees, blending into the thick underbrush with fur as black as the depths of the mountains at night. Its eyes, an unnatural yellow, glowed with a predatory intelligence as if it was aware of its role as the terror of these hills. That's what the guy said. Just like that. He said the creature had a face that's almost feline but twisted, and horns curved wickedly above its head, like a predator stitched together from every fearful tale in the Ozarks."

"And you heard that and said, 'Hum, let's hang around and chase the thing?'" Kahn shook his head. None of this made any sense.

"Not exactly," Ray said. "There was more. The guy said there was a kid named Stacey, and she ran into the woods, and he chased after her. To help, you know, and he ended up tracking the Howler."

"Unless the kid was yours, none of that explains why you're here over a year later, lying in the weeds with a gun," Kahn said.

"No. No, it doesn't." Ray stopped walking and examined the ground.

Another overgrown road, the start of which was barely discernable through the head-high weeds, trailed up the hillside to the north and disappeared into the thick forest of evergreens. Ray started up the trail, but Kahn didn't follow.

Kahn wasn't going any farther until he knew a little more about Ray. He'd been going on faith so far because that's all Kahn had, but this was all getting too strange.

When Ray realized Kahn wasn't following him, he stopped walking and turned to face his partner. "Cold feet?" Ray said. "I thought you wanted to find these things? For Misty and all that."

"I do, so stop lying to me and tell me who you are, why you're helping me, and what you were doing hanging around the interstate after the crash."

"I've been watching this section of the highway since last year, tracking Howlers," Ray said.

"Because now you're a big game hunter? What do you do for a living?"

Ray sighed. "Look, I get it. You don't trust me. Why would you? But ask yourself what motive could I possibly have for bringing you out here. What, I'm a crazed killer and I'm bringing you into the woods to murder you? Is that what you believe?"

"No, but—"

"I need you to trust me so I can trust you, O.K.?" Ray said. "When we get there, I'll—"

"What's your real name and where do I know you from?" Kahn said. He'd had just about enough mystery for a lifetime.

Ray's eyes went wide, and he pursed his lips but said nothing.

Kahn made a show of turning around like he was heading back to the car.

"How do I know I can trust you?"

"You don't," Kahn said.

"Do you want me to show you where I've seen the Howlers? Where they live?" Ray said.

"You know where they live?"

"They have more than one spot, but I know where the female births her young. I've been there." Ray let that sit out there like a fart in church, the trees cackling as the wind spoke of the past.

The partners were at a standstill. Kahn felt he could trust the guy, he gave off that vibe despite Kahn knowing most of the stuff he'd been told was bullshit—but still… Ray could have very good reasons for using a false name and not wanting folks to know who he was, and yet Kahn couldn't get over the fact that the man was trying to manipulate him in some way, though his motives were elusive.

Kahn said, "I understand privacy, but I'm not going on a hunt for an apex predator without knowing who is watching my back. Why do you care? Why are you hunting the Howlers?" Kahn's voice rose higher than he had intended, his frustration leaking through.

"Because I lost someone I cared about, O.K.?" Ray said, and his head jerked back like he'd revealed information he hadn't intended to provide.

"You saw it? How did the person die? Who? What—"

"Her name was Aniyah, and I…" Ray looked away.

"Was she your wife?" Kahn asked.

"No, but she could have been in another life."

"What about this life," Kahn said. "A Howler killed her?"

The man who called himself Ray nodded.

Kahn was a decent judge of character, and it had served him well over the years, even as his own life slipped away, his own compassion and strong ethical standards tumbling away with it. But that didn't mean he didn't believe there were honest people in the world. He felt most folks were honest—cheating on taxes and speeding notwithstanding, though he'd been forced to accept that nobody was perfect—nobody, certainly not him.

It was clear to Kahn the guy wasn't out to get him, but what his real motivation was he didn't know, and that made him nervous. "I'm sorry,"

Kahn said. "We should have had this conversation yesterday or at the very least this morning, but I can't go on."

"For starters—if I tell you my real name, can we get going?"

Kahn started to protest but Ray put up a hand.

"I'll tell everything to you," Ray said. "I just need... some time."

"Your name," Kahn pressed.

"My real name is Carter Renfrow."

21

"Who?" Kahn said. He'd heard the name, but he had no more luck pulling it from his memory than he had the guy's face.

Ray... Carter trekked through the weeds and Kahn followed. That was the deal. A metal gate blocked the way, but it was for vehicles, and Kahn and Carter walked around it.

The driveway climbed up, and there were steep sections where the partners had to go slow for fear of slipping. Kahn's nerves nagged at him, pulling and stabbing. Though he got good vibes from Carter, it tweaked him not knowing who the guy really was, but Kahn reigned in his indignation. What had he told Carter of himself? The man knew nothing of Kahn's past, his exile.

Carter picked through the tall weeds that clogged the trail, and after a mile or so the driveway angled sharply down. Vegetation and overgrowth made the ground uneven and maintaining solid footing required caution, so the duo's progress slowed. When Kahn reached the bottom of the hill he heard the rumble of cars, the whish and hum of vehicles driving on the interstate, but it was distant.

After cutting through a thicket of pricker bushes, the driveway twisted north, and the land climbed as Carter led Kahn up a gentle mountain slope, the forest thinning.

A howl echoed through the hills, followed by a series of laughing barks.

Carter and Kahn halted, surveying the area, though the cry sounded far off.

"These hills suck you in," Carter said. "From what little I know of you, it's clear you understand that. The Ozarks isn't a place to let your guard down."

Kahn was concentrating on putting one foot in front of the other.

"I'm sure you've heard the legends about this place, how it came to be known as Borderland Pass," Carter said.

"I've heard a few stories," Kahn said. He wasn't in the mood to talk, but if Carter wanted to talk, he'd listen. What else was there to do? And he might learn something about the guy.

"You know, then, that the Caddo and Quapaw tribes considered the deep recesses of Borderland Pass to be sacred territories, and both tribes shared a respect for a force in the valley they could neither understand nor control," Carter said. "The Native Americans believed Borderland Pass wasn't just a natural boundary but a place where the earth's spirit bled through to the world of men. In its shadows and among its twisted oaks, the Ozark Howler—part beast, part phantom—stalked the land, a creature born of dark legends and fearsome omens."

Kahn tripped over a root that snaked across the driveway, and he stumbled and squeaked as he regained his balance.

"The Howlers aren't simple mutants as others have claimed so they don't have to deal with reality. You know this or you wouldn't be out here. The Caddo believed the Howlers were a remnant of ancient warriors, beings who had betrayed the gods and were cursed to wander as fearsome, shadowy animals. In their new form, the Howlers guarded the earth, ensuring that no one would dare disturb the spirits buried beneath the ground. An Ozark Howler's eyes, it was said, glowed like fire, twin golden orbs that pierced the deepest darkness, and were visible through even the densest fog. Some claimed to have heard its roar—a deep, thunderous cackling bellow that chilled the spine and froze the heart as the sound reverberated for miles."

A thick tunnel of pines and junipers clogged the path, the opening to the green tunnel leading into near darkness. The forest around the natural tunnel was thick, the oaks thin and spaced close together.

Carter paused and stared forward into the gloom beneath the evergreens, his face a blank slate of nonemotion, as if he were engrossed in something Kahn couldn't see.

"Are you O.K.?" Kahn asked. "It jangles my nerves when you space out like that."

Carter chuckled. "Sorry... another bad memory." As he led Kahn off the driveway, the pair traversing the tunnel of pines and juniper, a guttural growl, a roar, then gurgling bark-like laughter floated up the path behind them.

There were Ozark Howlers near.

Carter's short, ragged breaths were like a metronome, but he set a steady pace, and as the partners slipped between tree trunks and avoided pricker vines, Kahn felt good about the decision to skip the tunnel, eliminating the potential for an ambush.

Back on the driveway, pine boughs drooped over the path, and the ruts of the road were gone, filled with weeds that had fought their way through the hardpan. Birds and squirrels crisscrossed the path, and Kahn judged a vehicle would just fit through the thicket of trees. The sweet scent of the conifer's terpenes was like perfume, and it reminded him of Christmas, but as Kahn stalked forward the rank stench of unwashed hair and sweaty skin overpowered the candle-like aroma.

A gurgle-growl carried on the wind and the partners froze, the echo of the wail hanging in the stillness. Once again, the chickadees went still, and even the wind seemed to die away, the hiss of leaves falling to a faint chatter.

"The Quapaw, they held a different view," Carter said, his need to speak soothing Kahn's angst. "To them, the Howler was a guardian of the earth itself, an ancient force that stirred whenever blood was spilled or whenever the land suffered an indignity. In times of peace, the Howlers' presence was merely a whisper among the trees, an eerie rustle in the dead of night. But when tribes fought, or when settlers trespassed with steel and fire, the Howlers' rage flared, and they would prowl the pass, black shadows among the trees, their haunting cry—not unlike the one you just heard—splitting the silence.

"The Caddo and Quapaw, who respected each other's domains, avoided claiming Borderland Pass for their own. It was a place of mystery and fear, and both tribes knew the Howlers would not suffer human presence within their territory lightly. Still, scouts or hunters would venture into the pass to seek omens or gain favor with the spirits. They went with offerings and prayers, for to enter Borderland Pass was to risk invoking the wrath of the Howlers."

Carter paused and made a sharp right turn and plunged off the driveway into the forest.

"Where... For shit's sake," Kahn said as he trudged after the man.

About fifty yards into the forest, an old wheel was propped against a giant white oak, its thick canopy rattling in the breeze.

Carter said, "We're almost to the fork. Come on." As the partners worked through the underbrush back to the path he continued, "There's much more to the legends, as you might imagine."

Kahn could imagine, but he said nothing, and Carter took his silence as a desire to hear more.

"Though there is little or no proof, the legends tell that one year, a fierce drought settled over the Ozark Mountains. The rivers ran dry, game grew scarce, and hunger gnawed at the people. The elders of the Quapaw and Caddo met beneath a great cedar near the edge of the pass, sharing visions and dreams that all pointed to one conclusion: the drought was a curse laid by the Howlers, who were angered by the tribes' trespass into their territory to seek water. Desperate to make amends, they called for a rare quest to the heart of Borderland Pass, where they would offer gifts and plead with the Howlers to restore the land's bounty.

"Two were chosen to make the trip. Hahtsi, a young Quapaw warrior who had once encountered a Howler and lived to tell of it. He was joined by a Caddo maiden named Nita, a healer whose skills were revered in both tribes. Together, they carried offerings—herbs, woven garments, and an obsidian blade, rumored to be forged in ancient fires. As they approached the pass, the air grew thick with an unnatural quiet. The usual chorus of night creatures was absent, and an oppressive weight settled over them as if the shadows themselves were watching."

"Tall tales," Kahn said, but he didn't mean what he said. He was enthralled.

"Really?" Carter nodded sarcastically. "Have you seen the ancient rock face carving at the heart of Borderland Pass?"

Kahn shook his head no. He'd never heard of such a thing.

"I've seen it, though its outline is badly worn. The years and weather haven't been kind," Carter said. "At the base of this sacred carving, Hahtsi and Nita laid their offerings. They recited prayers taught by their elders, their voices trembling as they implored the Howlers' forgiveness. As they finished, a low rumble shook the ground and a pair of yellow eyes emerged from the shadows, smoldering golden fires. The Howler stepped forward, its massive form cloaked in darkness, his fur bristling like the needles of a pine.

"As you would imagine, Hahtsi and Nita were transfixed as fear gripped them. They had been warned never to look directly into a Howler's eyes, for to do so was to invite madness. But the Howler stopped short of them, sniffing the air, its fiery gaze lingering on the obsidian blade they had offered. It was then that Nita understood the truth behind the ancient curse: the Howler's rage was not born of human trespass alone but of something buried deeper, something ancient and violated beneath the ground."

"That's crazy," Kahn said.

"Is it?"

Kahn said nothing.

The partners reached a confluence in the driveway, and with the heavy overgrowth, it was difficult to track the actual path. Carter bore left, the path plunging through thick evergreens as it headed north. "We need to pay attention now. The driveway becomes a warren at this point, backtracking and circling in odd spots."

"How do you know this?" Kahn asked.

Carter sighed. "I've been here before."

Kahn said nothing.

"If you've had a hard time believing the legend so far, what Hahtsi and Nita claimed happened next even the tribe elders questioned. The couple claimed that in a voice neither fully human nor animal, a Howler spoke, its words a rasping echo. 'The blade,' it growled. 'It is the blade that binds us.'"

Kahn scoffed.

"Confused, Hahtsi looked at Nita, but she had already begun to understand," Carter said. "The blade, passed down through generations, had once been used by a native warrior to slay a creature that had terrorized their ancestors. In taking its life, the warrior had bound the Howler's spirit to the land, trapping it within the pass to serve as guardian and watchman. But over the centuries, the spirit had grown restless, its connection to the blade a chain rather than a symbol of honor.

"Believing that the drought was a manifestation of the Howlers' suffering, Nita picked up the blade and raised it high. 'We release you from this bond,' she declared as she drove the blade into the earth, breaking its connection to the spirit within.

"The ground trembled violently, and a deep, mournful howl tore through the pass. The Howler's form shuddered, its eyes fading from blazing yellow to a cool, solemn glow. The creature looked at Hahtsi and Nita, its gaze softening as if in gratitude. With a final, earth-shaking roar, the Howler dissolved into a plume of dark mist, its shadow dispersing into the trees and the rocks, merging once more with the land."

Birds chirped, and insects buzzed and tittered. It was a nice story, for what it was, though Kahn didn't understand why Carter was telling him.

"The drought lifted soon after, and the rivers ran strong and full once more. Hahtsi and Nita returned to their tribes with the story of their encounter, and from that day forth, the blade was buried at the center of Borderland Pass, a silent reminder of the Howler's sacrifice and the price of wielding ancient power. The Caddo and Quapaw tribes honored the place with offerings each season, marking it as hallowed ground, a place where the spirit of the land watched over them, no longer bound, yet eternally present."

"I know the remnants of those tribes are still around," Kahn said because he felt like he had to contribute something to the conversation. "Do they still make an offering?"

"No," Carter said. "The spot is lost to time, but though the Howler was never seen again, the tribes believed its spirit had become one with Borderland Pass, a part of the mountains themselves. On certain misty nights, when the wind is right, it's said the Ozark Howler's cry can be heard echoing through the trees—a reminder that its spirit, freed but not forgotten, still guards the Ozarks."

"That's some story," Kahn said.

"Many myths have a basis in truth," Carter said. "And you've seen the beasts."

Kahn looked over at Carter and smiled. Sunlight angled through the trees and painted the side of the man's head white, and in profile, Carter looked like— He stopped walking so abruptly his rifle fell from his shoulder and dangled by its strap.

"What is it?" Carter said, his eyes darting about as he searched for the source of Kahn's concern.

But it wasn't the specter of a Howler that had made Kahn's skin crawl, it was the memory of how he knew Carter.

22

Kahn lifted his rifle but didn't point it at Carter.

"What is it?" Carter asked again as he stopped walking.

Kahn's tongue was dry and glued to the floor of his mouth. His lips slipped open, but he said nothing.

"Kahn?"

"You're..." Kahn still didn't want to believe but he couldn't deny the news report that was now clear in his head. He recalled the name of the man who had eluded authorities and escaped capture and now he saw his face. "You're wanted for murder."

Carter's mouth fell open as he sucked in a deep breath and looked at the ground, but he didn't protest.

"What was it you did?" Kahn said, and then it hit him like a shot of whiskey. "You gunned down your daughter's rapist in cold blood. Out on the street. That right? That you?"

Kahn's anger drained away. If some kid raped Jenna, he'd do the same thing, and it struck Kahn then that he and Carter weren't all that much different. They were both exiled from their former lives, and they were both bound by decisions that were understandable—forgivable, even, and yet those decisions were against the laws of man and they'd both paid the price for breaking them.

"That guy I told you about telling the story in the bar," Carter said.

Kahn nodded.

"He is me."

Pieces of the man's tragic tale came back to Kahn then and he felt sorry for the guy.

"I did shoot my daughter's rapist in cold blood. I've never denied that, and yes... I'm a wanted man. Got me. How do you feel now?"

"What a person does to protect their family..." Kahn wasn't sure how to feel. "I'm no cop, but..."

"Yeah," Carter said. "I understand. I do. First off, I have always intended to turn myself in, but things went sideways. I punked out a few times, but I have this fantasy where I turn myself in, go to court, and the judge lets me off with probation and I'm free. Thing is, that shit doesn't happen."

Kahn said nothing. What was there to say? Had this revelation changed anything for him? He wanted the Howlers, and what else mattered?

"The first thing you have to understand is that the COVID pandemic set me free," Carter said as he started walking again. "Having to wear masks. It was great because it restored my anonymity."

Kahn hesitated for a heartbeat before trailing after Carter.

"As to how I got here and why I'm here now." Carter's shoulders lifted as he threaded through the chest-high weeds. "I'd been driving for six hours, and my neck ached, and I was exhausted. I was heading to my son Tommy's away game in West Fork, which was the following day at 11 AM, and I wanted to get a good night's sleep so I could get up early and reconnoiter the location. It was harder than you'd think to stay in the shadows, even with many people still wearing medical masks." Carter paused and took a deep breath. "I also hoped to catch a glimpse of Katie, my daughter, and the ex-wife was going to be there, but... Well, let's just say she no longer factors into my plans. When the cops came for me, she left me for dead.

"Anyway, I was driving I-49 north and the radio goes silent and then starts beeping as visibility dropped to fifty yards, the whiteness ahead thicker than the deepest night. More beeping and a voice says, 'This is an NWS Severe Weather Update. Scattered whiteouts have been reported on I-49 north of Winslow. Reduce speed and use extreme caution.' I slowed, right? What else was there to do? Then pinpricks of red appeared in the gloom ahead, more beeping, and the message repeated.

"Dense fog obscured the road, and the horizon disappeared, the windshield a blank white canvas. Taillights appeared in the whiteness, and I heard the booms of collisions, and the sound of crunching metal carried over the interstate. Then I rear-ended the car in front of me and before I knew what was happening, I was at the center of a massive pileup. Uninjured, thankfully."

Kahn said nothing. He could have guessed much of what Carter had just told him, but there was more, and he waited for it.

"As you can imagine I was freaking out," Carter continued. "I had a gun in the glove box, and I was... am, a wanted man. When the emergency workers arrived an accounting would be done and that would have been the end of the road for me. Literally. My plan was to slip away quietly, but what is it they say about best-laid plans?"

"They never survive implementation," Kahn said. He knew that better than most.

"Anyway, I picked up two strays. A young girl named Stacey whose parents had been killed in the crash, and Aniyah who lost her husband."

"Is that the woman who could have been your wife in another life?" Kahn asked.

Carter nodded. "I was tracking a missing corpse and following a blood slick that led off the interstate when I found Stacey. I'll never forget it. She was wearing a blue ski jacket, a white medical mask with Dora the Explorer on it, and her blonde hair spilled out from beneath a white knit cap. She was staring into the forest at the edge of the interstate."

Kahn's stomach grew hot.

"Thick bloody tracks led into the forest, and fingers of fog reached out from the dark tree line, mist lifting from the snow-covered underbrush. It was spooky, I'm not going to lie. Huge crimson footprints trekked across the dirty snow and trailed into the forest.

"Then it roared, a bestial howl that echoed through the desolation," said Carter. He paused as if expecting Kahn to protest. When he didn't, Carter said, "I knew something was off then."

The weeds and overgrowth grew thicker, and the driveway was nothing more than a narrow field between the tall trees.

A cackle-bark carried through the forest, and it sounded near.

"It sounded just like that."

Kahn found himself nodding like Carter was an old mate and they were talking about a past hunt.

"Let's rest here," Carter said. He led Kahn beneath a tall conifer with spreading boughs that offered cover and a good line of sight in all directions. The partners settled in as Kahn checked his rifle and Carter drew out a Heckler & Koch VP9. "If we're lucky they might come to us. We are hunters after all." He smiled.

Lucky? Kahn said, "Where'd you get the gun?"

"I've had it for a while, though I ditched it a ways back and had to find it out here." Carter motioned expansively, indicating the Ozarks.

"Ditched it?"

In a whisper, Carter said, "We'll get there. You have to understand I was running through all the stages of denial back then—it was a mutant bear, I was seeing things, I was in shock from the accident, blah, blah, blah. But reality asserted itself fast. Huge four-toed footprints in the snow formed double tracks. Like a bipedal creature, and three-inch slices at the tip of each digit delineated claws.

"At this point, you might ask, 'why didn't you run in the opposite direction', and you'd have an excellent point. That was my plan, but see prior statement on plans. The Howler attacked a crash survivor, though I didn't know what the thing was until I met Jed."

The trees rustled to the partner's left, but it was a squirrel. Sunlight angled through the canopy onto the weed-covered driveway, birds chirped, and insects buzzed, but there was no sign of the Howlers.

"I knew something was up with Jed from the start, but..." Carter sighed. "I didn't follow my instincts, and when the kid ran off into the forest, and Aniyah insisted on finding her, I was sucked in. Jed said he would help, but the Howler had different plans, and it wasn't long before we were all separated, including Jed, who claimed he knew how to track the Howler."

"Why is that I already know Jed was full of Howler poo?" Kahn asked.

Carter chuckled. "So now I'm in the woods, unprepared, and the Howler is hunting me! Not the other way around."

"I know the feeling," Kahn said.

"Yeah, how's that?"

"Another time," Kahn said. He wasn't in the mood to spill his sorted history.

"I ended up by myself, in the woods, lost," Carter said.

The wind gusted and the pine needles sighed and whispered.

"This isn't working," Kahn said. "The Howlers must not be close."

"Patience," Carter said.

"You were taking me somewhere, right?" Kahn pushed.

Carter nodded and said, "I'm taking you to Jed's homestead, for starters."

"He can help us?"

Carter laughed. "Not exactly. He's dead."

That let the air out of the conversation and Kahn listened to the woodland band as he waited for something to happen.

An hour later Carter said, "Let's go."

Kahn's guide pressed through the evergreen boughs and fought his way back to the overgrown driveway.

"Things continued to go downhill for me, as you might imagine," Carter said as he flattened weeds. "The Howler was on my ass until Jed found me. The guy appeared out of nowhere and said he'd lead me back to the interstate. By this point, I just wanted out of the woods. I know this area well now, but then... In the darkness, with no supplies, I took the guy's help and that was the biggest mistake I've ever made."

"Ever?" Kahn was thinking about the murder he'd committed.

"I don't regret what I did, Kahn, not really," Carter said. "But if I had it to do all over again, I hope I would do it differently. I could've worked to put him in jail for life. Wouldn't that be a worse punishment? But I couldn't live with what happened to my daughter. I just couldn't, and I resolved that I'd rather be in prison than see the piece of shit that damaged my daughter for the rest of her life walk free. I made it about me. Not what was best for my daughter. Do you have children, Kahn?"

"A daughter."

"So you must understand."

"Better than you think," Kahn said.

"Why's that?"

"Let's just say my daughter was dealt a shitty hand also," Kahn said. It bothered him how close the guy was able to cut to Kahn's bones without even knowing him.

"Like I said, I had suspicions about Jed from the beginning, but I wasn't in the best headspace. I was worried about Stacey and Aniyah, and he said he could lead me to the road so I could get my bearings. My hope was Stacey and Aniyah would be there."

Kahn was having trouble believing, but why would the guy lie? "You just went with Jed?"

Carter nodded. "It's not that I didn't struggle with what he told me about the Howler. It might be hard to understand now—especially for you because you've seen the beasts, but as I shuffled my memories and tried to reorder things and think rationally it wasn't to be."

Kahn understood because he hadn't believed his own eyes. Was Carter to believe, with no real proof, that he was being tracked by a mythical creature part of a genus that included Yeti, Bigfoot, the Loch Ness Monster and its associated kin, Chupacabra, and the Jersey Devil? The idea of it was crazy, yet...

Ahead there was a gap in the trees, and blue sky and tattered clouds replaced the dark tree canopy.

"We're almost there," Carter said.

Kahn hadn't known Carter long, but he felt the tension rolling off the man in waves. "Everything alright?" he asked. "I'm getting that spaced-out vibe again."

"I haven't been here since..." Carter stopped walking and turned to face Kahn. "What I'm about to show you... Really bad things happened here. Aniyah died here and I've avoided this place until now, so you'll have to cut me some slack."

Kahn nodded. Suddenly he felt like an asshole.

"Jed took my gun without me knowing—" Carter put up a hand. "Don't ask. I tripped and he pulled a sleight of hand. Now, I don't consider myself to be a particularly smart man, but I'm not a dope. I see things, though sometimes those things don't register until later when new information comes to light. Jed's vibe hadn't been good, and it wasn't until I spoke with the man that my fears eased. He sold me. But then I remembered Jed showed me his pickup. If he lived in the Ozarks as he claimed, why did the red pickup have Oklahoma plates?"

Kahn stayed silent.

"All these ideas were too late in coming," Carter said. "He picked the perfect spot—I was all twisted around." He shook his head. "I don't have my gun, he points his rifle at my head and says, 'Don't worry, Mr. Renfrow. The Howler isn't around.' Like I don't need a gun. Now I'm freaking out. The guy knows who I am and wants some kind of hillbilly justice. I looked around for a weapon, but it might not surprise you to find out there's nothing lying around the forest floor that can best a bullet. Jed sees me freaking out and says, 'Take it easy, man. I'm a fan.'"

That made Kahn's chest hurt, and he said nothing as he focused his attention on an ant trundling through the weeds.

"Yeah," Carter said. "I gaslight the guy and say, what do you mean? He says, 'The way you took care of that punk. Put him down like a dog. They should've given you a medal.' Now I'm relieved, but totally spooked, so I ask, that's why you're doing this? He says, 'This country is a mess, and taking the law into your own hands is necessary sometimes. You can't let mutts take what's yours and do whatever they want, now can we? Question is, are you qualified to have such power?'"

"Damn," Kahn said. "At least you didn't have to worry about him turning you in."

"You would think," Carter said. "He said what he had planned for us was much more fun. I'm thinking I'm getting raped if I don't cooperate and then he drops a nuke. Says I have to cooperate because he has something I care about."

"The kid and Aniyah?"

"Just Aniyah," Carter said, his tone weak and saturated with sadness. "After that he brought me…" He paused and the partners walked on in silence for thirty seconds before Carter continued, "Here."

The overgrown driveway ended, the tunnel of greenery giving way to green foliage and blue sky. When the partners broke free of the woods yellow hazard tape blocked the driveway. It ran around the property, but in spots, it was broken and fluttering in the breeze. The driveway opened onto a homestead of roughly twenty acres comprised of overgrown fields, and an old, crumbling, white house at its center.

23

The property was carved from the forest and weed-choked fields surrounded the white house on three sides, the front yard filled with dilapidated buildings including a busted open woodshed, a large barn, and several smaller outbuildings the purpose of which Kahn could only guess at. The place reeked of desperation, loss, and finality.

Carter paused and put his hands on his hips as he surveyed the scene.

Kahn watched a range of emotions slide over his companion's face—anger, fear, and then sorrow. An old, rusted pickup sat on four flat tires, weeds hiding most of the vehicle from view. An animal path had been worn into the overgrowth and it split off in several directions. To Kahn, it looked as though the paths had been made by a baby elephant.

"This looked much different last year when I was here," Carter said as he oozed back into motion. "It was winter and..."

The barn was a traditional design, open at both ends with stalls lining each side of a central aisle. Bales of hay lay scattered around, but they had sprouted patches of fresh grass, and it looked like no animals had occupied the barn in quite some time.

Carter stuck his head into the barn and said, "There was a horse. I don't see its remains, so I guess someone cleaned up."

"Howler?"

Carter nodded. "Though thankfully I didn't actually see it."

Kahn looked over the man's shoulder and saw a large brown stain on the barn floor. "What happened here, Carter?"

"Come with me and I'll show you."

As the duo walked down a Howler trail the stench of raw sewage permeated the air, the weeds swaying in the gentle breeze.

"What in the name of—" Kahn covered his nose.

Under dark clouds of hissing and buzzing insects a mound of animal waste sat festering in the sun. It looked like a giant pile of chocolate soft ice cream with streaks of red—like jam, and tiny pieces of bones and sticks that might have passed for sprinkles protruded from the mound.

Carter used his shirt as a makeshift gator-mask as he examined the waste. "Definitely a Howler's. See the paw prints all around?"

Kahn did and he nodded.

As the pair advanced the smell didn't improve, but it morphed from sewage to the unmistakable scent of rotting flesh. Sweat dripped down Kahn's back as the buzzing grew to a fever pitch.

A gutted deer lay sprawled across the Howler path, its lifeless form twisted and mangled as if tossed by some primal force. Its once-glossy fur, now matted with blood, had been shredded in wide swathes across its flanks, torn open by deep, vicious gashes that revealed raw muscle, sinew, and bone. Jagged claw marks ran across its body, and the animal's head was twisted at an unnatural angle, its dark, glassy eyes staring blankly into the next world. Blood pooled beneath the corpse, while streaks of red splattered the bent weeds where the deer had been dragged or rolled during its final struggle.

Chunks of flesh had been ripped away and its belly torn open. The softer organs had been devoured entirely, leaving nothing but the remnants of ruptured tissue and twisted entrails. Bits of fur and bloodied flesh lay scattered around the corpse, and one hind leg was bent and twisted, bearing bite marks that dug deeply into the bone, as if the predator had clamped down and pulled with enough force to nearly snap the limb free. Splinters of antler lay nearby, each fragment tinged with a faint red hue, telling of a fight that was both brief and violent. Flies buzzed in a feverish cloud, settling hungrily on the blood and torn flesh, and the smell of death—thick, pungent, and metallic—filled the area.

"They don't waste much, do they?" Kahn said. He'd seen his share of animal kills, and what he was looking at was indicative of wild animals. What the hunter didn't consume was left for the next rung down on the food chain, and so on until there was nothing left but bleached bones.

"This kill is fresh, as I'm sure you know since you're a hunter," Carter said as he started working his way down the Howler path again.

"Not that it's a secret, but how do you know what I do for a living?"

"I asked around about you," Carter said. "I heard mostly good stuff."

"You were watching Misty and me?" Kahn asked.

"Little bit. I heard what happened at the game preserve," Carter said. "But the folks I talked to didn't know or wouldn't tell me why you're here in the Ozarks. Alone."

Kahn grunted.

"Hey, when you're ready," Carter said. "Who am I to demand to know anyone's background?"

The path split: the center track headed toward the house, the righthand path to the fields, and to the left, the third path trailed to the buildings at the front of the house. Carter took the lefthand path, and the weeds grew thicker, and he was forced to trailblaze.

"This is where Jed held me prisoner for a short time," Carter said. "Aniyah was already here when I arrived at these lovely accommodations."

The woodshed looked like it might fall down; its rotted gray boards and sagging roof a strong wind away from becoming firewood. Its door hung from broken hinges, and a strip of yellow hazard tape was strung across the opening. Stapled to the wall next to the door was a legal notice on state letterhead. It read, "WARNING: DO NOT ENTER. This area is an active crime scene under investigation. Unauthorized entry, tampering with evidence, or moving any items is strictly prohibited and will be prosecuted. The site is monitored, and law enforcement is collecting critical forensic evidence. For your safety and the integrity of this investigation, do not cross the marked boundaries or disturb the scene in any way. Any questions should be directed to the Arkansas State Troopers or the Stone County Sheriff's Office. Thank you for your cooperation in preserving the scene."

Carter leaned in through the open door, sniffed, and his face wrinkled with disgust. "Aniyah was in here longer than me because..." He shook his head.

Kahn saw no dried blood, no sign that anything horrible had happened here, so he didn't ask the question that kept elbowing its way to the front of his thoughts; is this where Aniyah died?

"She was the bait, as I've told you, and Jed had much grander plans for me, though, in the end, those plans were his undoing."

Kahn sensed he was being watched, but he saw nothing unusual, though his line of sight was limited in all directions because of the overgrowth.

"I was to play the most dangerous game, and thankfully for me and Stacey, I won."

There was no need to ask about Aniyah because Carter had already told him she was dead. It didn't take a great leap in logic to assume Jed or the Howler had killed the woman, and if Kahn was a betting man, he'd bet Carter had murdered at least two people in his life, one being Jed. Kahn felt the need to ask questions, to try and participate in a conversation that had so far been mostly one way. He said, "Like the short story? The Most Dangerous Game?"

Carter nodded. "Just like it. The asshole set me free and went and had a mug of coffee—gave me a head start so the hunt would be fair and more of a challenge. Fair!"

There was no animal path through the weeds from the woodshed to the house, so Carter took a roundabout way, staying along the edge of the shed and using the other building as markers.

All the house's windows were broken, and Carter and Kahn trod lightly as they crossed the dilapidated front porch, the old boards creaking and popping beneath their feet. The front door was swinging in the breeze and the same notice they'd seen on the woodshed was posted on it. Yellow hazard tape surrounded the entire place, but most of it was broken and in tatters, and huge paw prints marred the dirt and grit that covered the porch.

Carter eased through the open door.

"Is that a good idea?" Kahn said as he pointed at the yellowed legal notice.

"I haven't been here, but I've been watching this area. Nobody has been up this way in over six months. What happened here is forgotten, as are the people who died here."

Kahn followed Carter inside and closed the door behind him.

Carter paused in the living room, his gaze falling on gouges in the wooden floor. The furniture was overturned, all the light fixtures were shattered, and the deep, musky scent of greasy animals filled the room. There was a hallway that ran to a kitchen, a bathroom, and stairs that led to the second floor.

The bathroom door was splintered and broken, and Carter stopped before it and caressed the broken frame. "Jed locked Aniyah in here while we played our game." The toilet was smashed and the wall next to the door looked like it had been gnawed on by the largest rat to ever walk the Earth.

Carter continued down the hallway until he reached the back door. There he turned to face Kahn. The man's eyes were wet with tears, his face wrinkled and red. "This is where it happened."

The back door led to a stoop, and Kahn saw the remains of three large blood stains right away. Small red flags outlined the areas, the rain and snow having washed away most of the blood stains. Weeds distorted the shapes, but two of the outlines had clearly been placed around human forms while the third—it was larger and oddly shaped.

"I led Jed deep into the forest and then doubled back to help Aniyah," Carter said, his eyes locked on the smallest of the three marked areas. "There was a—"

As if on cue, an angry snarl carried on the wind, and it was answered by another. To Kahn, it sounded like one had come from the north, the other south.

Carter said, "They're tied to this place. One of them died here."

"Should we take cover? We'd have a good view from the second floor," Kahn said.

Carter nodded, and said, "Her body was right there the last time I saw it. One of the Howlers trailed Jed and I back here and..." He hiked his shoulders and opened the back door, but before he went into the house he turned back and said, "Then Stacey crawled from hiding, and thank the heavens she did." He shook his head as he stepped inside. "Jed took a couple of bullets, but he stumbled out this backdoor, and when he saw Aniyah, the bastard rotated his broken body like a zombie trying to work muscles that were no longer attached to bones. The Howler was charging from the woods—what was Aniyah to do? She bolted."

Kahn watched, pity leaking through him as Carter broke down, the tears flowing freely like they'd been dammed up for far too long. The partners went back inside, and Kahn flipped the old deadbolt on the backdoor.

"Jed shot her in the back three times," Carter said as he wiped away tears. "The first shot hit her in her upper left shoulder. The second tore through her neck, and the third took off the top of her head. She kept running, blood spraying the snowpack. Then her right leg gave out and she stumbled before collapsing face down in the snow."

Kahn wanted to console the man, say something to ease his pain, but he couldn't find the words.

"The Howler arrived and attacked Jed, who hadn't seen the beast in his fury to kill Aniyah. It pushed onto its hind legs, its claws tearing across Jed's chest. Then Jed and the Howler went down in a tangle, the creature's teeth tearing into Jed. Stacey was yelling and pleading for me to run away, but I couldn't. I didn't." Carter fell silent.

"You killed the Howler?" Kahn asked.

Carter shook his head. "I was lost in the fog," he said. "The same fog that allowed me to kill my daughter's rapist. I was gone. A different person."

Kahn said nothing.

"I went to Jed, stood over him, and I genuinely considered getting him help when he coughs up blood and sputters, "Do it.""

"Kill him?" Kahn said.

"He was already dead," Carter said. "He was asking for mercy, and I was prepared to oblige until I asked one final question. I had to know. I asked him why. Do you know what he said?"

Kahn stayed silent.

"Jed smiled up at me and said, 'Because I could.'"

Kahn sucked in a sharp breath.

"Yeah, my humanity fell away then," Carter said. "Jed didn't deserve death. That was too easy, and my mind flashed back to my daughter's rapist. Would rotting in jail have been more of a punishment? Like then, I was no judge, but I resolved to be the jury.

"I made sure Stacey had passed around the corner of the house because I didn't want her to think of me as a killer. She was... is like one of my children, and I—" His voice cracked and faltered. "I'd found this scythe on the farm and… I don't know how many swings I took, blood spraying my jacket and pants, specks of heat dotting my face, but when the job was done, I felt no guilt."

An unnerving heat pressed through Kahn, and for the first time, he was wary of Carter.

24

A crow cawed and a jetliner streaked overhead as the sun dipped below the tree line and beams of light streamed through the forest creating bright puddles on the overgrown fields. As dusk gave way to night, Kahn munched on a power bar and drank water. He'd known staying out late or even overnight was a possibility, but he'd still imagined himself going home and getting a good night's sleep in his bed. But it had taken too long to hike to the site and judging by the sounds emanating from the woods, things were just starting to get interesting.

The upstairs of Jed's house smelled of damp smoke and there were signs of teenage habitation. Food wrappers, beer cans, bottles, and cigarette butts littered the wooden floor, and though most of the furniture was broken, there were a few usable seats and couches that could have passed as art deco art installations. There were three bedrooms, and they all contained the shattered and picked-through remains of Jed's life. Everything of worth had been scavenged, and Kahn doubted Jed himself would find anything of value.

In the growing darkness, the duo cleared paths through the trash and clutter so they could watch from windows on all sides of the house. Then they settled into a shifting routine of covering each window and taking turns using Kahn's night vision binoculars.

"It's been eating at me," Kahn said as he offered Carter a power bar. "The girl that started your woodland adventure. Stacey. What happened to her?"

"After the massacre downstairs we lit out, Stacey and me," Carter said. "We left the bodies behind—everything, and I didn't come back."

Kahn could understand that.

"We were going to take that pickup out there, but things didn't work out and we fled on foot, down the same driveway you and I came in on," Carter said. "Then…" He shook his head. "One of the Howlers attacked us on the trail and Stacey saved my ass. Shot the beast dead." He sighed and laughed softly. "The kick of the gun knocked her on her ass."

"What? The little girl? How the hell did she get a gun?"

"The thing tossed me around and I lost this." Carter displayed his VP9. "She found it and shot the thing before it could put an end to me."

"That's…"

"Amazing?" Carter offered. "As I've said, I had made up my mind to turn myself in, though I hadn't decided how and when, and there were my wounds to consider. I was a bloody mess, and my arm was messed up, in addition to several other superficial wounds. If I walked out of the woods with Stacey I would have been arrested, and she would've been put into the system and be forever tied to a murderer. I didn't want that, but as I looked down at the child I didn't know if I could let her go. Do you feel me? She was like... She was my responsibility."

Kahn nodded. He understood all too well. Jenna was his responsibility, and though he hadn't given her cancer, he sure as hell hadn't prevented it, and who knew how his genetics factored into the equation?

"I'd already lost one family, Aniyah was dead, and I didn't want to lose Stacey," Carter continued. "Then there was the scene at the farm to consider. Jed's body, Aniyah's, and the Howlers'. I knew there would be questions and investigations, and the police would look to lay blame. I didn't want Stacey to have any part in that, and that meant I needed to let her go."

"What did you do?"

"The same thing I always do," Carter said. "I ran, but not before taking care of Stacey. I gave her a story to tell the cops. It was mostly true and included me, but she was to tell the police that I didn't give her my name. I know she stuck to that because in all the news coverage following the accident and what the troopers found here on the farm, my name was never mentioned.

"I sent the child up to the interstate as I watched," Carter said. "I gave her my ex-wife's name and told the kid to tell whoever picked her up that she'd been separated from her mother during the accident, and she wanted to call her. Once she had my ex on the phone, she would drop my name and try to get her to help. I also took the risk of a message to my ex to explain things."

"She's with your ex-wife?"

Carter shook his head no. "You've got to remember, COVID was just ramping down, and the country was still in turmoil. Stacey's mother had family up in Montana, and last I heard that's where she was."

"Have you seen her? Contacted her?"

A dark cloud leaked over Carter's face. "No. I can't until I settle my own shit."

Which wasn't going too great from what Kahn could see, yet he still felt a kinship with this man. A bond.

"I watched from a distance as Aniyah's body was collected. I didn't dare go to her funeral. Too risky, and we hardly knew each other, and I would've stood out. It was clear she'd been murdered, and though I could identify her killer, I had no proof and Jed was... well, dead."

"That must have been hard. Not being able to pay your respects and say goodbye."

"You know what the bigheads say," Carter said. "Relationships that start during stressful or traumatic experiences build quickly but fall apart just as fast. What was there to gain by being there? You recognized me right off without a mask, and it's been a few years."

Kahn nodded as he finished his power bar and dropped the wrapper on the floor. "At least you did right by the girl in the end and she wasn't even your blood. Me? I couldn't even…"

A cackle-howl carried over the homestead, but the call wasn't answered, though it sounded close.

The gloom pressed in on the pair like they were the last two people alive.

Kahn felt the urge to tell this man everything, to unburden himself of a weight he could no longer carry. So, Kahn told his story to Carter, the two outcasts making their penance. He told Carter about the diagnosis, the endless meetings with Jenna's doctors, how he handled it so poorly his wife left him, and he lost everything.

"She… left you?" Carter said, the tone in his voice supporting the look of anger and confusion that slid over his face.

Kahn's stomach burned. He hadn't told anyone why his wife broke it off or why he left his family behind, but Carter was like him. Heat built in his chest, his stomach a churning beehive. "I… I couldn't… didn't visit her."

The old house moaned, the wind whispered, and the forest answered with faint creaks and pops.

"I just couldn't bear it, Carter. I know it sounds… crazy, like I'm the biggest wimp alive, but surely you understand? I couldn't see her like that. My baby skin and bones and dying right before my eyes and there was nothing I could do about it. I was… am, weaker than weak, and my wife was right to kick me to the curb."

"What did your ex tell your daughter?"

Kahn shrugged in the darkness. "Something along the lines of 'dad is also sick'. Not too far from the truth."

"I do understand," Carter said.

"At least you did something," Kahn said. "I slinked away like a coward, unable to face my kid. I do pay her medical bills, but most days that feels like a copout."

"Did I?" Carter said. "Do something? Now my daughter lives without a father and the scars from what was done to her are still there. So what did I accomplish other than making myself feel better and powerful?"

"I don't know," Kahn said. "I couldn't even visit my dying daughter. The image of her in a coffin just won't leave me alone and I deserve to die. That's what my actions as a father have earned."

"You certainly don't deserve death," Carter said. "Is that why you're out here? Hoping you get killed by a Howler?"

Kahn said nothing.

"It seems to me that you've paid a dear price already," Carter said. "Why not go home, Kahn? Push through it. Figure it out."

That was the question Kahn thought about every day. "I don't know. The situation is like a tumor that just keeps growing and growing and growing. I know it's gonna kill me, so I just ignore it." He shook his head. "Then there's the—"

A shrill howl, a piercing primal cackle, carried from the forest to the south.

"Do you hear that?" Carter said.

Kahn chuckled. "I heard it. It sounded close. But their—"

"Not the Howler. Listen."

The partners moved to the master bedroom, which had two large windows overlooking the southern expanse. Darkness pressed in on the land, and nothing could be seen in the blackness beyond except the faint shadows of swaying trees against the star-filled sky. There were no lights on in the house, so Kahn used the night vision binoculars to scan the tree line. Nothing moved except the weeds as the wind played with the evergreens and the tinkle and pop of branches swaying and pine needles rustling carried on the breeze. Beneath the arguing night, Kahn heard a rumble, a popping, an artificial sound. "I hear it," Kahn said.

A glow blossomed in the woods to the southeast. It started small as if it were no more than a flashlight, but soon became a large cloud as the woods filled with harsh white light. The low rumble grew and transformed into the scream of a small engine, and Kahn had visions of law enforcement acting on a tip and coming to get... Who? Kahn looked over at Carter, who stared out the window into the darkness, his face smooth and free of worry.

A huge shadow emerged from the forest to the southeast. It flowed to the front of the barn where it paused.

The forest was alive with white light and dappled green shapes, and the cackle of the engine had driven out all other sounds. Two round headlights plowed down the weeds that covered the driveway and an ATV with two people on it came into view.

With an unnatural speed, the shadow bolted forward, becoming one with the night as it raced toward the house.

Bathed in the green and white of night vision, an Ozark Howler stood just beyond the reach of the trees, its shadowed form looming in the stark headlight beams of the oncoming ATV.

The beast's shadow approached, broad and powerful, its figure blurring the line between a massive wolf and some forgotten predator. Its shoulders were hunched and muscular, leading to a thick neck that supported its cat-like head, which was adorned with short, coarse fur that bristled in the growing light.

Yellow eyes that appeared star-bright white glowed with an unnatural light, a sinister intensity piercing the night with a depth that Kahn felt as much as he saw. It was an ancient and knowing gaze, as if the Howler held the forest's deepest secrets. The creature's maw hung open, revealing long, jagged teeth that glowed green with saliva as its nostrils flared.

With the tearing of dirt and the whine of ripping weeds, the ATV skidded to a stop and its engine's cackle faded to a dull rumble. Dust and grit filled the air, and tall weeds partially obscured Kahn's view. Everything was moving too fast, and both people were wearing helmets so Kahn couldn't tell who the newcomers were.

One of the new arrivals leaped from the jumpseat, the form of a person taking shape as he raised a gun in a doublehanded grip.

Shadows danced and frolicked as they became one with the Howler's dark, nearly black coat. The fur was thicker around the neck and shoulders, forming a mane-like ruff that ran along its back, the fur bunched into untamed ridges, giving the impression of spines or the remnants of a prehistoric mane.

The Howler moved with a strange blend of grace and power, and its form was almost spectral as it faded in and out of the shadows. Bathed in the cold, sterile green light of night vision, Kahn saw a creature bound to its environment, yet fearsome in its isolation.

"Let me see if I can get a bead on it. There might be enough time to—" Carter said.

A deep thumping erupted from downstairs as wood cracked under enormous weight, each impact like a miniature concussion bomb. Hinges screeched as something massive threw its body against one of the doors, relentless and unyielding.

"Shit!" Carter said. "Thankfully they're too big to squeeze through those windows."

"Do you really think it matters?" Kahn said, his eye sockets throbbing with pain from pressing the binoculars to his eyes too hard.

Shadow man fired. Three fast shots echoed over the Ozarks and whizzed through the vegetation. The Howler didn't slow, yelp, or show any sign it had noticed the gunshots, and as Kahn tried to aim his gun he soon gave up.

Yelling and screaming as the hunter jumped back onto the ATV.

Downstairs wood crunched and shattered, and a hollow, booming thud resonated with each strike. A final blow landed with an explosive crash, and wood shattered, followed by the sound of heavy breathing—a low, primitive exhalation that made Kahn's skin crawl.

25

"It's happening again!" Carter yelled.

Darkness snaked through the house, and the anguish in the man's voice brought Kahn's stomach to a full boil. Having just heard Carter's tale Kahn was having a bit of déjà vu himself.

Outside the ATV raced toward the house, its headlights blazing across the overgrown fields, but Kahn could no longer see the Howler.

"What should we do?" Carter asked. "We can try and hold the staircase and maybe get some clear shots, or..." Carter stared at the broken window and the porch roof beyond.

Kahn wasn't thrilled with the idea of climbing out onto what was surely a rickety roof. In the dark. Carrying gear and weapons. He said, "If we hold the steps, we'll have it in a confined area."

"That's what scares me," Carter said. "Have you ever gotten a solid shot on one of these things?"

Kahn said nothing. He was a good marksman, but trying to hit the Howler was like trying to shoot smoke.

A loud sniffing, followed by a low-throated growl, echoed up the steps, accompanied by the crack and whine of the stairs as an Ozark Howler came calling.

With the element of surprise and the advantage of the stairs lost, Kahn slung the Remington over his shoulder and climbed through a broken window onto the porch roof.

Stars blared down, the moon three-quarters full, and below the ATV came to a stop at the front of the house, its headlights illuminating the front yard of dirt and outbuildings. The roof popped and flexed, roof shingles giving way as Carter climbed through the window and joined Kahn.

"This could work," Carter said as he crouched before the window, using its pane for support as he aimed his H&K at the open bedroom door. "Come on. Show yourself!"

Out front, the passenger jumped off the ATV. It was Buck, and he moved toward the front door of the house, gun up.

A surreal silence engulfed the homestead as the ATV's engine fell dead and Maddox dismounted the machine. He took up position behind the quad and covered Buck.

Buck saw Kahn before he passed beneath the porch roof, and he gave him a thumbs up.

Kahn wanted to scream a warning, but then he remembered Buck was an experienced hunter, and the man knew what he was getting into. How he and Maddox were here, on Kahn and Carter's asses, well, that was a different issue.

The front door creaked, but Kahn heard no other sounds. Even the night symphony had paused to watch the spectacle.

With the darkness pressing in the next four seconds felt like four hours to Kahn.

Carter whispered, "It's coming."

A growl carried up from below, followed by a single gunshot.

Though he couldn't see it, Kahn heard the front door fall back on its hinges and slam the side of the house. Something thumped the porch, and boards creaked and cracked.

Buck flew off the porch and crashed down the steps onto the hardpan.

Kahn fumbled to aim his rifle, but the Howler didn't make an appearance.

"Shit! Shit! Shiiiiitttttt!" shrieked Maddox as he left the cover of the ATV and went to Buck's side, his gun aimed at the front of the house as he moved.

Gunshots rang in Kahn's head as Carter fired into the bedroom. Wood splintered and sheetrock dust eddied from the broken window, crawling over the roof like smoke.

Kahn shifted his position to get a better view, but the roof shingles beneath his feet gave way, causing him to slide across the sloped roof. The rifle fell from his grasp as his arms shot out for balance, and the weapon hung from its strap around Kahn's neck, pulling him forward. He managed to regain his balance, and he teetered at the edge of the porch roof, Maddox standing over Buck's fallen form twelve feet below him.

"I can't see it!" shrieked Carter.

To Kahn's amazement, Buck was sitting up.

There was a break in the action, and for a full twenty seconds, Kahn neither heard nor saw any sign of the Howlers. The heat of rage built in Kahn's stomach. He and Carter had been hunting, waiting patiently, when Maddox and his lackey busted into town like a freight train.

Maddox was helping Buck to his feet, the front of his hunting vest drenched and glistening with blood, when a Howler streaked from the porch into the cloud of light created by the ATV's headlights.

Kahn struggled with his rifle as he slipped and braced himself on the roof.

Carter eased away from the window, gun at his side as he inched toward Kahn.

145

"Did you hit it?" Kahn said.

"I don't think so," Carter said. "I drove it off, though, so maybe—"

A great rending crack, like the largest redwood in the world was being felled, pierced the chaos.

The roof beneath Kahn's feet vibrated and shook, and then he was falling, roof shingles, broken plywood, and rotten beams engulfing him as he and Carter plummeted.

It was only twelve feet to the decking below, but it felt like a mile to Kahn. His mind spun with the idea of being buried alive as the Howler dug for its prey. A nail bit his arm, and a piece of wood smacked his head. He pressed his eyes closed as he saw stars, tiny pinpricks of light pulsing in the darkness in rhythm with the stabbing pain exploring the outreaches of his body.

Carter and Kahn landed with a crash in a tangle of debris, a large section of the roof cushioning the partners' fall and helping them avoid the numerous nails and spear-like shards of wood.

Kahn coughed and sputtered as he flexed his fingers and toes. Everything was there and still worked, despite the pain filling all his empty spaces. His head thumped with the worst headache he'd ever had, and blood dripped down his cheek from where he'd been nicked with a board.

The Howler shrieked, its cackle-like howl bringing Kahn back to the here and now. He struggled to sit up, the beast's breathing in his ears, the creature's greasy scent driving out the smell of pine.

Carter shed debris as he pushed to his feet, the H&K still in his hand. With his free hand, he reached out and helped Kahn up.

The section of the roof beneath the pair's feet shifted. Carter fell, and that probably saved his life.

With a screech that would have shattered glass, had there been any left in the windows, the Howler jumped onto the debris pile, its right front paw lashing out like a boxer trying to deliver a death blow. The massive, clawed paw raked through the air a foot above Carter's head.

"Move! Move!" shrieked Maddox, who stood at the base of the steps with Buck, his gun trained on the chaos, but unable to shoot for fear of hitting Kahn or Carter.

Carter rolled across the broken section of roof onto the pile of rotted wood and broken roof shingles.

The Howler shifted and dodged, flitting in and out of shadow as Kahn tried to track the beast.

Whether it was a safety feature or a low battery precaution, the ATV's headlights dimmed, blinked three times, and then winked out.

Moonlight painted the scene in harsh black and white as Kahn leaped from the debris pile and down the steps. As if the night hadn't delivered enough blows, he tripped and fell, landed on all fours, and pushed to his feet. Everything ached, but other than some bumps, bruises, and cuts, he'd escaped the roof's collapse without major injury.

A flashlight bloomed in the darkness, and Maddox panned the light around as he held it atop his gun like a sight.

The Howler's massive form rose over the debris pile like Godzilla rising from the ruins of a building. It thrashed and lurched, wood flying through the darkness, the beast's black fur blending into the night as its yellow eyes searched for prey.

From the field to the east a low growl built to a full-throated roar, and four heads turned toward the sound.

Buck screamed.

The male Howler, its twisted horns gleaming in the moonlight, attacked.

With the female approaching from the east, panic and chaos ensued as the foursome tried to bring their weapons to bear on both beasts at once.

But the companions were packed too tight, a knot of humanity that couldn't be separated from the attacking Howler.

It was every man for himself, and Kahn threw himself to the ground as he drew his Beretta. From his prone position he had no shot, but he saw Carter position himself behind one of the porch's support columns, gun up as his partner scanned the maelstrom.

Maddox stood frozen, gun out, his head jerking around like he didn't know which Howler to concentrate on.

Buck stood before him in a daze, the guy wilting like a week-old cut flower, the front of his hunting vest drenched in blood.

Like a living shadow, the male Howler lunged at Buck with explosive force, its jaws gaping wide. The beast struck with its right front paw, claws extended, driving deep into Buck's chest.

A loud gurgle escaped the dying man's lips as he collapsed, his body hanging from the Howler's claws.

The beast struck a second blow with its left paw, claws scraping over Buck's face. He went down like a sack of potatoes as the beast pulled its claws free.

With Carter and Kahn out of the line of fire, and Buck as good as dead, Maddox opened up, the crack and pop of his shots filling the night.

The beast took a bullet or two but made no sound as it darted like a focused column of smoke behind the debris pile. Shadows frolicked like an attacking enemy, and everything went still except Buck's final death wail as the Howler fled into the house. It shrieked and whined as it ran.

In their eagerness to deal with the male, the female stalking through the tall weeds filling the eastern fields had been forgotten.

Kahn pressed to his feet, his gaze locked on the trail of black drips—blood, trailing into the house. His head was ringing, and his muscles ached from the fall, but he was coiled like a spring, ready to fire at the first sign of a Howler.

Maddox dropped to his knees next to Buck, the gun still in his hand. The a-hole looked genuinely upset, and Kahn wondered if it was because Buck was dead, or because the lodge manager was concerned that he'd lost several key people in the last few days and finding henchmen... and henchwomen, wasn't easy or cheap.

Buck's corpse lay next to the pile of debris from the collapse, and the wood and metal popped and creaked as it settled.

Carter got low, his gaze shifting from the house to the fields in the east. He hissed, "Kahn. The night vision? Do you still have the night vision?"

He did, and Kahn dug the binoculars out of his pack, hoping beyond hope that they hadn't been damaged in the fall. They weren't, and Kahn used them to scan the weeds for the female Howler, but he saw no glowing yellow eyes, no great hulking shadows.

A guttural choking, followed by a deep, wheezing puffing emanated from the house. To Kahn, it sounded like the labored breathing of an injured animal, or one that felt scared or threatened. Either way, that didn't bode well for Kahn and his companions. What was the beast waiting for? Kahn knew. He knew all too well. The Howlers were smart, and they'd already proven on this night that they could work together.

"Rrraaawwwwwrrr... hrrrrnggg," carried from the weeds like rolling thunder, deep and guttural, almost a growl but stretched, drawn out, ending in a huff like distant rocks tumbling.

From inside the house came the response of the male. "Awwwrrr-rrrawrrrr!" The call was louder, almost a snarling scream, rising in pitch with a brutal edge. The cry ended in a stuttering, rough series of clicks like stone grating against bone.

The partners exchanged glances. Kahn was thinking it might be time to give up the hunt, and the grim look on Carter's moonlit face suggested he was wrestling with the same thought.

A heavy snorting, as if huffing in agreement or reassurance, then, "Hawwwwr-hawwwwrr." It was a bellowing, horse-like sound, like a tree bending against the wind.

The male growled briefly, low and mournful, trailing into a final low, hissing snarl, almost as if the creature was whispering through its teeth.

As the beasts fell still, the forest and its creatures held their breath as they absorbed the fading echoes of the Howlers' primitive voices.

26

Ozark Mountains, Arkansas, U.S.
1:19 AM CST, August 25th, 2022

"What the hell are you doing here?" Kahn said.

"Same thing as you. At least that's what I thought," Maddox said, his gaze shifting from Kahn to Buck's corpse. "I was told you were an expert hunter and so far all I've seen is incompetence that's led to several of my people pushing up daisies."

Kahn took a fast step forward and Carter stepped between the two men.

"Right," Carter said. "You guys know each other."

Kahn reached past Carter and stabbed Maddox's chest with his index finger. "Me? You're trying to lay this on me? First, you push the creatures out of their habitat, and then—"

"What?" interrupted Carter.

"Oh, did I leave out that part?" Kahn said. "Sorry. Yeah, dumbass here and his band of merry misfits drove Howlers onto the game preserve so they could offer high-priced hunts to their truly pathetically rich clients."

Now it was Carter's turn to step back. "Well, then kick his ass."

Maddox laughed. "How'd that work out for you last time?"

Kahn's head pulsed with pain, but so did his jaw and the bruises Maddox had given him during their fight. "Then you race in here on an ATV—a loud ass ATV! Carter and I have been patiently waiting on the beasts for hours. For a guy that runs a game preserve you sure as shit don't seem to know much about hunting."

"We were following your trail, and we had an opportunity to track the creatures," Maddox said.

"Why? What the hell do you want with the Howlers?" Carter asked. "I'd think after the beasts ripped your lodge apart, you'd be happy they were back on this side of the interstate."

Maddox turned his cold eyes on Carter and Kahn would swear the man flinched. "And you are?"

"Mr. None Of Your Business," Carter said with a sidelong glance at Kahn that said, "Tell this man who I am and you're dead."

"Do I know you?" Maddox asked Carter, his head tilting like he was examining an exotic bug.

"No. Are we going to just sta—"

The Howler prowling the overgrown field hissed and cackled.

Maddox went to the ATV, started it, and turned the headlights back on.

The cloud of severe LED light extended to the house, blaring through the broken windows, but it faded into blackness in all other directions.

An angry growl leaked from the house, then the distinct sound of a door falling back on its hinges.

"It's going out the back," Maddox said as he headed for the rear of the house.

Kahn started to follow, but Carter grabbed his arm, shaking his head as he pointed to the field to the east.

Maddox got to the corner of the porch and skidded to a stop.

A dark shadow galloped across the open area at the side of the house and darted into the weeds to the east.

Maddox fired, but Kahn didn't see the point. In the dark, with the weeds and shadows, and the beast running at full speed, he didn't see how the preserve lackey could hit the thing.

The field to the east stretched wide under the cold grip of night, tangled with waist-high grasses and thorned brambles that would snag clothing and skin. A low mist clung to the earth, glowing faintly under the wan moonlight. The air smelled of damp earth and decay, carrying the faint, wild musk of something that didn't belong.

Kahn adjusted the strap of his rifle and glanced at Maddox and Carter. Maddox gazed east, his dark eyes scanning the expanse like a hawk searching for prey. Carter, lean and sharp-faced, nervously ran a hand through his unkempt hair, the VP9 at his side.

"This doesn't feel right," Carter muttered, his voice barely audible over the symphony of crickets and the occasional hoot of an owl.

"Nothing about this is supposed to feel right," Kahn replied, his voice steady but low. "Stay sharp. Mom and Dad are out here."

Maddox grunted, hefting his gun and nodding toward the tree line at the far end of the field. "If they show, aim for the head or chest. Anything else won't even slow 'em down much."

"We know," said Kahn and Carter in unison.

When Carter and Kahn didn't follow Maddox, he turned and said, "What? You're giving up now? After everything?"

"Why the hell do you care?" Carter asked.

"It killed my people. Destroyed my lodge!"

"You put us in a position where we had to kill its child," Kahn said. "A child that wouldn't have been on the game preserve's land if you hadn't brought it there."

To that, Maddox had nothing to say.

Carter advanced and joined Maddox. "He's right," Carter said. "I'm in too deep and so are you."

"Fine," Kahn hissed. "But I'm on point."

"Be my guest," Maddox said as he made a sweeping gesture.

As the three hunters moved forward in a loose formation their boots crunched on weeds, pebbles, and debris. The overgrown field seemed to stretch endlessly, bordered by ancient evergreens and white oaks whose gnarled limbs reached out like tentacles.

Somewhere in the distance, a branch cracked.

The sound froze the trio in place.

Kahn raised his hand signaling for his companions to stay motionless as his eyes darted toward the source of the noise. The darkness was alive with an unnatural stillness, as though the creatures of the night were waiting for the second act of the show to start after an exciting first act.

"There," Maddox hissed, pointing to his left.

A shadow slithered through the mist—large, low to the ground, and impossibly quick. Another shadow mirrored it to the right, circling like a predator assessing its prey.

Carter muttered, "They're watching each other's back."

The silence shattered as a guttural growl rolled across the field, deep and resonant like the rumble of distant thunder. It vibrated in Kahn's chest, a sound that promised pain and death. The grass rustled violently to their right.

Kahn swung his rifle, finger hovering over the trigger.

Maddox and Carter followed suit, their weapons aimed and ready to fire.

The female Ozark Howler emerged first, its massive frame cutting through the mist like a ship through water. It was twice the size of any bear, with thick, matted fur that rippled in the moonlight. Its eyes glowed a sickly gold, and they were fixed on the trio with a predatory intensity.

Kahn aimed his rifle.

The male followed, stepping into view with a slow, deliberate gait. It was even more massive, its muscular frame bristling with raw power. Its horns shone in the moonlight, sharp enough to pierce steel.

"Jesus," Maddox whispered, the word barely escaping his lips.

"Fire!" Kahn barked.

The night exploded in a cacophony of gunfire. Carter's gun cracked first, followed by the booming blast of Maddox's weapon. Kahn's rifle spit out bullets in a steady rhythm, each of the four shots aimed squarely at the creatures.

With the fluidity of smoke, the female Howler leaped to the side as the male charged forward, barreling toward the trio through the dense overgrowth.

"Cease fire!" Kahn shrieked.

Five seconds dripped away as the companions frantically searched the weeds as the grunts and growls of exertion grew.

"I don't like this," Carter said.

"Move!" Kahn shouted.

The trio plowed forward into the weeds, Kahn on point with Carter and Maddox flanking his sides and watching his back.

"Look out!" Carter yelled as he shoved Maddox out of the way just as one of the beasts exploded from the vegetation. Its claws raked the air, cutting through the mist like knives.

Maddox stayed on his feet, raising his gun and firing, but the shots only cut down weeds.

As fast as the Howler had appeared, it was gone.

"Easy!" Kahn yelled. "You'll hit one of us!"

The male Howler roared, the sound so loud and primal it seemed to shake the ground. It charged from the weeds right at Maddox, its massive horns gleaming as it plowed through weeds.

Maddox fired as he dove to the side, narrowly avoiding the beast's charge.

The Howler skidded to a halt and dropped to all fours, its claws gouging deep furrows into the earth.

From behind, the female Howler emerged—a slightly smaller, sleeker figure with the same glowing eyes. She glided through the tall grass like a Titanoboa as she stalked the trio.

Carter fired, but the creature was too fast. It lunged at him, jaws snapping, claws out as the Howler pushed off on its powerful hind legs.

Kahn slung his rifle over his shoulder, drew down his Beretta, and fired, the bullet grazing the female's flank.

The beast snarled, spinning toward him as Kahn stood his ground, firing another round that struck the creature in the shoulder. It stumbled but didn't fall.

Above, the moon slipped behind a cloud, plunging the field into impenetrable darkness.

Kahn's skin crawled in the blackness. He had a flashlight, but it was in his pack, and the precious seconds it would take to retrieve it might cost him his life.

Weeds snapped and bent as the trio searched for targets other than themselves, the wind chuckling as the trees snickered.

His heart thumping, skin prickling, Kahn turned three hundred and sixty degrees, gun up.

A crow cawed, and the night symphony started to come back online, then fell silent like nature's conductor wasn't pleased with the sound.

Then everyone was moving, a chaotic churning of panic and fear. The threesome shuffled around, aiming at nothing.

Kahn felt the creatures drawing near and heard their gurgling communication. What the hell was he doing out here? He didn't know how many times he'd asked himself that question, but the answer always came in the form of Misty lying in a hospital bed clinging to life.

Carter tried to reload in the blackness, but Kahn didn't. The three men put their backs together as they stared into the swaying weeds, the mist thickening as the night grew colder and the dark clouds in the west advanced like an approaching army.

Time stretched out and Kahn was left to his thoughts. To his right was a man Kahn had tried to pummel just a couple of days prior and now he was counting on the guy to watch his flank. On the other side was a man committed to his own sorrow and had found solace in the pursuit of the Howlers who had killed someone he loved and driven him further from his family. Not exactly the team he would have chosen to go to war with, but beggars can't be choosers, and though he—

A set of glowing orbs appeared in the weeds to the east. Kahn could tell by the height of the eyes from the ground that it was the female. She circled wide, her gaze locked on the hunters, but the male was nowhere to be seen.

"Hold your fire until I give the order," Kahn said. Weeds rustled and shook, and Kahn saw tiny pinpricks of stars all across his field of vision.

The eyes disappeared in the darkness and Kahn's nerves burrowed deeper beneath his skin. Hunting was about being in control. Being the smarter, stronger, superior species. All animals, humans included, hunted for food. Most humans did so in a market with money as their weapon. Beasts big and small, plant eaters and carnivores, knew that obtaining food required patience, persistence, and sometimes, courage.

Thick clouds rolled in from the west like a dark tide, their advance heralded by a low rumble that seemed to vibrate through the ground. High, wispy tendrils of cirrus clouds streaked across the star-filled sky like ghostly brushstrokes, and behind them, towering cumulonimbus clouds reared up, their bases shadowy and dense, blotting out the moonlight and casting an ominous gloom over the forest. The clouds boiled upward and out, their edges crisp and dark against the moonlight, but within them, the hues shifted—layers of charcoal gray and deep indigo.

Kahn felt a tightening in his joints, his eyes stinging as he searched the overgrowth to the west, but there was no sign of the Howlers.

A flash of light lit the leading edge of the storm as the clouds surged closer, spreading like spilled ink over the horizon. Tendrils of mist skimmed the treetops, merging sky and earth in a seamless dark blur. Lightning flickered again deep within the cloud mass, illuminating its interior with fleeting, electric veins. The distant growl of thunder followed each strike, like a predator stalking closer. A faint scent of ozone mixed with the earthy aroma of the decaying vegetation, a warning of the storm's imminent arrival.

A flash lit the night for a heartbeat and two elongated shadows fell across the weeds.

"Fire!" Kahn screamed, though his targets were fleeting.

The hunters unleashed another barrage of gunfire, the flashes of their weapons lighting up their faces.

Both creatures retreated, their glowing eyes disappearing into the shadows. The hunters stopped firing and stood frozen, weapons still aimed at the darkness, waiting for the next attack.

But the night settled, the night symphony returned, and no attack came.

Seconds ticked away, a minute, as the clouds obscuring the moon moved on and the world was once again painted black and white, the dark collar of the approaching storm boiling over the western horizon like black rapids. Kahn peered through the night vision binoculars, which had managed to remain unbroken.

The weeds at the edge of the forest wavered as the female Howler let out a piercing yowl that echoed over the field.

With a muscle-shuddering motion, the male came into view, his glowing eyes locked on his mate.

She backed away slowly, her gaze never leaving the hunters.

The male stood frozen, as if reluctant to retreat, but then followed her into the mist.

Kahn lowered his gun. His leg throbbed with pain from the fall, but he didn't let it show.

Carter slumped to the ground, his hands shaking as he fumbled to reload his gun. "I don't know how much more of this I can take."

"As much as it takes," Maddox snapped, though his tone lacked its usual bite. He looked at Kahn. "Are you hurt?"

"I'll live," Kahn said, brushing off the concern. He glanced at the field, scanning the darkness. "They're testing us."

Carter nodded grimly.

The three hunters rested in the overgrown field, their breaths coming in ragged gasps as their heart rates slowed and the adrenaline retreated. A chill swept through Kahn as the mist thickened, swallowing the world around them.

In the distance, to the east, a howl echoed through the forest—lonely, haunting, and full of hatred.

"We better get after it," Maddox said.

Kahn and Carter shared a knowing glance as they walked through the field toward the forest's edge.

27

The forest brooded, gnarled limbs and deep undergrowth casting jagged shadows that clutched at the tree trunks and wrapped the Ozarks in fatal secrets. White oaks and towering pines choked the way forward, their dense, intertwined branches forming a tangled barrier that snagged, pulled, and scraped at the party as they tracked the Howlers. Pines outnumbered the oaks, the bark covering the evergreen trunks marked with dark, resinous veins that glistened faintly in the dim light. The sharp, tangy scent of turpentine lingered in the air, wafting from the oozing sap and mingling with the earthy aroma of the forest.

As the wind whispered and cajoled, urging Kahn forward in his obsession and denial, the underbrush quivered, carrying with it the first breaths of the approaching storm. Turning back was always at the forefront of his thoughts now, but like leaving home he'd gone too far, extended himself too much to retreat, and admit that what he was doing was… stupid. He could think of no better word for it. Like abandoning his daughter, chasing the Howler was for him, not Misty. Kahn knew this. Was certain of it, and yet…

Carter led Maddox and Kahn down a series of animal trails that wove aimlessly through the trees, each path narrowing into tunnels of thorns and shadow that disappeared into the deepening gloom. Somewhere, a crow cawed—a sharp, defiant cry, as though the bird resented the intrusion. The underbrush seemed alive, and Kahn's nerves tingled with the anticipation of the hunt.

A distant rumble, low and guttural, like the growl of a waking beast, vibrated through the bones of the hills. Soon the storm would arrive, and the forest and the creatures within would bear witness to its fury.

Tracking the Howlers' faint blood trail in the darkness was an arduous task, made even more challenging by the shifting shadows and uneven terrain. Just as Kahn began to worry they might lose the trail, Carter would spot a broken branch, a glistening drop of crimson, or a stray clump of fur, reigniting their pursuit. The forest reeked of the creatures, although the companions hadn't seen or heard the beasts since they'd left the farm.

"They're probably heading right for their closest lair," Carter said.

"Lair?" Maddox asked.

Neither Kahn nor Carter responded. Maddox was on a need-to-know basis, and Kahn was starting to wonder why the man was on the hunt with them. The dipshit only cared about the lodge and the game preserve, and only because that's how he made his money. Maddox's motivation for being on the hunt had always been clear: he wanted a pelt for himself. Something to bring back to the lodge to ease fears and stoke the flames of the Borderland Game Preserve's mythical standing among hunting enthusiasts, though most real hunters wouldn't be caught dead hunting there.

Carter said, "If we continue on this course we'll go by the Quapaw memorial wall. The one I told you about from the legend of Hahtsi and Nita."

The tree canopy blocked what little starlight and moonlight leaked through the thickening cloud cover, and the party climbed steadily, the dark shadows of the Ozark Mountains growing on the eastern horizon. Ahead there was a break in the woods where a cliff rose above the trees.

"We're here," Carter said. "Let's risk a little light."

Kahn's Maglite revealed a memorial out of place and time.

The Quapaw rock face monument towered over the Ozarks, a natural marvel turned sacred testament to a bygone era. Rising nearly sixty feet above the surrounding woodland, its surface, naturally weathered by centuries of wind and rain, was a blend of warm, earthy tones—reddish-browns, soft grays, and hints of golden tawny that gleamed faintly in the gloom as the flashlight struck the deeper angles. The cliff's texture was rough and jagged in places, yet the central section of the monument was surprisingly smooth, as if meticulously chiseled and sanded, its surface streaked with veins of quartz and darker mineral inclusions. Its edges were framed by nature—gnarled oak and pine trees clung precariously to the rocky terrain, their roots weaving into the cracks as if holding the cliff in place. Vines cascaded down portions of the rock face, their dark green leaves contrasting starkly with the muted tones of the stone.

The monument's center was a natural canvas for the Quapaw's intricate petroglyphs, their sharp lines and curves etched deeply into the stone. Ancient symbols covered the lower third of the monument, displaying a range of images from geometric patterns to depictions of humans and animals, seamlessly blending artistry with storytelling. Figures of great buffalo, stylized birds with outstretched wings, and abstract spirals dominated the upper sections. The lower half was filled with more complex scenes. Depictions of hunters wielding spears, gatherings around mysterious symbols, and what appeared to be mythological creatures—giant feline forms with fangs, horns, and long tails.

Time and weather had worn the edges of the carvings, softening their outlines but leaving the petroglyphs intact. Spirals, zigzags, and concentric circles hinted at celestial or spiritual significance, while abstract humanoid forms and animal figures leaped from the rock, frozen in perpetual motion.

Above the petroglyphs, the rock face was rougher and less uniform, its surface pitted and furrowed with centuries of erosion. Ledges and shallow overhangs broke up the vertical expanse, creating shadows that shifted throughout the day. Here and there, small pockets in the stone held tufts of stubborn vegetation—ferns, lichens, and hardy wildflowers that thrived in the thin cracks between worlds where rainwater collected.

Toward the top of the wall, a horizontal crack split the cliff face, forming a narrow ledge. The break was worn smooth as if it once served as a perch or ceremonial platform. Above it, the cliff extended to a jagged, overhanging edge that framed the uppermost glyphs.

At the monument's base, large boulders partially encircled the site, roughly arranged to form a meager natural amphitheater. The stones were etched with symbols, smaller and simpler than the towering glyphs above. Between the boulders, vegetation had reclaimed the ground, with moss creeping up the base of the cliff and ferns sprouting from cracks in the stone.

There was a flat altar stone at the center of the natural theater, and upon it lay what appeared to be offerings.

"Are you sure modern Quapaws don't still make offerings to the Howlers like in your tale?" Kahn asked.

Carter shrugged. "Like I told you the first time you asked, not that I know of, but given this new information I'd say I'm wrong."

Kahn said nothing.

The trio pushed through the last of the underbrush, mist coiling over the cliff's upper ledge and slithering down the monument's face.

Maddox and Kahn crowded around Carter as the triad stared down at the offerings.

The hand-carved cedar box rested on a woven grass mat dyed in earthy tones of orange, green, and deep brown, its lid adorned with traditional Quapaw motifs etched in delicate, swirling patterns.

Carter retrieved the box and opened it.

Inside bundles of sage, sweetgrass, and tobacco were tied together with thin strands of leather, each meticulously arranged. Among the sacred herbs were quartz crystals, their edges catching the LED light which created sparkling rainbows inside the box.

In addition to the box, there was a clay bowl, fired in muted tones of red and brown. It held dried corn kernels and crushed sunflower seeds, offerings of sustenance. Feathers from eagles and hawks, wrapped in red cloth, framed the display.

Carter said, "The feathers symbolize prayers carried to the sky."

Behind the bowl a circle of burnt-out beeswax candles contained a meticulously crafted sculpture, standing about a foot tall and made from polished black stone. Its surface was smooth and cool to the touch, and it was intricately engraved with ancient Quapaw motifs—spirals, river waves, and the outlines of rising flames. The statuette was shaped like an abstract representation of a sacred fire, its pointed edges curling upward and reaching for the sky.

At the base of the sculpture, inlaid with shimmering mother-of-pearl, was the symbol of the Great River, its winding flow capturing the LED Maglite and creating the illusion of moving water. Small turquoise stones arranged in concentric circles surrounded the base, their vivid blue contrasting with the dark stone. Carved into the hollow center of the sculpture was the depiction of a tiny obsidian blade surrounded by feathers carved from white marble.

The remains of a ceremonial fire looked fresh, the stink of smoke still hanging in the air which was pregnant with the approaching rain. Kahn couldn't escape the sense of overwhelming peace and harmony. He felt the knots in his neck ease a little as if the physical manifestation of the Quapaw's devotion to their gods bought him favor with the earth, water, fire, and sky.

"How isn't this place well known?" Maddox asked.

"We're deep in Borderland Pass now," Carter said. "I didn't find this place until much later. After…. I don't think Jed even knew about it, and he'd spent his entire life in these hills."

"Jed?" said Maddox. "Who the hell is—"

The Howler gave no warning.

A thump echoed off the cliff face as the male Howler exploded from the vegetation with a roar of rage.

The trio was caught unawares, and as Kahn drew his Beretta the beast swiped at Carter as it lunged for Maddox.

Chaos ensued as the Howler pushed back onto its hind legs, jaws flexed open, saliva dripping through spiked teeth, its golden eyes filled with fury. Sections of black fur were caked with dried blood, and it was clear at least one bullet had punctured the Howler's tough hide.

Carter took cover behind a boulder and used it for support as he aimed his gun.

Everyone was in tight, most surfaces prone to ricochets, and the beast shifted and dodged as it attacked Maddox.

Kahn aimed and fired, the heat of anger driving him, Maddox as collateral damage, not a consideration.

With a gurgling howl-bark, the beast dropped to all fours, avoiding Kahn's shots which stitched across the top of a boulder.

The beast didn't slow, its dark fur rippling with raw power as the Howler surged forward. It collided with Maddox, slamming him to the ground with a bone-jarring thud, as though the weight of the forest itself had come alive, relentless and unstoppable.

A loud crack reverberated off the cliff face, and Kahn's mind spun back to the collapsing porch roof.

Maddox vanished behind a blur of fur and muscle, the massive beast towering over him. Its front appendages struck with the precision and fury of an enraged boxer, claws slashing relentlessly as Maddox struggled to defend himself.

Carter still held his fire. Shooting at the Howler risked hitting Maddox, but if something didn't change soon it wouldn't matter, and ricochets be damned.

A calm engulfed Kahn. He didn't want to risk his life for Maddox—hell, he didn't even like the guy, but some folks run toward danger, and some flee, regardless of feelings or intentions. Kahn took three steps toward the Howler, arm straight, gun out before him gangster style as he pumped three shots into the Howler's rear flank.

The beast let out a piercing shriek, a mix of pain and fury, as it darted to the left, vanishing into the tangled vegetation, leaving a dark trail of glistening blood in its wake. Moonlight filtered through the tree canopy, casting shifting shadows as the Howler escaped into the dark embrace of the night.

Kahn's chest ached and his heart pounded as he and Carter went to Maddox's side.

The hunter lay next to a boulder, his vest torn open, his right leg twisted at an angle it wasn't designed to accommodate.

"Shit," Maddox said. His hunting vest had absorbed some of the attack, but a rib bone poked from his chest, there were bloody gashes all over his body, and a section of skin had peeled away from his jaw and bone glowed therein. Between breaths, Maddox said, "Get it. Kill it."

Kahn shook his head. He hated the guy, but he was no murderer. The thought made him look at Carter, who gazed at the flattened section of greenery where the Howler had escaped.

A hyena-like laugh carried through from the forest, and it was answered by a pain-choked howl that sounded close.

"Leave me," Maddox said. "I'll be fine." He raised his phone. "I've got good service. They'll come get me."

"We can't—" Carter started but Maddox held up a hand.

The lodge director pushed himself into a sitting position and propped himself against a boulder. "Go, otherwise all this is for nothing."

Kahn and Carter exchanged a glance that asked, "Do either of us give a turd about this guy?"

"There's nothing you can do anyway," Maddox added. "Go!"

So the partners went.

Maddox called for help, and with the cavalry on the way Kahn followed Carter around the cliff face to a path that led deeper into Borderland Pass.

The storm bubbled over the western horizon, and the stars and moon were hidden by dark gray cotton candy clouds.

"This would be easier if we had some daylight," Kahn said.

Carter said, "Don't hold your breath. There will be no dawn."

28

Carter raised his hand and pointed north toward a jagged cliff face where a massive section of the mountain had fractured and tumbled into the valley below. The peak jutted upward like a shattered tooth, stark and sharp against the backlit clouds. Amid the rolling hills of the Ozarks, the fractured mountain stood out as an imposing anomaly, its scarred face visible at a distance, and Kahn didn't think it was too far away.

"I hope… well, hope isn't really the word, but I don't want Maddox to die," Carter said.

Kahn never wished anyone dead, but he wouldn't attend the funeral if the lodge director shuffled off his mortal coil. Still, if he died that would mean an investigation; names, and past deeds would come to light. "What could we have done? Waited with him?" Kahn said, justifying a decision he wasn't thrilled with, either. "His people know where he is. He'll probably be at the hospital before we could have gotten him there." Kahn felt lighter of foot without Maddox around because he'd never trusted the man. He trusted Carter—it was a gut thing, and that same gut had told Kahn that Maddox was an ass the first time he'd met the man.

Carter said, "You got a point there, I guess."

Wind gusted and twisted through the trees, weaving its way into the underbrush like a restless spirit. Kahn felt the faint glow of dawn creeping toward the lip of the eastern horizon, though the sky remained dark and choked with dirty clouds.

The pair followed a well-worn deer path, their steps careful and deliberate, as if performing a balance beam act on the thin strip of exposed hardpan. Buzzing, chirping, a cooing carried on the restless wind as the forest began to thin, the white oaks giving way to rugged terrain—tumbled boulders, patches of devil grass, and stunted evergreens emerging like animals in the encroaching darkness.

"Maybe Maddox will look at things differently after today," Carter said.

Kahn snickered. "There're only two things that motivate people like Maddox and they go hand in hand. Money and exercising power over others."

The path splintered into multiple directions, branching out like the arteries of a living, untamed highway. It was a chaotic intersection of trails, each one etched into the earth by the relentless passage of countless hooves. Mixed within were giant paw prints, and the partners paused briefly to examine what looked like a drip of blood before continuing toward a slope blanketed in loose scree.

Kahn followed Carter up the incline of jagged, tumbled stones toward a path flanked by massive, cracked slabs of stone. He wasn't a geologist, but the story of the cliff face was plain to see. The entire Ozark region bore the scars of relentless erosion. Water had cleaved the mountain long ago, the crack widening over centuries until an enormous chunk of the southern mountainside broke free and collapsed into the valley.

"What I can't deny is how much the Ozarks changed me," Carter said. "I was a different person before that accident. You can't tell me you don't understand what I mean."

Kahn nodded and said, "I understand it. So what? What does it mean? Nothing. We both know what we need to do and we're not doing it. No magic there."

"What's your plan, Kahn?" Carter's tone was aggrieved. "Are you going to stay out here keeping people's land free of nuisance animals for the rest of your life?"

"Assuming we get through the day, that was the plan," Kahn said, unwanted anger creeping into his voice. "And what about you? When do you plan to start your stroll down the road to prison?" Kahn was sorry he said it as soon as the words escaped his lips. This man was helping him, had saved his ass, and he'd been nothing but good to him and the last thing he deserved was snark. "Sorry," he added. "I'm getting hangry."

"No worries," Carter said. "You're not wrong. These are touchy subjects, my new friend. Maybe we can help each other through. As to what I'm going to do…"

A crow cawed.

Kahn's partner didn't continue, and he let it go. For now. Plus, the hunt wasn't about Carter.

As Kahn drew closer to the Howlers' lair, he couldn't help but sense he was also getting closer to his own reckoning. The sins of the past, the ghosts of those he'd wronged, and the raw, unyielding truth of who he had become fighting for control of his future.

As the pair moved along the uneven path, Carter in the lead, the fissure in the mountainside widened, revealing the shadowy maw of a cave, the dark opening looming against the gray and black stone like a portal to another world.

Near the entrance, there were four-toed footprints, each toe marked by a thin line that could only be from claws. The tracks clustered around the cave's threshold, but Kahn saw no sign of blood—no drip trail, no splatter. Vines and weeds tangled across the mouth of the cave, and several white oaks leaned precariously over the opening, their gnarled roots exposed as they clung stubbornly to the mountainside.

A faint tinkle of water carried on the breeze, mingling with a strange, rhythmic clicking—a metallic sound, like a lead line striking against an aluminum flagpole. The noise emanated from within the cave, but it wasn't just the sound that unnerved Kahn. A stench seeped from the dark hollow, a nauseating cocktail of decay, feces, animal musk, and the damp, earthy tang of mold. Red warning lights flashed all over Kahn's mental dashboard.

"I don't think the Howlers are in there," Carter said.

"But do we want to stink the place up? A confined space like that might hold our scent," Kahn said. The hunters were dusted like donuts with scent repellant, but so far it hadn't helped much.

Carter nodded.

"If the Howlers are like most wild animals, and we both know they are, the beasts will flee if they catch our scent."

Carter nodded faster and harder. "What do you propose?"

"I propose we hunt," Kahn said. "The Howlers might come back here to spend the daylight hours resting."

The duo found a boulder partially hidden by a bent evergreen and they climbed atop it. From the raised vantage point, the partners had a good view of the cave mouth and the path that approached it.

"Do you mind if I catch a bit of shuteye?" Carter asked.

Kahn was exhausted himself, the night an endless array of stress and exertion that had drained his physical and mental batteries. "Good idea. I'll wake you in an hour and you can take a turn watching."

"Deal."

With the plan set, Kahn settled in to wait, the Remington loaded and ready to fire.

The pair got a little rest, ate, and drank water, but of the Howlers, there was no sign.

Kahn knew the sun had risen because he trusted in the cosmic scheme of the universe, but other than the faint glow that leaked through the storm clouds there was little sign of it. Thick mist working to become rain snaked and eddied through the boulders and cascaded down the mountain face. The sky was black, and occasional puffs of white shone through as lightning backlit the clouds. Faint booms, like an approaching battle, echoed over the Ozarks, and the air thrummed with menace.

As the partners put themselves together and prepared to head into the cave Carter said, "Do you think our scent kept them away?"

Kahn shook his head no. "The wind is coming in hard from the west. But who knows? These things are... advanced."

"You're probably right," Carter said, but the guy didn't sound convinced.

The partners made their way to the cave mouth, where they stood side by side, like frightened children frozen at the edge of a dark room, half-expecting the bogeyman to lunge out from the black depths and drag them into the unknown.

"Let's do this," Kahn said as he flicked on his flashlight and plunged into the blackness.

Darkness fled and a rancid scent assailed the duo as the cave filled with harsh LED light.

The clicking the partners had heard was a dead branch hanging from a root just inside the cave entrance. It swung back and forth in the breeze, tapping the stone wall. Shadows danced, thin rivulets spidered down the cave walls like snot, and the sound of dripping water accompanied the wind, which played the cave like a broken bassoon.

"Most caves in the Ozarks aren't much more than cracks in the limestone created by erosion," Carter said. "But some of them, like this one, have flowstone, stalagmite-like formations made of calcite or other carbonate minerals, formed from flowing water."

The formations were stunning, and as Kahn panned the flashlight across them, the rank scent of death filling Kahn's nostrils, he waded deeper into the cave.

Not unlike the Quapaw rock face monument, the cave featured drawings on the walls, primitive stick figures wearing Native American garb, and praying to the moon, which was represented by a huge, pocked circle. The figures danced, and several symbols that looked like Mayan writing ran below the drawings like a narrative. Kahn recalled what Carter had said about the ancients in the area, the warring tribes believed to have originated in South America.

"Why do they pray to the moon? I learned the Egyptians, who lived way before, prayed to the sun," the Kahn asked.

"The moon represented night, which was cooler. The sun was an enemy, as it can get very hot in most of the southwest United States." Carter chuckled. "At least that's what I remember. Who knows?"

Kahn stopped arcing the flashlight around, and its beam illuminated a disturbing image.

The scene depicted four stick figures elaborately clad. Feathers of blue and red festooned their heads, and they wore black loincloths that had squiggly white lines running across them. The figures held spears, and the hunters were arrayed around a beast that could only be an Ozark

Howler. The bear-like form was three times the size of the stick figures. It stood on its hind legs, front paws up in attack position, dark smudges of paint depicting drool or blood seeping from a tooth-filled mouth. But it was the yellow speck-like eyes. They seemed to follow Kahn's every move.

A rank wind wafted from within the mountain, and the hairs on the back of Kahn's neck stood on end.

The deeper the pair delved, the more disturbing things became. The sound of trickling water reminded Carter that the cave might have another outlet. Limestone caves created by water often had many side passages, and the cave they were in most likely had tributaries, but what were the odds one could lead them out? Slim.

Daggers of light filtered through cracks in the rocky ceiling, illuminating what could only be the Ozark Howler's birthing nest. It was a rough yet carefully constructed depression in the dirt floor, its edges lined with a mix of matted fur, dried moss, and fragments of bark.

The floor surrounding the nest was uneven and covered with gravel compressed by years of weight. Claw marks scored the rock walls, and bones were embedded in the earth around the nest, varying in size and condition. Some of the long bones were cracked and splintered, their marrow sucked clean, while smaller fragments were piled like trash. Ribs and skulls rested on ledges like macabre trophies, while others were half-buried.

Ragged teeth marks scarred most of the bones, and the dried remnants of flesh clung to a few, though decomposition had taken its toll, leaving the air thick with a faint metallic tang.

Overhead, stalactites dripped water into a shallow pool that reflected the fractured images of the bones. In spots the walls glistened, streaked with mineral deposits, but here and there, dark smudges of dried blood stained the stone—a grim reminder of violence.

Clawed pawprints fanned outward around the nest—some large, while others were smaller, newer prints—perhaps from cubs. The entire place felt decayed and neglected, and there was a thin sheen of dust atop everything.

"The Howlers haven't been here in some time," Carter said. "Last birthing season, maybe, whenever the hell that was." He sighed. "I thought, maybe because they were wounded, they'd come back to a place they knew, even if the female wasn't pregnant."

"Is she?"

Carter hiked his shoulders. "It's possible. From what I've seen their gestation period is about ten months, so the odds are good. How far along? That's another question altogether. But if the Howlers are similar to most other creatures, winter isn't the best time to bring calves into the wild."

"Do these things hibernate?" But before Carter could answer, Kahn answered his own question. "Of course they don't. Your struggles with the beasts were during the winter."

Kahn nodded and said, "I'm surprised birds and other animals haven't encroached on the Howlers' cave, especially when they're not around."

Carter harrumphed. "Maybe a bear would have the stones, but I don't think there's a—"

A cackling laugh-howl carried into the cave and choked off Carter's words.

"Sounds like you might have been right after all," Kahn said.

"We need to get out of here before we get trapped," answered Carter.

29

As the partners fled the Howler's lair the sky opened up.

Rain came in torrents, a deluge that turned the ground into muddy rivulets as water drummed against stone and pine needles. The scent of wet earth filled Kahn's nostrils, mingling with the sharp odor of crushed vegetation as the storm battered the hillside.

Dark clouds churned and folded into a boiling cauldron as huge shadows danced on the rugged mountainside, their craggy silhouettes melting into the gloom. Lightning sizzled with a crackling fury, illuminating the forest below in a ghostly white.

Then came the howling wind, a banshee wail that swept through Borderland Pass, driving the rain sideways. Tree branches swayed violently, and some snapped under the onslaught, their falls punctuated by sharp cracks that echoed like rifle shots. In the distance, thunder rolled—a low, guttural growl that seemed to rise from the depths of the Earth.

The partners took shelter beneath a stone outcrop as they scanned the path that ran down the mountainside. Flanked on both sides by vertical slabs of split stone, the path was now a shallow rushing river that carried twigs, dead leaves, and bronze pine needles. Kahn saw no sign of the Howlers, and whatever trail they might have left was being washed away.

Both men checked their weapons, and Kahn's rifle and Beretta were locked and loaded. Kahn fished in his pack for his rain parka, and he stowed the night vision binoculars before trussing the pack, shrugging it on, and putting on the rain gear. Keeping the guns dry would be a challenge. Neither Kahn's Beretta nor Carter's H&K VP9 were law enforcement grade, and though the manufacturers claimed both weapons could fire underwater, neither man had tested the theory, and the duo had no urge to.

The rain let up a little as the partners settled back to wait.

There's nothing to do on the hunt except replay memories, calculate new angles and dream. With the rain pattering on the brim of his hat, water leaking into his hunting vest and boots, and a summer chill seeping into his bones, Kahn thought of his daughter. He tried to envision where she was, and what she was doing, and his mental camera placed him at her side. But the image always transformed like a horror movie, his little girl shrinking before him as her muscle mass was depleted and her skin hung from her bones.

These thoughts usually turned to self-pity, which was why Kahn never brought alcohol on hunts. The temptation to give in to despair was too great, and even when the red fox was your only prey, unexpected guests were always possible, and being sharp was a prelude to survival.

"What's that?" Carter said as he pointed. Like Kahn, the man had been marinating in his thoughts, most likely reliving nightmares he felt he still needed to atone for.

A large boulder marked a turn in the path, a spray of pricker bushes at its tip. Two yellow eyes peered at the partners through the leaves and rain. The beast threw back its head and roared a mighty warning, then disappeared into the vegetation.

The duo aimed their guns into the rain-clogged gloom, waiting for the beast to show itself.

It didn't. Five minutes slipped away... Ten. Fifteen. It was as if Kahn and Carter didn't want to address the Howler in the room: was it time to turn back? The beasts were on the run, the male's warning clear. Follow and die. Still... not hunting the Howlers would mean dealing with the future, and Kahn would do anything to avoid that.

"We need to finish this if we can," Carter said.

Kahn nodded and pushed out from cover into the driving rain.

Both Howlers were wounded—at least that's what Kahn believed, but the beasts hadn't slowed much. They fled down the path, their huge paw prints easy to see in patches of thick mud.

It was a one foot in front of the other situation, and when the partners broke free of the mountain pass Kahn saw the dark shapes of the Howlers tracking north along the forest's edge. It was hard to tell in the rain, but it appeared to Kahn that the smaller beast was moving slowly.

The partners pressed on, the trail clear, the Howlers intent on moving north into the heart of Borderland Pass. Tall trees rose around the duo as the hills in the east gave way to forest, thick mist snaking through the pillar-like trunks.

"There's a hint of a path," Carter said. "Do you see it?"

At first, Kahn didn't, but like one of those puzzle pictures that only becomes clear when you stare at it, the faint outlines of a trodden path became visible through the undergrowth; a freshly snapped lower branch, a tuft of fur, and pawprints drawing the partners on.

Gun raised but concealed within the sleeve of his raincoat, Carter took point. As the partners pushed through a tangle of branches and circled a massive boulder, they stumbled upon a pile of stones stacked in the shape of a pyramid, crowned by a prominent red ochre-colored rock.

Carter reached out a hand in reverence before remembering he was on the hunt. His head jerked around, searching the surrounding vegetation, but when he saw no sign of the Howlers, he said, "It's a cairn."

"A warning?" Kahn said.

"Probably. Red ochre is a sacred American Indian color symbolizing life and death," Carter said. "Cairns may mark boundaries, with the paint signifying a spiritual or blood price for those who pass. Also, red ochre was used by the Quapaw in burials and sacred rituals."

"Great."

The rain eased to a steady drip that was just enough to be annoying. Kahn was drenched through, and his feet were starting to chafe in his boots. He was tired, hungry, angry, and he needed a drink. Something with an olive or cherry in it.

For once the sheer size of the Howlers helped because within the tight quarters of the forest, their trail was easy to follow, and there were no clear breaks in the greenery that ran along its edge. If the Howlers had left the trail, they'd done so without leaving a trace.

Carter screamed, "Hold up!"

Kahn dropped to a knee and brought up the Remington, rain pelting the barrel as he searched for a target.

Carter stood before a large oak tree, arms at his sides.

Kahn lowered his weapon and joined him.

A haunting face was carved into the trunk of an ancient oak.

"I think it's a Quapaw Indian chief," Carter said, rain splattering his face.

Weathered by decades of rain, sun, and wind, the chief's features retained a sense of solemn dignity despite the erosion. Deep-set eyes gazed forward with an unyielding intensity, their carved sockets shadowed by natural grooves in the wood. Etched fine lines suggested wisdom and age, the crow's feet at the corners of the eyes radiating outward like sunbeams. The nose was broad and strong, its bridge slightly flattened, blending seamlessly into the tree's grain. High cheekbones jutted proudly, giving the face an air of authority and resilience, while the mouth, with its downturned corners, spoke of quiet determination and sorrow.

The chief's cascading hair merged with the oak's natural ridges as if the tree itself had grown to accommodate the image. Above his brow, a feathered headdress had been etched with delicate precision, the feathers fanning out in a semicircle that framed the chief's stern visage. Lichen and moss crept along the lower edges of the carving and cracks cut across the wooden face like scars.

"Another warning?" Kahn asked.

171

Carter nodded, rain sluicing off his coat. "Effigies like this are common markers warning intruders of the spiritual danger lurking in the area. Like the Ozark Howler."

Time slipped away as the forest got deeper and the day darker.

Rhythmic murmurs wove through the trees as the storm eased and raindrops tapped against the tree canopy. A breeze rustled the wet leaves, adding a faint whisper of despair. Amid the rain's melody, the forest breathed, alive, but beneath the subtle undertones a violent clicking disturbed the storm's soundtrack.

"Dear God," Carter said as he made the sign of the cross.

The partners came upon a series of bone assemblages hanging from the trees that lined the path. They clattered in the breeze, striking each other with a brittle, hollow sound. Macabre works of art, each one consisted of animal bones meticulously strung together with sinew and twisted vines.

Skulls of deer, their antlers jagged and broken, formed the centerpiece of several of the macabre ornaments, their hollow eye sockets gazing downward as if in eternal warning. Around them, smaller bones—ribs, femurs, and vertebrae—had been arranged in intricate swirling patterns. Some of the deadly windchimes featured sharp, pointed ends, and feathers, blackened by soot or age, were tied to certain pieces, twisting like dark omens among the pale bones. Fragments of predator skulls—wolves or mountain lions—with their gaping jaws set open, teeth bared in silent aggression, were interspersed with talons and claws. Splashes of red ochre stained the bones, and some crude charms made of bird bones and hollowed-out shells swayed, emitting haunting chime-like whistles.

It was a stark, visceral warning.

Kahn said nothing as his heart tried to escape his chest.

"The Quapaw really don't want anyone in this area," Kahn said. "Do you think i—"

The male Howler bounded from the undergrowth on all fours, mouth agape, teeth bared.

Carter dove off the trail into the underbrush and disappeared into a cloud of green.

With the swiftness and ease of a cat, the massive beast charged Kahn.

Twenty feet stood between Kahn and certain death. As he raised the Remington, a strange sense of freedom leaked through him, as if in this fleeting moment, he controlled his fate. If he died, he died. He shrugged off the thought. This time he wouldn't miss.

The Howler surged onto two legs as its paws lashed out, its cackling laugh-like shriek cutting through the dying rain.

Kahn fired, pulling the trigger as fast as he could until the rifle clicked empty.

Like the beast had hit an invisible wall, the Howler skidded to a halt and reared back as bullets plunked into flesh.

Kahn dropped the Remington and drew down the Beretta.

The Howler backpedaled as it roared, its giant paws cycling through the air as it stumbled.

Fury engulfed Kahn, a hatred he didn't quite understand. It was as though the Howler now represented his entire failed life. The beast was responsible for every wrong, and it was time to pay the piper. He aimed the Beretta at the Howler and fired, slow and steady as he fell into rhythm with the storm.

The first two shots hit the Howler in the right shoulder, blood flying as the creature retreated. Kahn saw himself standing in his kitchen, taking the call from Misty, breathing a sigh of relief that he'd be able to pay this month's medical bills.

Kahn squeezed the trigger four more times, the shots punching into the beast's midsection as the Howler staggered back, its horns glinting in the gloom. He saw Blair die, her bloody face staring at him through the rain.

The Howler moaned and huffed, blood spouting from the gunshot wounds.

More shots thundered over the scene as Kahn's mind exploded with images of the massacre at the lodge and Slade's death.

He screamed with fury, pulling the trigger as fast as he could, the image of Misty lying in a hospital bed merging with his fall through Jed's porch roof as Buck's corpse laughed.

Kahn stopped firing, the rage momentarily subsiding as Maddox's crumpled form filled the center ring of his mental circus. Then Kahn took three fast steps forward and emptied the gun into the Howler's head.

With a massive exhalation of breath, the Howler collapsed, its massive frame heaving with labored breaths. Its once-majestic black fur, thick and matted with dirt, was now soaked in blood, a deep crimson pool forming beneath it and mixing with the wet earth.

The Howler's powerful legs trembled, ripped muscles and shattered bones visible through punctured skin. One paw, massive and tipped with claws like curved daggers, twitched as the last vestiges of the beast's strength waned. Its barrel-like chest rose and fell unevenly, the deep rumble of its breaths reduced to a ragged wheeze, punctuated by wet, gurgling sounds as blood bubbled from its open jaws. The beast's shaggy mane was damp and tangled, its glowing, golden eyes now dulled with pain and fading life, flickered weakly as they stared at Kahn. One horn was broken, and one ear was torn, dangling limply, while the other twitched faintly, reacting to distant sounds even as it died.

Kahn felt like shit. He was a professional hunter, but this was something else. This was a reckoning, not a triumph, but a sorrowful end. As the Howler took its final breaths, Kahn felt an undeniable truth settle in him: he and the beast were now bound together, their fates forever linked. The air was heavy with the understanding that what had been taken could never be undone.

With its final surge of adrenaline, the Ozark Howler shrieked a final warning before it deflated and fell still.

The male Howler's final wail echoed through the forest, a haunting sound that carried both pain and finality. Moments later came a mournful cry from its mate, resonating with raw fury and grief.

30

Kahn and Carter gathered their courage for the final push. The rain came in a steady stream, though the thunder and lightning had diminished as the hidden sun pressed on the top of the cloud cover. Kahn felt the sun there and knew the sky was bright above the clouds, but the knowledge provided little solace as the partners tracked the female Howler deeper into Borderland Pass.

The sounds of the beast's passage were unmistakable now despite the rain and wind. She huffed and puffed as though winded, and she was making no attempt at stealth. The Howler drove forward with a singular purpose that set Kahn's nerves on edge, but not enough to make him pause to reconsider the hunt. That time had passed.

As the rain eased the mists thickened, ghostly tendrils intertwining and twisting with the shadows that fought beneath the tree canopy. The rumble and static of running water filled the woods, and when the partners broke free of the forest they stood on an outcrop of stone overlooking a shallow sinkhole.

The rim of the sinkhole was jagged, with uneven limestone edges streaked in shades of pale gray and weathered white, and in places, moss clung to the wet rock. Dead leaves collected in pockets around the rim and weeds sprouted from every crack. The earthy scent of decaying foliage and cool stone permeated the air, the undercurrent of mist breaking over the hole like a wave. The sinkhole's sides sloped gently inward, the walls dotted with outcroppings of limestone that descended into the basin. Thin vines with large deep green leaves snaked over most surfaces, and Kahn saw a path leading into the hole hidden by a curtain of tangled foliage that swayed in the wind.

Boxed in by a vibrant mosaic of towering oaks and evergreens, their gnarled roots gripping the sinkhole walls, the basin felt confined, like an outdoor room. Faces were carved into many of the trees, their solemn visages staring into the gloom as they protected the site.

At the sinkhole's southern edge, a delicate waterfall spilled over a ledge, the stream narrow but persistent. The water cascaded in a silver thread that crashed on a pile of stones before tumbling gracefully into a shallow pond. Smoothed by time, the rocks beneath the waterfall glistened in the gloom, while rivulets of water trickled off to either side, feeding the surrounding moss and ferns. Mist rose from where the falling water penetrated the rain-dimpled pond, curling in wispy columns before being scattered by the wind and rain.

"Care to take a dip?" Carter said.

Kahn said nothing. The pond looked like the Kraken might live at its bottom.

The pond's surface was pinpricked from the rain and reflected the canopy above like a broken mirror. Small ripples turned into tiny waves that broke with a gentle whoosh that drove dead leaves and debris to the shoreline, which was framed by a crescent of dark rocks and patches of vibrant ferns and marsh grasses that thrived in the perpetual dampness. The water was a dark emerald hue, its rumpled clarity revealing distorted submerged stones and a scattering of sunken leaves and tree branches, and algae bloomed in shades of jade and green-gray on the pond's edge, blending seamlessly into the surrounding foliage.

At the northern end of the pond, a shadowed tunnel yawned like the mouth of some ancient, sleeping creature. The cave's entrance, framed by jagged rocks flecked with streaks of damp mineral deposits, was partially obscured by a tangle of vines, roots, and hanging moss. The opening was low and irregularly shaped, and water flowed into the tunnel and faint ripples suggested an unseen current.

The female Ozark Howler's head bobbed above the surface of the pond as the beast dog-paddled toward the cave mouth.

Kahn raised his rifle.

Carter found his voice. "Do you—"

"Do not fire," said a shrill mechanical voice.

Kahn lowered his rifle, his gaze shifting to Carter, who shrugged.

People stepped from the shadows all around the sinkhole. Most were clad in hunting garb, their faces covered with paint or ceremonial masks, and some wore the traditional accouterments of Native Americans.

Unlike the Quapaw tribe of old, it wasn't a huge deerskin-clad chieftain who called out to them, it was a woman with a bullhorn. She stepped from the greenery not far from where the partners stood.

Kahn started and took a step backward.

"We mean you no harm." The woman chuckled softly. "I should have come up with something better than that."

Kahn glanced around at the people standing guard around the rim of the sinkhole. Some had weapons, but they were in holsters or slung over their shoulders.

The female Howler disappeared into the cave at the far end of the pond.

"Who are you and what do you want with us?" Carter said.

The woman lowered the bullhorn and stared at the duo. She had sad eyes, and the lower portion of her face was hidden by a bird mask with a long curved beak. She wore jeans, a camouflage jacket, and a ring of colored feathers decorated with beads of many colors sat atop her head, soaked by the rain.

"I am Tiana, the Chieftain of the remnants of the Quapaw Nation," she said. "Surprised I'm a woman?"

The partners said nothing.

"Things are... different these days, and yet some things haven't changed," she said. "We are here because of you. Despite the many warnings not to enter this sacred place, you ignored the totems."

Kahn shifted on his feet. She had a point there.

"You will leave and never come back here or tell anyone of this place."

"Or?" Carter said defiantly.

"Or fate will see to your punishment. I am but a servant, as are all the people here." She lifted the bullhorn and added, "Now go. Leave the beast in peace so it may fulfill the prophecy and protect the pass."

The sound of metal sliding over metal echoed through the rain as the Quapaw drew their weapons and prepared them to fire.

Kahn wanted to laugh, but was what the woman said so much different than the prattle preached in churches all over the world?

Carter put a hand on Kahn's shoulder and said, "Looks like the end of the road."

Kahn met his friend's eye and nodded. Sometimes having no choice was the best choice of all.

When the partners turned their attention back to the sinkhole, the leader of the descendants of the Quapaw and all her followers had disappeared back into the mists.

Two days later Kahn and Carter sat across from each other at Betty's Diner sipping coffee, daylight draining from the world outside. The duo had been sitting in silence for over an hour, and when Kahn finished his coffee, and the waitress attempted a refill, he put his hand over the mug and shook his head.

"They say Maddox is going to live," Kahn said.

"That's what they say," Carter said. "Did you hear he's four rooms down from Misty?"

Kahn laughed. The deputy sheriff was going to be fine. She was through the hard part and was up and about. The doctors were starting to complain that if they didn't get rid of her soon, she was going to take over the joint. That made Kahn's insides feel warm and almost justified his obsessive stupidity.

Carter finished his coffee and also begged off another cup. "Where do things stand with the sheriff?" he asked.

Kahn leaned back and stared up at the water-stained ceiling, the jiggle of his reflection in the old mirror mounted on the wall at his side catching his attention. He looked into the mirror and saw his younger self for a heartbeat. The wrinkles had smoothed, the gray hair was once again black, his standing worry face gone. Could he be that person again? Did he want to be?

"Are you alright, Kahn?" Carter asked, his tone heavy with worry.

"Yeah, yeah." He wasn't fine, but he answered Carter's question anyway. "The staties have all the material, and Maddox is going to be investigated and charged with some crimes. But he didn't murder anybody, and as you know much worse things happen out in the Ozarks than messing with wildlife, cryptid or otherwise." Kahn sighed. "He'll most likely get some form of probation and he'll be fired as director of the lodge. But he's been there a long time and there are rumors that he's connected to the owners somehow, so he'll probably end up a guide. At least for a while until the stink blows over and he can be reinstated as the lodge director without any fuss."

"So, basically no ramifications," Carter said.

Kahn's gaze shifted to his empty mug as he said, "It's not your fault, you know? Nothing that happened out there is."

Carter threw up his hands. "Who knows? The cops will head back out to Jed's place for sure, right? They won't find a hell of a lot there, except some blood and disturbed dust. It'll all be forgotten just like before."

Kahn nodded. On a base level that was correct, but he was thinking about the big picture. "What do we do about the Quapaw? Do we tell somebody what we saw? What we think we know?"

"No," Carter said wistfully, without hesitation. "What purpose would that serve? We think we know what happened to us out there, Kahn, but we don't. Our fear, luck… Shouldn't we leave it be? And who knows? Maybe part of that old legend is true. I vote we leave them alone. Forget what we saw and never go back there again."

"Fine by me, I guess."

With that, the conversation ran out of gas. The two men stared at each other for two long minutes before Carter pressed to his feet and extended his hand across the table.

Kahn locked eyes with his partner and nodded as he shook his hand.

"Good luck, Kahn," Carter said. Then he turned on his heel, strode toward the exit, and left the diner without looking back.

As people ate and laughed, Kahn sat alone as his thoughts poked, prodded, and pushed. He felt lost. Though he hadn't known Carter long, in that short time the guy had been Kahn's rock. A real friend. A compatriot he could count on, and now he had nobody.

He thought of Snoop. What would happen to the cat if he left the Ozarks? Would he come with him? Kahn didn't see it. The coon had survived for years without him and could do so again, but maybe he could persuade the feline with a trail of the treats he coveted like they were made of catnip cocaine.

Kahn turned his gaze toward the front of the diner, his eyes fixed on the windows. He searched for any sign of Carter, clinging to a fragile hope that he might return. Instead, all he saw was the deepening shadows of night.

But as the darkness came, so did the light.

Kahn saw what he should do. Wanted to do. What he needed to do. The blur of his life had transformed into the clearest picture he'd ever seen. He would go home, find a job, pay his taxes, and give all his money to his daughter. He would do all that after he went to see her, even if it killed every bit of life left within him. Because it wasn't really about his life any longer, it was about hers.

31

Borderland Pass, Ozark Mountains, Arkansas, U.S.
11:12 AM CST, September 3rd, 2022

The Ozark Howler lay sprawled in her birthing nest, her massive, muscular frame heaving with each labored breath. Her thick, shaggy fur was matted with sweat and streaked with dark, glistening patches of blood.

Two gunshot wounds marred the beast's powerful body. One was a jagged hole just below her left shoulder, its edges singed and blackened. The second bullet was buried in the Howler's hindquarters where the flesh was torn and puckered around the entry point. Both wounds oozed a mixture of blood and yellowish fluid. Torn scabs marked her movements as the wounds reopened under the strain of her labor, and the Howler's golden eyes were so red they looked like they might bleed.

Her body trembled with exhaustion. The beast's barrel-like chest expanded and contracted, each exhale a low, guttural growl that echoed off the cave walls. Ribs shown faintly beneath dense fur, evidence of the toll her injuries and pregnancy had taken, and her powerful shoulders, built for crushing prey, sagged under the weight of pain.

As a contraction wracked her body, the Howler released a guttural, bone-chilling howl of defiance and agony that sent the small creatures scurrying deeper into the cave. Her jaws flexed open revealing yellowed teeth, and foam gathered at the corners of her mouth as she endured waves of pain.

Swollen with the burden of life, the beast's abdomen looked out of place against the rest of her battered body. The taut skin beneath the fur stretched with the effort of her contractions, rippling as the time drew near. Her belly heaved, the muscles quivering with exertion as if her very essence was being pulled in two directions—toward life and death simultaneously.

Her face was distorted in an agony-twisted blend of primal beauty and savage menace. The angular, cat-like face was framed by a mane of bristling fur that stood on end, and her pointy ears twitched toward every sound. She braced herself against the sides of the birthing nest, the claws at the ends of her paws chipped and bloodied from her desperate scrambles through the wilderness to reach the safety of the cave. Her tail lay limp behind her, twitching occasionally with the rhythm of her labored breaths. Dark, congealed blood pooled around her hindquarters, the coppery scent mixed with the musk of her sweat and the earthy tang of the cave.

As the moments stretched on, the Howler's body gave way to instinct. Her haunches shifted, muscles visibly straining, and her tail lifted, revealing the raw, bloodied area beneath.

The cave floor beneath her was suddenly drenched with a mixture of blood, amniotic fluid, and sweat. As the walls closed in on the Howler a sliver of moonlight angled through a narrow opening in the ceiling. Shadows danced on the walls as she shifted, her enormous frame casting distorted, spectral shapes that made the cave appear alive with her struggle.

Another contraction wracked her body as the beast bucked and heaved.

The moment came suddenly. Her body arched, every muscle taut and straining as a final, piercing howl escaped her lips. The air grew charged with heat and energy as she bore down, her wounds forgotten in the primal drive to bring new life into the world.

As the birth canal widened and shrank in grotesque spasms, a cub appeared—a slick, blackened head, crowned with a membrane of slime. The mother shrieked, a sound that rose and fell like a siren, her claws tearing at the birthing nest. Each forced breath sent tremors through her as the beast's growls deepened and mingled with her panting gasps.

The head emerged slowly, the glistening skin stretched taut around the malformed skull. It was too large, its outline grotesquely exaggerated by the nubs of horns just beginning to form beneath the surface of the skin.

Blood and amniotic fluid pooled beneath the Howler, and with a final, guttural scream, she pushed free the first cub, a wet, writhing mass that slithered into the nest. Its body twitched as it drew its first shuddering breath, the sound a sharp, high-pitched screech like glass scraping against stone.

But before the mother could rest, the contractions resumed, and the monster's glowing, blood-spidered yellow eyes rolled back in her head.

The second cub came faster, its emergence heralded by a gush of dark liquid. This one was smaller, though no less monstrous. It slid free with a sickening squelch, landing beside its sibling.

A convulsive tremor ran through the mother Howler, and then her muscles relaxed as she licked the cubs clean, her tongue rasping against their raw, newborn flesh.

The cubs were not the fragile, mewling things of ordinary predators, but horrors born of darkness, their forms distorted as though shaped by malice itself. The first cub's fur was a deep, inky black, streaked with a sheen of crimson that refused to fade even after the mother's ministrations. Its body was thick and muscular, its limbs unnaturally long, ending in budding claws that were already sharp.

Cub one's eyes opened, burning coals set into a malformed skull. He blinked once, then twice, as though testing his sight before unleashing a growl. The beast's toothless jaws snapped at the air, and its movements were jerky and unrefined, but there was nothing infantile about its presence.

The second cub was different. The beast was leaner, almost skeletal, and there were no nubs foretelling horns. Her fur was silver-gray, mottled with patches of black that seemed to shift like shadows. Unlike her sibling, she made no sound, her movements silent and deliberate. The cub's sickly yellow eyes glowed faintly in the dark, unblinking and eerily intelligent as she writhed in her mother's blood, tail lashing like a whip.

As the mother Ozark Howler lay motionless, the two cubs regarded each other, their gazes locking in a way that suggested a deep bond. The male snarled, but the female held her ground, her silence more unnerving than any growl. They circled each other for a moment, their movements already predatory, before turning their attention to the mother.

She watched her offspring with a mixture of pride and fear, her breathing labored, her strength draining away.

The male moved first, crawling toward her teats, his emerging claws digging into her flesh as he fed greedily.

Eager yellow eyes studied the mother with a disconcerting intensity as the female cub hesitated. Seconds dripped away, and as if she were satisfied her mother's milk wasn't poison, the female cub joined her brother.

As they fed, the mother shuddered, a low growl rumbling in her chest.

The cubs were relentless, their hunger insatiable, and the sounds of their feeding filled the cave—wet, sucking noises that echoed louder than they should have. The male cub's tail lashed as it drank, its movements frantic, while the female remained eerily still, drinking with a precision that felt predatory.

When they were done, the den fell silent save for the ragged breaths of the mother. The cubs sat back, their faces smeared with blood, their glowing eyes fixed on their mother.

The male cub explored the birthing nest, while the female remained near the mother, watching her with an unsettling stillness.

Sensing the danger, the mother Howler let out a warning growl, but her strength was waning, and the cubs did not heed her. The male pounced on her tail, biting down hard, its stubby new teeth sinking into flesh. Mom yelped and jerked away, but the female cub was already moving to help her brother as the siblings tested their mother's power.

Outside, the forest grew still, as if holding its breath, and the only sounds were the arguing trees and the complaining wind. Time seemed to pause as the Ozark Howler cubs took their first breaths, and in that fleeting moment, a new nightmare began—a nightmare that would stretch across years, haunting Borderland Pass with the weight of what was to come.

THE END

Other Severed Press novels by Edward J. McFadden III: TRAGIC (#1 Amazon Bestseller Tag), Purgatory Beach, Time's Claws, Landfill Lizards, CRICS, Terror Lake, Predators & Prey, Wolves of the Sea (#1 Amazon Bestseller Tag), Fortune's Cypher, Crimson Falls (#1 Amazon Bestseller Tag), Hell Creek, Barracuda Swarm, The Cryptid Club, Dinosaur Red, Drop Off (#1 Amazon Bestseller Tag), Jurassic Ark, Keepers of the Flame, Throwback, Sea Tremors, Primeval Valley, Shadow of the Abyss (#1 Amazon Bestseller Tag), Awake, and The Breach (#1 Amazon Bestseller Tag, Amazon #1 Hot New Audio Release Tag). His other novels include: Just Beneath the Skin, Terror Peak (#1 Amazon Bestseller Tag), the Theo Ramage Thriller series: Quick Sands, Sandbagged, and Too Much Grit, and Dogs Get Ten Lives, The Black Death of Babylon, and HOAXERS. Ed lives on Long Island with his wife Dawn, their daughter Samantha, and their cats Snoop and Skittles.

CHECK OUT OTHER GREAT CRYPTID NOVELS

BIGFOOT WAR
by **Eric S. Brown**

Now a feature film from Origin Releasing. For the first time ever, all three core books of the Bigfoot War series have been collected into a single tome of Sasquatch Apocalypse horror. Remastered and reedited this book chronicles the original war between man and beast from the initial battles in Babblecreek through the apocalypse to the wastelands of a dark future world where Sasquatch reigns supreme and mankind struggles to survive. If you think you've experienced Bigfoot Horror before, think again. Bigfoot War sets the bar for the genre and will leave you praying that you never have to go into the woods again.

CRYPTID ZOO
by **Gerry Griffiths**

As a child, rare and unusual animals, especially cryptid creatures, always fascinated Carter Wilde.

Now that he's an eccentric billionaire and runs the largest conglomerate of high-tech companies all over the world, he can finally achieve his wildest dream of building the most incredible theme park ever conceived on the planet...CRYPTID ZOO.

Even though there have been apparent problems with the project, Wilde still decides to send some of his marketing employees and their families on a forced vacation to assess the theme park in preparation for Opening Day.

Nick Wells and his family are some of those chosen and are about to embark on what will become the most terror-filled weekend of their lives—praying they survive.

STEP RIGHT UP AND GET YOUR FREE PASS...

TO CRYPTID ZOO

CHECK OUT OTHER GREAT BIGFOOT NOVELS

THE BEASTS OF STONECLAD MOUNTAIN
by Gerry Griffiths

Clay Morgan is overjoyed when he is offered a place to live in a remote wilderness at the base of a notorious mountain. Locals say there are Bigfoot living high up in the dense mountainous forest. Clay is skeptic at first and thinks it's nothing more than tall tales.

But soon Clay becomes a believer when giant creatures invade his new home and snatch his baby boy, Casey.

Now, Clay and his wife, Mia, must rescue their son with the help of Clay's uncle and his dog, a journey up the foreboding mountain that will take them into an unimaginable world...straight into hell!

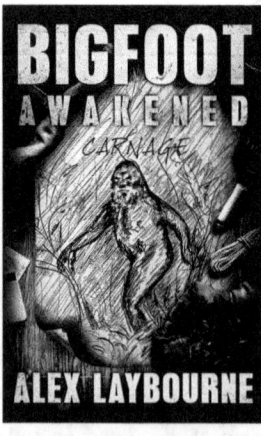

BIGFOOT AWAKENED
by Alex Laybourne

A weekend away with friends was supposed to be fun. One last chance for Jamie to blow off some steam before she leaves for college, but when the group make a wrong turn, fun is the last thing they find.

From the moment they pass through a small rural town they are being hunted by whatever abominations live in the woods.

Yet, as the beasts attack and the truth is revealed, they learn that despite everything, man still remains the most terrifying evil of them all.

CHECK OUT OTHER GREAT CRYPTID NOVELS

RETURN TO DYATLOV PASS
by J.H. Moncrieff

In 1959, nine Russian students set off on a skiing expedition in the Ural Mountains. Their mutilated bodies were discovered weeks later. Their bizarre and unexplained deaths are one of the most enduring true mysteries of our time. Nearly sixty years later, podcast host Nat McPherson ventures into the same mountains with her team, determined to finally solve the mystery of the Dyatlov Pass incident. Her plans are thwarted on the first night, when two trackers from her group are brutally slaughtered. The team's guide, a superstitious man from a neighboring village, blames the killings on yetis, but no one believes him. As members of Nat's team die one by one, she must figure out if there's a murderer in their midst—or something even worse—before history repeats itself and her group becomes another casualty of the infamous Dead Mountain.

DOVER DEMON
by Hunter Shea

The Dover Demon is real...and it has returned. In 1977, Sam Brogna and his friends came upon a terrifying, alien creature on a deserted country road. What they witnessed was so bizarre, so chilling, they swore their silence. But their lives were changed forever. Decades later, the town of Dover has been hit by a massive blizzard. Sam's son, Nicky, is drawn to search for the infamous cryptid, only to disappear into the bowels of a secret underground lair. The Dover Demon is far deadlier than anyone could have believed. And there are many of them. Can Sam and his reunited friends rescue Nicky and battle a race of creatures so powerful, so sinister, that history itself has been shaped by their secretive presence?